THE PRICE OF DEATH

S.J. ROBINSON

A NOVEL

BridgewayBooks

The Price of Death
Published by Bridgeway Books
P.O. Box 80107
Austin, Texas 78758

For more information about our books, please write to us, call
512.478.2028, or visit our website at www.bridgewaybooks.net.

Printed and bound in the United States of America. All rights reserved.

Library of Congress Control Number: 2008926854

ISBN-13: 978-1-934454-30-5
ISBN-10: 1-934454-30-3

This is a work of fiction. All of the characters and events portrayed in this book are fictional, and any resemblance to real people or incidents is purely coincidental.

Front cover design by Kristy Buchanan

10 9 8 7 6 5 4 3 2 1

Preface

Dear Reader,

The Price of Death is about two ordinary lawyers who become involved in a very extraordinary endeavor—finding out how a forty-year-old accountant in the prime of his life died suddenly in a hospital emergency room. The plot thickens as the two stumble onto a scenario of international intrigue and find time to fall in love along the way.

The book explores the difficulties of proving culpability in medical cases and includes some detail in doing so, with substantially more information in the author's note, if you are a skeptic. If you aren't a skeptic and you don't need this detail to be convinced, you don't need to understand the detail to enjoy the book. There is no test!

I hope this book helps you appreciate that there are some good trial lawyers in this country who help the survivors of the more than 98,000 people who die every year due to medical errors, and who risk hundreds of thousands of dollars of their own money in doing so. Incredible as it sounds, victims' lawyers in malpractice suits must advance out-of-pocket cash in amounts varying from $75,000 to more than $300,000 to get a case to trial. This money is not repaid unless the lawyer wins or settles.

Much of this expense could be avoided if another method of determining responsibility and compensation were available, but our system of insurance does not make that possible at this time. This may change in the future, and I have every confidence that it will.

This book is also a celebration of the American culture, the belief in the importance of each individual, and a commitment to the ideal that one person can make a difference. I hope you find this as exhilarating as I do.

S.J.R.

Chapter One

"He can't be dead," Mary sobbed, as she laid her head on Brad's chest, almost expecting to hear his heart beating. She didn't hear it, and she sobbed even harder. What had she done wrong? She had convinced Brad to go to the hospital in time, but it didn't save him. Mary thought back over the last few hours.

When Brad and Mary Thompson arrived at Peoples Hospital of Seattle, the emergency department was packed. The woman at the desk took Brad's insurance information and asked about his symptoms. Her expression clearly said that she was not impressed by mere light-headedness and heart palpitations. Hearing that Brad had been having the symptoms for an hour and a half, her original demeanor of cool efficiency turned to downright disgust. She directed Mary and Brad to sit in the waiting room. After sitting several minutes, Brad's pallor traveled from white to gray and then almost blue. He fell out of his chair onto the floor and didn't move. Mary couldn't even see him breathe.

She jumped out of her chair and made the distance to the un-caring woman at the desk in two strides. "Get someone now!" she shrieked, pointing to Brad. It took the woman at the desk a few seconds to register the problem, but when she saw Brad on the floor, she picked up the phone and quickly punched in some numbers. Within seconds, a woman in green scrubs burst through the doors from the treatment area followed by a stretcher and a man in matching scrubs. The next minutes for Mary moved in slow motion—the stretcher was lowered, and Brad was lifted onto it and whisked away.

She sat in the waiting room for what seemed an eternity. Looking at the clock, she discovered that it had only been an hour and fifteen minutes since they had taken Brad through the doors from which his rescuers had come. Just then, a dark-haired man—short, slight, and dressed in scrubs—came out of the treatment area, stopped at the desk for a minute, and then walked over to Mary. He introduced himself as Dr. Haseem.

He spoke English with a heavy accent. It was difficult to understand him, but he looked distraught. In fact, he was speaking so fast that Mary could understand very little of what he was saying. He had tears in his eyes, and the best Mary could understand was, "Resuscitated...normal sinus rhythm...acidosis...so sorry...shouldn't be happening...protocol."

Mary didn't have much time to talk with Dr. Haseem, because just after he came out of the treatment area, a tall, blond-haired man in a sport coat approached them from the hallway. The man introduced himself as Lars Hansen, chief executive officer of Peoples Hospital. He apologized profusely for interrupting and pulled Dr. Haseem aside. After a short conversation that Mary couldn't hear, Dr. Haseem walked back into the ER treatment area.

At first Mary was glad to see Mr. Hansen. He was much less agitated than Dr. Haseem, and English was obviously his native language. His tall stature and polished manner was comforting. He explained that Dr. Haseem was needed back in the emergency room and that he was here to help her understand what had happened. He sat down with Mary, took her hand, and spent almost twenty minutes with her explaining that the hospital just couldn't save her husband. Though the doctors did their best, sometimes they just weren't able to save even young men like Brad suffering from cardiac arrest. Hansen was silently congratulating himself on his success in smoothing over the incident, when Mary interrupted him.

"But they did save him!" Mary protested. "Dr. Haseem said that he was resuscitated. He said that this shouldn't be happening. You have the wrong person! You weren't there, were you? You came from the hallway." Mary couldn't believe what she was hearing. Mr. Hansen was telling her that Brad didn't recover from the cardiac

2

arrest. Mary told herself, "This patronizing guy has the wrong man! He must! Brad cannot be dead!"

Mr. Hansen patted Mary on the hand for what seemed like the umpteenth time and said, "I know it's very hard to understand." "Hard to understand! I know what he told me. *You* don't understand!" Mary noticed that her voice came out much louder and higher than she intended. She jerked her hand away from Mr. Hansen.

Again he said, "You're very upset. I have called our grief counselor, Mrs. Thomas; she is very experienced in these matters. I know that it's very hard to accept the death of a loved one." Hansen was also thinking, "I need to go talk to Haseem before he finishes charting."

As Hansen stood up, Mary noticed a kindly-looking, overly plump woman with blue-gray hair arriving from the same hallway that had produced Mr. Hansen. He introduced her as Mrs. Thomas, made apologies for having to leave so quickly, and left. Mrs. Thomas too took Mary's hand. Mary wanted to pull away again, but by this time she was beginning to believe that she wasn't acting rationally. She allowed Mrs. Thomas to repeat the platitudes that had flowed so easily from Mr. Hansen's mouth. Mary just really wanted get away from this place of crazy people, but she couldn't leave Brad there alone.

Despite Mrs. Thomas urging that she have a cup of coffee instead, Mary insisted that she see Brad. She and Mrs. Thomas arrived in Brad's treatment room just as two men in scrubs were taking him out. Horrified that the hospital would move Brad without telling her, Mary lost her temper again. She screamed at the orderlies to put Brad back in the treatment room, followed his stretcher into the room, and told Mrs. Thomas to get out. Mary closed the door and, lowering the railing on Brad's stretcher, leaned over his body and kissed him. "He can't be dead," she thought. "We have so many plans. We're going on vacation next week. This can't be happening!" She sat in the treatment room for about half an hour. The same thought kept running through her mind, "How could Brad be dead? He cannot be dead!" As she sat with Brad, occasional sobs escaped her lips but didn't relieve the growing knot in her chest. She found that it was hard to even move.

Eventually she did agree to let Brad be taken to the morgue. On the way out of the ER, Mary saw Dr. Haseem and Lars Hansen through the window of a door to what appeared to be a conference room. The door was closed, so she couldn't hear what Hansen was saying. She could tell, however, that they were having a serious conversation. The doctor was holding some paper tape stretched between his hands. Hansen grabbed it and tore it up. Mary wanted to open the door and demand that they explain what happened, but she just couldn't listen to that patronizing speech or endure any more hand holding right now. "These people are crazy!" she thought again.

The one thing that Mary could handle at this time was to make sure that Brad had an autopsy. She went to the reception desk and asked for an autopsy request form. The receptionist looked at her with a blank stare. "That isn't my job, ma'am," she said.

That was too much for Mary. "Not your job, you idiot! What do you do here? You don't take care of people! I don't care if it isn't your job! Get me the form!" she yelled.

Hearing the yelling, Hansen looked out the window of the conference room and rushed over to Mary. "I want an autopsy," she demanded, this time in a lower voice. Hansen tried to put his hand on her shoulder, and Mary drew back. "Please don't do that anymore. I want an autopsy. Give me the form, and I'm going home." Hansen indicated that he would be right back. He entered the conference room, leaving the door ajar. While Hansen rifled through a file cabinet, Mary could see that Dr. Haseem was still in the room, now sitting with his head in his hands.

Indeed, Hansen did come right back, holding out an envelope that Mary assumed contained an autopsy request form.

"I'm sure you'll feel better about this later. Here's my card. Please feel free to call me if there is anything I can do," Hansen said.

Mary took the card, mumbling, "Thank you." She knew that she wasn't thinking well and probably wasn't up to driving. Hell! Mary was *sure* that she wasn't up to driving, and she didn't want to leave Madaline without a father and a mother. She pulled out her cell phone and called a cab to take her home.

Mary didn't see the streets rolling by on the way home, and she didn't respond to the taxi driver when he tried to talk to her. People often tried to make conversation with Mary. She had soft, blond hair; a pleasing face with high cheek bones and a turned up nose; and a pleasing figure, which she dressed with modest but tasteful clothes. "Pleasing" was a word that fit Mary well—you would believe it instantly if you were told that she was a kindergarten teacher. To many who knew her, her behavior at the hospital today might have seemed out of character. But it wasn't really out of character at all—every mother bear would do the same.

Now Mary alone was responsible for Madaline, a three-year-old miniature of her mother but with darker and thicker hair that came from her father. Brad, a rising young partner in a regional accounting firm headquartered in Seattle, had always been so proud of Mary and Madaline when they went out in public—Mary for the reasons just described and Madaline because everyone commented on what a pretty little girl she was. Now there would be no Brad to proudly respond to those comments or to hold Madaline's little hand. Another tear wandered down Mary's cheek. Mary didn't give it notice—there had been too many tears today.

Mary was still trying to determine how things could have gone so wrong when she was only trying to protect Brad. She had insisted that Brad go to the emergency room. He hadn't felt well since lunch—he had been dizzy, had a thumping feeling in his chest, and had looked pale. Mary recognized the signs; they were the same as those his father had just before he died.

The story Brad's mother had told her of his father's death was etched in Mary's memory. He died of cardiac arrest, and Brad's mother found out afterward that he might have been saved if he had gone to the hospital. She never forgave herself for not insisting that he go to the hospital. She wanted Mary to know this because she had read that the predisposition to cardiac arrest could be hereditary. But Mary never could convince Brad to have his heart checked; after all, he was only forty years old.

Mary, a thirty-five-year-old kindergarten teacher, didn't often contradict her husband. But this time, she got backbone. She called the young woman next door to sit with Madaline and then drove Brad to the hospital even though he didn't want to go. It was Sunday afternoon, and he had a major project due at work on Monday—he didn't have time for this. Though she knew she had done everything she could to help Brad, Mary couldn't help but blame herself.

Chapter Two

Brad's death occurred in late February 2006. Mary made an appointment with Jessica Lamm's office just six weeks later. She had checked with one of Brad's partners at the accounting firm, and after consulting with his lawyer, the partner had recommended Jessica B. Lamm, a successful medical malpractice attorney who had won some very difficult cases. When she first met Jessica, Mary was glad that she had checked for a recommendation first. Though Jessica was businesslike, she was also so downright striking that Mary's first instinct was that she couldn't be very good at her job. Mary did not think of herself as antifeminist, but this was no ordinary job. Mary would be entrusting discovery of what had happened to Brad to this attorney's care. Would this woman be up to the task? This concern melted away, though, as they worked through Brad's medical records. It quickly became clear that Jessica knew what she was doing.

Jessica, or Jess as most people called her, was reluctant to take the Thompson case at first, but her reluctance was more than matched by Mary's insistence and organization. Unlike most potential clients, and despite the fact that she had been extremely distraught at the time, Mary had made notes about the hospital episode when she returned home. She brought those notes and the hospital records, including the autopsy report, when she met with Jess. Mary had read and reread the records until they were so dog-eared that the paper was falling apart. Jess ran two sets of copies—one for herself and a new one for Mary, who Jess realized would be reading and rereading the records until this case was done.

Mary fervently insisted that the records didn't tell the whole story and, therefore, Jessica thought, was unlikely to be swayed on cross-examination. By the time she met Jess, Mary had already spent a considerable amount of time thinking and rethinking the episode at the hospital. She acknowledged that she had been very distraught, but she couldn't get over the surreal nature of the doctor's anguished confession and the hospital personnel's patronizing insistence that there was nothing more they could've done.

Chapter Three

Jess, concerned that Brad's death simply might have been un-avoidable, ran the records by Dr. John Peterson. John was an old friend of Jess's. They first met when she was fresh out of law school and just starting out with her old firm, and he was just finishing his residency in vascular surgery at the University of Washington. He was appalled at the sometimes sloppy care that he observed and agreed to work with Jess on a case that two other physicians had already reviewed for her. The others had told her that the care was sloppy, but in the end it didn't make any difference. The patient, a sixty-two-year-old man who was a smoker, was overweight, and didn't get regular medical care, had undiagnosed coronary artery disease and probably wouldn't have lived but a couple more years anyway. Jess didn't see this as a reason to write the patient off and was pleased when she found a doctor who agreed.

When John and Jess met, he was a muscled, five-foot-eleven thirty-something with short brown hair and a smile that spread across his face when he uncovered the solution to a problem. Over the years John had developed a few streaks of gray hair and had mellowed a little in his willingness to accept imperfection, but he hadn't lost his intensity or the smile. He still worked long hours, focusing on providing the careful treatment that he thought his patients deserved. Jess wondered how he found the time to maintain his muscled physique, which seemed to hold up pretty well even though he was now in his late forties. She had noticed that this generation of doctors seemed to appreciate the importance of exercise and weight control, even if they didn't live the balanced life of work and play that they all recommended.

That latter flaw, if it was a flaw, worked to Jess's advantage, so she wasn't about to criticize. John didn't live his life much differently than she did hers, and she enjoyed that balance, or lack of it. Besides, balance—like art—is in the eye of the beholder.

Early in their relationship, John had encouraged Jess to meet with him after work, since his schedule was often disrupted by delays in surgery. It wasn't uncommon that Jess would have to wait an hour or two at John's office while he worked on a patient who apparently wasn't aware that he was only allocated one hour and thirty minutes for surgery. Jess thought the after work idea seemed reasonable since twiddling her thumbs in John's waiting room wasn't her idea of fun. After a couple of times, however, Jess realized that the informal nature of the setting, sometimes coupled with a glass of wine, made her appreciate John's muscled physique more than she was comfortable with. She was pretty sure that this attraction wasn't lost on him. But John was married, and being "the other woman" didn't strike her as a good situation. After a couple of uncomfortable moments at evening conferences, Jess decided that she could live with the unscheduled periods in John's waiting room.

During one of these many office visits Jess corralled John into reviewing Brad Thompson's records. Fortunately these records were fairly short, so John merely reviewed them with her while they visited and didn't charge her the huge upfront fee that a doctor unfamiliar with her would have.

He confirmed her hunch that the autopsy findings were skewed by the report of pre-death events. The coroner depends on the hospital record to determine what happened and what to look for during his autopsy. Since Brad didn't survive the code, it wasn't surprising that cardiac arrest would be reported as the cause of death.

"This is odd," John said as he skimmed the autopsy report. "The coroner noted evidence of what might have been a large premortem infarct—a pre-death stroke. Apparently he didn't think it affected the cause of death, but the heart has to continue beating for the stroke-induced changes in the brain to show up. That means that the stroke must have occurred at the beginning of the code, which is rare. In fact, I've never seen that happen before.

"The coroner took a good look at Brad's heart, since he died during an apparent cardiac event. There was no appreciable atherosclerosis in the coronary vessels, which means that the heart palpitations Brad had were not the result of myocardial infarction, or death of the heart muscle.

"That means that Brad's ventricular fibrillation was probably due to a primary disturbance in the electrical impulse, which wouldn't show up on an autopsy. Ordinarily, chance of resuscitation from cardiac arrest isn't good unless the patient gets immediate—and I mean *immediate*—resuscitation. But Brad's heart appears to have been in pretty good shape, and his wife brought him to the hospital, so he should have had immediate attention. They should never have let him sit in the waiting room with his symptoms. Assuming he was only in tachycardia, or rapid heart rate, when he came in, he might not have gone into arrest at all, if he had been treated right away. They might have avoided doing a full blown code.

"You know that the coroner also noted that Brad had a patent foramen ovale, or PFO."

"Right," Jess said. Jess knew that a PFO was a hole in the heart that should have closed at birth, but didn't.

"Often, a PFO doesn't cause any real problems. In fact some of them only show up on autopsy, but it can be significant in an attempt to resuscitate in a code. The resulting pressure changes can cause the blood to bypass the lungs and go directly to the head. The coroner mentioned the PFO but apparently didn't think that it had anything to do with the cause of death either."

After reading the report, John philosophized, "Medicine is an art, not a science."

"Meaning what?" said Jess.

"The human body is a very complex organism, and we only understand parts of it. Medical science tries to explain what it sees through a prism of imperfect knowledge and experience. Doctors are taught to look for the common explanation, not the most extraordinary. The cardinal rule is 'When you hear hoof beats, think horses—not zebras.'"

John also reviewed the emergency room record and commented on the care to Jess as he read. The record indicated that when Brad was taken into the ER treatment room, he was in ventricular fibrillation.

"This is what I was talking about," John said. By the time he got into the treatment room, his heart was in V-fib, no longer just a rapid heart rate but an uncoordinated quivering mass of muscle. If they had gotten him in right away, they might have prevented that.

"Anyway, let me check the care," John said. Reviewing further, he began again. "As soon as IV lines were inserted, he was given two amps of bicarb followed immediately by epinephrine. The bicarb was administered to correct the blood chemistry due to the failure of the heart to pump correctly, of course. When the heart isn't functioning well enough for the body's needs, waste products build up. The patient gets acidosis—acidic blood. Uncorrected, acidosis leads to shut down of the body organs and to death, so obviously it must be corrected.

"The epinephrine was administered to raise the blood pressure, which obviously goes down when the heart isn't beating correctly. We also think that epinephrine prepares the heart for better chance of success with defibrillation.

"I don't know how up to speed you are on physiology, but the purpose of defibrillation is to reset the conduction of electricity in the heart by causing the whole muscle mass to discharge and then, hopefully, restart in normal rhythm. It's sort of like rebooting your computer. Brad got 200 joules, which is a good strength for a first shock.

"During the code process, a breathing tube was also inserted into Brad's throat to help him breath. The respiratory therapist hand pumps a bag attached to the breathing tube. It is still the old Ambu bag that the operator uses to force air into the lungs that you probably saw when you were nursing."

John paused. After a moment, he said, "This can't be all there is of Brad's record. After the start of the code, Brad's chart is really bare. There are a few general notes on the cardiac rhythm at the beginning, but there isn't a cardiac strip. I can't believe the ER doc didn't order any print outs of the EKG. Maybe he did, but they're not here. If he didn't, you would at least expect to see ongoing notes about whether defibrillation was successful. But there's nothing here until about five minutes before Brad died, when they shocked him again. This suggests that the first shock was successful; otherwise they would have retried it right away. If it was successful, that would change everything; it suggests he should have survived. But we just can't tell from what we have.

"You can tell that the acidosis didn't go away...or at least it came back. Toward the end of the code a blood gas showed that the blood pH was 6.9. Normal is 7.35, you know.

"There's a note that Brad's heart was going back into tachycardia. Obviously, that also reinforces the assumption that the first attempt to defibrillate was successful. Apparently thinking that the changing heart beat was due to the bad blood pH, the ER doc gave another dose of bicarb. He also gave more epinephrine—probably to bring up the blood pressure, although there is no note about what the blood pressure was. Apparently Brad's heart progressed to fibrillation again because they tried to defibrillate. They made one attempt at 200 joules and then two at 300, with epinephrine in between. It looks like they were getting pretty desperate. Thompson died one hour and fifteen minutes after collapsing on the waiting room floor.

"Sometimes the EKG strips don't make it into the file or get separated," John said, "but we really need them here to know what Brad's heart was doing. Even the notes are sparse, which might suggest that tapes were run and they were relying on those for a record. I can't say for sure—this care could be reasonable. If I were the ER doc, I'd be having a fit about where the strips are, assuming he had some run."

Chapter Four

Because of the many questions raised by the sparse record, Jess wrote the hospital a letter. She questioned the implication of a pre-mortem stroke, and she also asked why there weren't any notations or EKG strips showing that Brad regained normal sinus rhythm, or—if the first defibrillation had not been successful—why the doctor didn't give more sodium bicarbonate and immediately attempt another defibrillation. She also asked about Mary's recollection that Dr. Haseem mentioned recovery.

Jess received a scathing letter in return, from an attorney on behalf of Peoples Hospital. The attorney, William Baker, accused her of trying to take advantage of an unavoidable death and suggested that Mary Thompson's recollection had been affected by her emotional distress.

The hostile response to her letter only heightened Jess's interest. Since the letter came by e-mail, she checked it for metadata—information that shows who typed each part of the text available when a "soft copy" of a letter is received.

"Interesting," Jess thought, "the major text of the letter actually came from Lars Hansen, Peoples' CEO. Mr. Hansen seems to be a *really* hands-on kind of guy. He not only shows up at a code death on a Sunday afternoon, but he also personally writes responses to inquiries about hospital care. Doesn't this guy take a day off?"

Several weeks later, after discussing the situation with her client, Jess filed suit against Dr. Haseem and Peoples Hospital. She wasn't sure exactly what went wrong, but Mary's report and the sketchy record suggested that something did; this wasn't a normal code death. At the very least, Jess thought that there was a good possibility she could rely on the theory of *res ipsa loquitur*.

The theory essentially puts the burden on the defendant to prove that he wasn't negligent if good care would have produced a different result. Someone shouldn't go into the hospital and have a massive premortem stroke with no atherosclerosis, or die of lingering acidosis because of administration of inadequate amounts of bicarb. The problem is that sometimes people do die of acidosis from cardiac arrest, and sometimes they do have strokes after cardiac arrest, though the emphasis is on *after*. Here the record was so bare that it was impossible to tell what really happened. Jess was pretty sure that she was going to have to sue to get the information to prove it.

One additional concern about the case was that the Washington legislature passed a law earlier in 2006 that was going into effect in June. While the legislation was well-intentioned, this case was an illustration of the problems it creates. The new law would require that a claimant in a medical malpractice case file a certificate of merit before filing suit. This certificate, a statement signed under oath by a "qualified expert" who verifies that malpractice was committed, was already required to prove a case of malpractice, but not before the facts have been discovered if the hospital does not want to give them up. Lawsuits give the opportunity to force the hospital to provide the facts of the case, at least theoretically.

One problem with the new law is that sometimes an attorney won't know what kind of expert is needed until the missing facts of the case have been obtained. In this case, the "qualified expert" would probably be a doctor, but maybe a court would decide it should be an admitting clerk. The delay in treatment might have reduced Brad's chance of resuscitation, but the inadequate record and the lack of EKG strips made it tough to be certain.

There were too many open questions. Jess knew that if she waited to file until the law became effective, the defendants' attorney would insist that she have the right certificate from the right kind of expert and would take the position that any certificate she filed was inadequate. If she waited until the law applied, the downside risk would be that her case could be dismissed for lack of whatever the judge later decided was the correct certificate of merit. Malpractice cases are fought with a "scorched earth" type of defense. Such a dismissal could even be "with prejudice," meaning that the case couldn't be refiled except under very rare circumstances, even if Jess was able to find out what actually happened outside the normal discovery process afforded by lawsuits. What better way to take care of a suit that you don't want to deal with than to challenge the adequacy of the certificate of merit?

Chapter Five

Someone was fiddling with the front door lock. It couldn't be anyone familiar with the condo door lock; no one she knew would have that much trouble with it. The fumbling stopped, and the door opened. It was hard to see who it was at first because Reesa couldn't see into the hallway from where she was in the living room.

As he stepped inside, she noticed his shoes first. It looked like they had never been polished, and they were huge. Of course, most people's feet were bigger than hers. She sat perfectly still, hoping he wouldn't see her. She could smell his sweat and see the stains on his pants, several streaks of black that made it look like someone had unsuccessfully tried to clean them.

From her vantage point behind the end of the couch, Reesa could now see him clearly. His pants were part of a suit, and the jacket had more streaks near the pockets. She could see why; his hands had black on them too, buried in the skin around the finger nails. Either he had not washed them in weeks, or the stain just wouldn't come out. As a "clean freak," Reesa noticed those kinds of things.

There was something more in his hands! As Reesa stared at it, a blade popped out. She had never seen anything like that before! The man started slashing the top of her favorite couch, stabbing and stabbing and stabbing into it, working his way down to the end of the couch where she crouched. As he approached, the sweat smell became overpowering. The stench of it was surpassed only by the fear starting in the back of her mind and welling toward the front. What if he saw her! People often overlooked her because she was small and could be really quiet. She hoped that this was one of those times.

The stabbing stopped just feet from Reesa's hiding place at the end of the couch. Fortunately, he turned away and started stabbing the love seat and throwing a lamp and pillows on the ground. Then he came forward again toward the end of the couch where Reesa was. She would have to move, or he would surely see her. She silently went around the corner of the couch on half-bended legs, like her ancestors had done for centuries when stalking prey. Only this time, she might be the prey. Just in time! He seemed to be reaching down under the bench-shelf along the windows. Reesa couldn't see what he was doing; she was just staying as still as possible. He was working there for a long time along the underside of the shelf.

Then he went into the kitchen and pulled open the cupboards. Dishes and glasses crashed to the floor—those special glasses that people gave Reesa's mother when she started her law firm. Reesa knew about those glasses because she had broken one once, and her mother got really mad. She hoped her mother wouldn't think it was her fault this time. The noise stopped, but Reesa could tell he was still there because the door hadn't opened again, and the condominium still reeked of his smell. She thought that he must be in the bedroom, because she heard noises in there from time to time. She couldn't tell what he was doing, but at least he wasn't throwing things out of the cupboard and stabbing things.

After what seemed like hours, Reesa heard him walk to the front door again. The door opened and closed. That could mean that he had left, but she sat very still for a long time to make sure. There was no more human sound, and the terrible smell seemed to be going away. He must have left.

Slowly, because her whole body was still shaking, Reesa walked over to her "Good Kitty" dishes. She was so nervous that she gulped down the tuna flavored Indoor Cat Science Diet that her mother had left that morning, hardly taking time to breath between gulps. That was a mistake! She threw up all the way into the bedroom on her way to the queen bed that she shared with her mother.

At first Reesa hid under the red-and-gold-striped bed skirt, but that didn't seem safe enough. She found the opening where the quilt met the bed skirt and crawled under the quilt to the middle of the bed, hoping that she was invisible. At least it was dark. She couldn't stop the uncontrollable shivering that had overtaken her body from the tip of her nose to the end of her tail. Her mind screamed, "I want my mom!"

Chapter Six

It was six o'clock Monday evening as Drew Stewart entered McCormick's Fish House and Bar on the Fourth Avenue side of the Columbia Tower. The building actually had been renamed a few times—first to "Bank of America Tower" and then to "Columbia Center." None of the Seattle natives called it by its new name, and Drew was a Seattle native.

Coming in through the main entrance, Drew noticed, as he always did, the tiny, white, hexagonal tiles interspersed with an occasional black one. He wondered if they really put those tiles in one at a time. That portion of the building, historically designated, sure gave the impression that it had been built long before tiles came in sheets. The tiles contrasted with the black paneling, creating the impression of an old-fashioned men's club, completed by the green half-curtains on gold rails and the wooden tables and chairs. The place was a "watering hole" for downtown office workers, and they had great oysters.

Drew noticed immediately that Jessica Lamm was one of the patrons. She was sitting at a table in the back corner by herself. He saw her look at her watch and frown. Evidently she was waiting for someone.

Jessica and Drew had previously said hi to each other since they both had offices on the forty-second floor of the Columbia Tower. The offices were part of the suite offered to professionals that provided a café of services from which they could select anything from telephone, voice mail, reception, conference rooms, use of a cyber café/lunch room, and even word processing and filing—if they wanted it. Drew's office faced out on the water of Elliot Bay and was on the same hallway as the Lamm Patrick firm. Lamm Patrick consisted of Jessica Lamm and Danielle Patrick, both attorneys, whose offices overlooked the I-5 freeway. Lorraine, their secretary, sat across the hallway in an internal cubicle. Drew didn't know Lorraine's last name and didn't want to know it. He got the impression that she didn't approve of him using what she seemed to view as her hallway, even though it was a semi-public area.

Drew had discovered Jessica's firm on his way to the lunchroom to get a cup of coffee on the first day in his new location. Ever since, he had been taking that route and occasionally ran into Jessica, who was a Seattle attorney of local fame. She had been featured in the *Washington State Bar News* several times and even once in the *Seattle Times* for spectacular results representing plaintiffs in her personal injury practice. What Drew hadn't learned from the news articles was how attractive Jessica was. And having discovered this, he didn't mind walking down that hallway toward the lunchroom on a regular basis—for the purpose of getting a cup of coffee, of course.

With his six-foot frame and muscled body, brown hair and startlingly blue eyes, Drew didn't have trouble talking to women in bars. This time though, he hesitated because he knew that lady lawyers have minds of their own, and he didn't want to mess up a chance to get to know Jessica Lamm. After a moment's thought, he decided to walk over to her table.

"Mind if I join you?" he asked tentatively.

Hesitating just a bit, Jessica said, "No problem…but you should know that I'm waiting for my friend Shelly from the prosecutor's office." Actually Jess had wanted a chance to talk to Drew outside of work, but she didn't want him interrupting what Jess thought was going to be heavy girl-talk with her friend Shelly.

She and Shelly often had trouble getting together with their busy schedules. Shelly often worked late into the evening at the prosecutor's office, preparing for last-minute trials or finalizing emergency briefs. This was one of those times that they had penciled in on their schedules a month in advance to try to keep the time open. "I assumed you must be waiting for someone," Drew said. "I don't think I've ever seen you here alone."

Jess, to her chagrin, blushed slightly. She had always had this inability to keep a bland face when she saw attractive men, and every time she saw Drew in the hallway, she had noticed that he was attractive. "Well, I mean, I don't want you to be surprised when Shelly comes in," she added.

"That's what I thought you meant," Drew said, as he pulled out a chair and sat down. Just then, Jess's cell phone rang with a "meowww." Again Jess blushed, but this time it was more pronounced. The specialized ring for her friend Shelly had seemed like a good idea when she put it in her cell, but she really hadn't counted on it coming up when she was talking to an attractive male lawyer who made her want to avoid looking like a frivolous female. She usually put her phone on vibrate once the workday was over, but she hadn't done it tonight because she wanted to catch any calls from Shelly. Even though the two of them had planned this get-together well in advance, on weekdays things often came up for Shelly, and they just hadn't been able to get together on weekends lately.

"Oh," Jess said. "That's my friend Shelly. She's a cat lover too." Opening the phone, Jess answered, "Hello…? Not again! Sometimes he should lean on someone else. You know he does that because he knows you'll rise to the occasion…Okay…Lunch sounds good. I'll check my schedule and call you tomorrow. See you later then."

"Shelly's boss is always assigning her last-minute trials. She's a great trial lawyer and an even better team player, but there's a limit!"

"From what I've read about her in the bar journal, she is a great lawyer. I can see why her boss depends on her," Drew agreed.

Jess smiled. She liked the fact that he appreciated lady lawyers.

"Well, let's have a glass of wine," she said and waived at the waitress. But as usual, the waitress was studiously listening to the bartender. "Funny," Jess thought, "that she's so much more interested in him—perhaps his curly brown hair and charm have something to do with it."

"Miss?" said Drew. "Miss…We would like a glass of wine over here." The bartender said something to the waitress. She looked over, picked up her tray, walked over to Drew, and said, "What can I get for you two?"

"I'll have a Hogue chardonnay," said Jess. The waitress glanced at her, made a note of the order, and immediately turned back to Drew.

"I'll have your house merlot," he said.

The waitress walked off, placed their order on the remote order device, cleared off a nearby table, and then walked back to the bar. She seemed to have a special attachment to that bar.

Jess frowned. Reading her mind, Drew said, "Right. Customer service isn't her first priority."

Turning back to Drew, Jess changed the subject. "Well, I know that you're J. Andrew Stewart, because I've seen your name on the office directory. I'm Jessica Lamm."

"Nice to meet you, ma'am! I actually know your name too. It's hard to miss your accomplishments. I've noticed a few articles in the bar journal about you too. I know you're a former-nurse-turned-lawyer, that you used to work for the Simon Grade firm, and that you started your own firm three years ago with Danielle Patrick. Impressive!" Drew also thought about, but didn't say, how hard it was to miss that perfect figure; the curly but professional-looking chestnut-blond hair ala Paula Zahn; and the earnest, almost sweet-looking face. "No wonder juries seem to like her," he thought.

Jess blushed again. "What's the matter with my face," she thought. "I must be going through premature menopause!"

"So, what does the 'J' stand for?" Jess asked to direct the conversation away from herself and her blushing.

"When I tell you, you'll understand why I don't use my first name," Drew said, and paused. "It's James. My folks used to call me 'Jimmie.'"

Jess chuckled. "Jimmie Stewart…he has a sense of humor," she thought to herself, "which isn't so common for a guy who has a good job and is good-looking too. Well," she thought, "he's more than just good-looking—he's a downright hunk." Jess found herself wondering if his abs looked like what she envisioned. Then she said, "I guess your parents had a sense of humor. I can see why you had to go to law school. It was either that or acting."

"No joke! I actually did give acting a lot of thought. But I find that make-believe isn't my thing. I'm much more convincing when I'm not trying to make things up."

"Hmm," Jess thought and couldn't come up with a smart retort for that comment.

The waitress broke the silence, bringing their wine to the table. "Your merlot, sir," she said, looking directly at Drew. "And your chardonnay, ma'am," she said, looking at the table.

The waitress walked to the next two tables, delivered the remainder of the drinks on her tray, and walked back to the bar.

"I've always thought that Lamm was a deceiving name for you. Though it fits your appearance, I'll bet your opponents think it doesn't suit you at all," Drew said.

Again, Jess blushed. She wished she hadn't worn her white "L.A. Law" blouse today. She was sure the white only accentuated the red that kept coming to her face and was now spreading down into her throat and beyond.

Coming to her rescue, Drew said, "So it's Jessica B. What does the 'B' stand for?"

"Call me Jess...and, well, my parents had a sense of humor too. The 'B' stands for Bonnie, but it almost sounds like a command when you use the initial with the first and last name. I always wondered if they thought about that when they came up with the middle name." Thinking to herself, she added, "But I didn't have time to ask my dad before he left."

Jess took another sip of her wine. Maybe it was the wine or maybe Drew just had a way of making people relax. Jess began thinking it wasn't so bad that Shelly's boss depended on her, at least this one time.

It was an hour and a half and two glasses of wine later that Jess said, "I've got to go home! My cat is very possessive. She'll be scolding me all the way from the front door to the kitchen for coming home late." She also thought to herself, "I have to stop here, or I'm going to lose sight of the fact that I hardly know you and that we work in the same office suite!"

"Oh," Drew said, "you have a cat! I used to have a cat, but I lost it in the divorce. She's a gray tabby."

"Yet another positive feature about Drew," Jess thought. She found it not unusual for married men to be as friendly as unmarried men. To put it mildly, she preferred the latter. "A lot of those good points right in a row—it has to be the wine. If I have more, I'll be in big trouble," she thought to herself.

"It's nice to have a warm, furry person at home," she said. "Even though I say that Reesa is possessive, she's also very affectionate. The good thing about having a cat is that when I have a tough day in court, she doesn't care, unlike some of my clients. And even though she sometimes needs a babysitter, she doesn't want to go to college."

Drew smiled and Jess fumbled in her purse for her keys. She wanted to make sure she got downstairs to her car and made it home alone. She liked Drew, but it wasn't as though she didn't get frequent offers. The law business is still a man's world, so Jess met many men in her job, and many of them, even some opposing lawyers who had an opportunity to meet her socially, were not bashful about making passes at an attractive, accomplished lady lawyer.

"Thanks so much for the wine and hors d'oeuvres, Drew. It was very pleasant and nice meeting you officially. I have a brief to get out tomorrow, and I need to be up and at it early in the morning. See you later." She stood up and walked out at what she hoped was a dignified pace, although after two glasses of wine, she wasn't positive that it was. Drew's eyes trailed her out.

Chapter Seven

Jess got out of the garage elevator on floor F. She was glad she'd gotten in early this morning and had been able to park where she didn't have to walk far from the elevator to get to her car. She preferred not to come down to the garage after six thirty in the evening when it was devoid of humans except for the occasional workaholic like her. She walked quickly to her silver Toyota Camry, opened the door with the remote control, got in, and pushed the lock button.

As Jess drove out of the Columbia Tower underground parking, she was glad that she was familiar with the route. Streets in downtown Seattle are often designated one-way streets. The designations alternate either east and west or north and south, *mostly*. Just to make it difficult, though, the city throws in a few two-way streets and some streets in succession designated the same way. A person could find herself driving around in circles if she didn't know where she was going. "I would have had a little trouble negotiating the one-ways tonight if I wasn't so familiar with the streets," she thought.

Jess turned left out of the Columbia Tower lot, going up the hill on Cherry. Since her condominium was on First and Blanchard, the first turn up the hill and away from the waters of Puget Sound was counterintuitive. She turned right on Sixth, right again on James, and down the hill to First. "It's the scenic tour of downtown Seattle," she thought to herself.

She often thought of the phrase she had learned in law school that helped her negotiate the streets of downtown Seattle: "Jesus

Christ made Seattle under protest." When going south to north on the numbered streets of downtown Seattle, which are labeled avenues, not streets, a person first passes James, then Cherry, Columbia, Marion, Madison, Spring, Seneca, University, Union, Pike, and Pine, in that order. "Such valuable things you learn in law school," she chuckled. Thankfully, all the streets in the mnemonic are actually labeled "streets." It's a difference of little note, except when you find yourself on a "street" looking for an address that's really on an "avenue" of the same name somewhere in the Seattle area.

On nights like these Jess was really glad that she had driven to work rather than walking and that she could leave from one garage and arrive in another. It's typically raining in Seattle, sometimes even in July, and tonight the rain was being driven by wind. It was blowing hard enough that the umbrellas of most of those walking on the sidewalks were either inverted or totally closed because their owners had given up trying to keep them right side out. "The wind usually doesn't blow this hard until October or November," Jess thought.

Well past Pine Street, Jess turned left on Blanchard toward the water and then into the alley, opening the garage door with her remote control. Inside the garage, the driveway was winding, so she had to be on the lookout for cars coming around the corner. She never really got used to using the mirrors that were supposed to let you look around the corner, and she was *really* not very good at using them after two glasses of wine.

On the way up the elevator, she was thinking about her conversation with Drew. "Maybe it wasn't *just* the wine. Maybe he really does have a way of making people feel comfortable."

As Jess approached her door to her condominium, she paused. Was it partially ajar? The door sometimes didn't latch when you closed it, so people who weren't familiar with it might not be aware that it didn't latch. "But then, why would someone unfamiliar with the door be using it?" she thought. She certainly wasn't expecting anyone. "And I'm pretty sure that it wasn't Reesa," she thought. Reesa could open doors with oblong handles by jumping up and catching them with her paws. Knowing this, Jess always locked the deadbolt from the outside when leaving. "No one gets past the doorman and up to the twenty-seventh floor in a high-rise apartment," Jess thought to herself. Security was the main reason she had bought this particular condo.

Just the same, Jess pushed the door forward to see if it would open without her key. "It is open!" She hesitated slightly and made the split-second decision to shove the door open hard. "If someone is in there, he would have heard me open the door, and might even be standing behind it." The wine clouding her judgment, she began to think about Reesa. "Where is she? Could someone have hurt her?"

When the door banged against the doorstop, she considered what to do next. Just then Paul and Teresa, her twenty-something yuppie neighbors, came out of the elevator. Paul was a regular visitor to the condo gym and looked like he pumped iron when he was there.

Relieved, Jess turned to Paul and Teresa and said, "Hi, I'm your neighbor Jess Lamm in 2703. I just got home, and I'm a little worried to go into my apartment because the door wasn't fully latched. It's probably just because I didn't pull it closed this morning, but I don't really think I did that. I usually pull it closed pretty hard. Would you mind standing here at the doorway while I go in and make sure that no one is in there?"

Teresa said, "Sure, we know who you are. We've seen you coming and going. Paul, I have my cell phone. Why don't you go in with Jess, leave the door open, and I'll get ready to call 911 if anything happens." For a split second, Paul looked as though he wasn't so sure he wanted to be the hero, but he screwed up his courage and said, "Sure." Even as recent as a few years ago, Paul had been known to get into scuffles on early Saturday mornings when the bars were closing, and he had never felt over-matched.

Jess turned on the light, and she and Paul crept down the hallway. She laughed at herself as they went. "As though a burglar wouldn't know we were coming after I turned on the light," she thought. Reaching the end of the entryway, she gasped at what she saw. The couch and loveseat were slashed to bits, and the pillows were all over the floor. "Reesa can be peevish when I come home late, but she isn't this strong," Jess thought. Proceeding around the next corner to the kitchen, she peeked over the granite counter top. One cupboard was open, and she saw her Waterford glasses in pieces on the floor. Fortunately, they were well into the kitchen, not at the refrigerator where Jess kept Reesa's Good Kitty dishes. Jess thought about Reesa lapping up food or water with glass in it. "Reesa! Reesa!" she shrieked. "Where are you, kitty?" There was cat vomit on the floor leading into the bedroom. Forgetting again that she should be cautious, Jess tore into the bedroom and saw a lump in the middle of her bed. It was right where an X would cross if you drew it from corner to corner. Jess hesitated a second, and then, gathering her courage, she pulled the quilt up and saw two yellow eyes looking back at her.

She reached in and pulled Reesa out from under the quilt. Reesa was so pleased to see her mom that she didn't dig in her heels as much as she usually did when being pulled out of a hiding place. "She's a good guard cat, but I'm glad she prefers to guard from a secure location," Jess thought.

Even though Reesa was very opinionated, she got over things easily, and soon Jess heard and felt Reesa's "motor" purring. Reesa was clearly saying, "Glad to see it's you, Mom!" She jumped out of Jess's arms onto the carpet and started diligently cleaning herself. Jess tried hard not to show the lump in her throat and the tears in her eyes. She hoped Paul wasn't noticing what a crybaby she was over a mere cat.

In short order, Jess and Paul checked out the rest of the condo. It didn't take long because the condo was only 825 square feet—essentially an open circle around a central core, with glass hip-high to the ceiling on the two outside walls. Built for no more than two, or two and a pet, the only room in the condo with doors was the bathroom.

After Paul and Teresa left, Jess called the police and a locksmith. She also decided to find out how the heck the intruder got past the doorman. One of them was on duty twenty-four hours a day. Obviously they weren't the secret service, but the building also had security cameras in the garage, which was a principal reason she bought this place right out of law school. It had cost her an arm and a leg, and there was no way she could have afforded it if she hadn't had the gift from her uncle as the down payment. Deciding to use the money as a down payment had been a tough choice, since at the time she also had thousands of dollars of student loans to pay.

She'd never had a problem with security before. "My god, the condo is on the twenty-seventh floor!" she ruminated again. "How could anybody get in?" As an attorney, Jess was used to dealing with threats. Lawyers often play games in the course of their jobs as advocates for their clients. Those games were at work, though—having your home invaded was something entirely different.

Chapter Eight

Both Jess and her partner Danni were used to the rough and tumble of the law business. A lawyer doesn't survive in personal injury and medical malpractice work without learning how to handle the lawyer tactics, or as Jess and Danni called them, the "lawyer crap."

But early in her career, Jess had found lawyer crap amazingly stupid. "Stupid, stupid, stupid, stupid!" was the best description she could come up with one day when she'd had a particularly difficult deposition during which the defense lawyer tried every trick in the book—yelling, pounding on the table, shaking his fist, and constantly interrupting her questioning with objections and instructions to the witness. She knew his actions were designed to make it more difficult for her to discover the facts, but it seemed just plain stupid to live your life this way. She wondered if she was really cut out for this work.

Jess had decided to get into the field of medical malpractice because she was impressed by her uncle, the same one who had given her the gift when she graduated from law school. Uncle Frank had been a malpractice lawyer most of his career, and Jess was secretly proud of how he really helped people. She kept her thoughts to herself because most non-lawyers that she knew bought into the cliché promoted by insurers, that malpractice attorneys were greedy, ambulance-chasing ghouls.

But after spending a day at the end of an entire week of depositions filled with lawyer crap, Jess decided to call Uncle Frank and ask him if he thought the job was really worth it. He was an advocate through and through and really did believe the effort was worth it.

"In 1999, even the Institute of Medicine agreed there were 98,000 premature deaths a year caused by medical errors," Uncle Frank told Jess. "You know that they weren't reporting high. It's not getting any better, probably worse. If we don't keep 'em honest, who will?" Uncle Frank gave his usual pitch.

"I know, but there has to be a better way. This is stupid! Most of the defense attorneys I deal with would never do what they do in front of their mothers!" Jess said.

Uncle Frank smiled. He'd had the same thoughts when he was a young lawyer. "Look, Jess," he said, "you know they're not the only ones. We do it too."

Jess turned slightly red. She knew she had tried these games. Most everyone did, so why not?

Uncle Frank continued, "We aren't trying to change the whole world, just the portion that we can affect. We can affect how patients and how malpractice victims are treated, and in order to do that we have to work within the system. We didn't create the judicial system, they did. You think the people who make the decisions at insurance companies don't plan on making it as hard as possible to build a case? You think the fact they chose defense lawyers who are best at hiding facts is by chance? You think if they really wanted to change things with the number of lobbyists there are in Washington, it wouldn't happen? No, they fight tooth and nail until the last dog is dead, and then they point the finger at us and claim we're making health care too expensive. Some day it might change, but I'm not holding my breath."

Whenever she had a particularly tough day, Jess thought about the people that she helped. Most of the time she thought the job was really worth it. In fact, when she had talked Danni into starting a practice with her, Jess had used the same logic that Uncle Frank had.

Jess knew Danni from law school She was a dark-haired version of Jess, though she was a little more athletic, and she kept her curly hair shorter, no longer than her jaw. Danni and Dave, her husband, spent a couple of hours a week in the gym and a few more outside on bikes. Her athletic build further accentuated her buxom figure. Immediately after graduation, Danni had gone to a large insurance defense firm in town, or as Jess liked to call it, the "dark side." Despite her job, Danni had the same fever for helping people that infected Jess. While working for the defense firm, Danni concentrated on the difficulties the medical care system placed on her own clients, the nurses and doctors.

Because of her focus on the defense side, Danni saw the justification for the tactics she had learned to use, the tactics to hide the "bad facts." Jess insisted that every case she brought had bad facts. "Hell," she said, "you think that we can afford to bring a case that doesn't have bad facts? These cases cost a fortune! You know that, but you may not have focused on it since the insurance companies pay defense counsels' costs. We advance anywhere from $75,000 for a relatively simple case to $150,000 or more for a complex one."

Danni insisted that there weren't bad facts—that there were only people caught up in situations that they couldn't control. The nurse who gave the wrong drug, didn't use the sterile technique when changing a bandage, or didn't turn the patient often enough to prevent a bedsore usually really wanted to do things right. She just didn't have the time to do all that she was supposed to do. Sure, there were a few bad apples, but that was far from the norm; people going into health care generally wanted to help others. Sometimes the errors in care didn't make a huge difference, making it even easier for Danni to justify their defense. Her clients certainly wanted to downplay or even hide the bad facts because they didn't want to advertise these errors. They were embarrassing and might even lead to the defendant losing his or her job.

Jess's clincher, the argument that convinced Danni to come over from the "dark side" was this: "I know they're just trying to do their jobs, but why should their jobs be so tough so a fat cat CEO can make a big bonus. I know from when I was a nurse! There just isn't time enough to do everything. I didn't realize until I went to law school that it was actually the duty of corporate CEOs to make profit for their shareholders.

"People don't seem to understand that corporations aren't supposed to be run for the benefit of the public and certainly not the employees. It makes me especially mad when I think about the effect of cutting corners on patients' health. Unfortunately, when things go wrong, it starts out at the level of the nurse or doctor who is sometimes just a cog in the corporate wheel of an increasingly crazy medical care system. I know you read Robin Cook. He agrees and he's a doctor!

"You have to keep your eye on the system. No one is going to change it unless someone brings the facts to light. If we don't show the public what really happens in these situations, they won't know. Most people wouldn't think that someone's bonus is worth the risk of death to their loved one. She finished with Uncle Frank's favorite argument. "We can't change the world all at once. We have to do it a little at a time."

"Boy, when you get on your soap box, you're really convincing," Danni said. After discussing the logistics of setting up their own firm, primarily the huge amount of money necessary to carry the firm between recoveries, Danni agreed to come over from the "dark side."

Being a plaintiff's firm, Lamm Patrick didn't recover a fee unless Jess or Danni won or settled a case. This contingent fee system developed because most people live paycheck to paycheck, and by the time the out-of-work victim makes it to an attorney, he generally has no money. The attorney must bankroll the huge fees of the expert witnesses who aren't willing to help victims' lawyers for nothing. These doctors get nothing but crap from their colleagues for helping them. At the very least they can be socially shunned, and they may suffer financially if their colleagues decide to send them fewer referrals. There are some "hired guns," doctors who testify against doctors for a living, and these guys in particular aren't willing to work for nothing.

The lawyers take their fee from the money paid by the defendants' insurance company. It always aggravated Jess that the insurance companies tout how much money trial lawyers make. They don't talk about insurance company profits or how their scorched earth tactics drive up the cost of lawsuits.

Since a new case represents a huge investment of time and money, Danni and Jess always review the medical information with great care before filing a suit. When they started their own firm, Jess—with her nursing background—tried to do a lot of the record review to avoid unnecessary cash outlay, and Danni had developed a fair amount of medical knowledge through on the job training. As they got busier, Jess and Danni had less and less time to review the files themselves, so they generally liked to consult with a nurse. At $150 to $300 an hour, her time was a lot less expensive than a doctor's time.

Fortunately Jess and Danni had been in the medical malpractice business long enough to have developed relationships with some physicians who would give them an overall view of a case without requiring big money up front. But even these more helpful physicians wouldn't sign affidavits for court filing without being paid large fees because of the potential risk to their social and financial well-being.

Chapter Nine

Since their income was tied to the case results, Jess and Danni often discussed their cases with each other, particularly when the case was new or when problems developed. These discussions not only kept each partner up to date on the financial situation, they also provided a listening post for problem issues. Jess often repeated the old axiom, "When you're up to your ass in alligators, it's hard to remember that you came to drain the swamp." Of course, Jess talked to Danni before taking on the case of *Thompson v. The Peoples Hospital of Seattle and Haseem*, in particular because the record was too sparse to tell what really occurred. They knew this meant the financial risk was more serious than the normal case, but they decided to go ahead.

Jess and Danni were both familiar with the background of Peoples Hospital. It had been named by the Catholic nuns who had run it before it was purchased roughly two years ago by a for-profit hospital group headquartered in Virginia. Virginia-American Hospital Corporation, frequently called VAHC, had started in Virginia and rapidly grown into a nationwide organization, acquiring failing hospitals as it spread. Its critics claimed that the acronym VAHC aptly described the way the corporation sucked charity out of the hospitals it acquired. Its supporters countered that VAHC had just learned to operate hospitals like a business.

The name of the local hospital—Peoples Hospital—described the goal that the Catholic nuns had set in operating the hospital. They had concentrated on providing care to anyone who walked through the door. Unfortunately that model no longer worked for Peoples Hospital in the modern health care environment—the hospital was hovering near bankruptcy when VAHC purchased it. VAHC didn't change the name of the Seattle hospital, but it certainly had changed its method of operation.

Danni and Jess also discussed the effect of the new law coming into effect in June with the sparse hospital record. Jess hardly had to explain to Danni what her concerns were. They agreed that they should file the suit and include the hospital and the doctor before the law became effective, even though they would have preferred to investigate further.

After discussing the case, Danni asked Jess, "Do you know who will be representing Peoples?"

"I think it's going to be Will Baker," said Jess. "He appeared in the last few cases I've had against that hospital. This is going to be a tough one."

Danni knew what Jess meant. Baker was one of those guys who was really good in the litigation war. Danni had once joked that his name was Will "No-fishing" Baker, after the standard argument that defense lawyers make when trying to prevent disclosure of bad facts. Jess just called him "asshole." Baker was one of the best at thinking up reasons for not producing information. Opposing counsel could always count on two or three trips to court before forcing him to hand over the information they needed and had a right to obtain.

Just to keep his opponent off guard, Baker sometimes changed from asshole mode to nice guy mode. That was when you really had to be careful, because Baker could change his approach within minutes. This was especially disarming because Baker's appearance was that of a nice guy. He was about five-foot-seven, probably weighed a hundred and fifty pounds, had brown hair with specks of gray around the sides, was in superb condition, and generally wore slacks and a sweater for depositions. The relaxed appearance was especially effective because it belied the relentless nature underneath. It also lent credibility to the outrage that could rear its head at any moment. The uninitiated and sometimes even the pros tended to believe that anger in such a nice guy must be warranted. In court, of course, a male attorney wouldn't consider wearing anything less than a sport coat, and Baker usually appeared in a dark suit to emphasize his professional nature.

Jess wondered if he really wasn't just schizophrenic.

Chapter Ten

It was Tuesday morning, the morning after the break-in at Jess's condominium. She thought about her discussion with the officer as she drove to her office. Since nothing seemed to be missing from her condo, he had questioned her about angry boyfriends. The officer seemed pretty insistent about it since this would also explain why the doorman didn't notice any strangers passing through the lobby on the way to the elevator. The problem with that theory was that at present Jess didn't have any "significant others"—as she preferred to call them—and hadn't been serious about anyone for at least a year.

Jess formed the strong impression that her report to the police would go nowhere. That made her doubly glad that she had insisted that the locksmith come out last night to change the lock and install another deadbolt that worked from the inside only, for when she was at home. Her front door was beginning to remind her of the doors she had seen in movies about the rough side of New York. The emergency call for the locksmith had been expensive, but at least it gave her some peace of mind. Now she only needed to get a new couch and let her friends and family know that her Waterford glasses were gone. That would give them an easy gift for special occasions.

Well, mostly she would have to let her friends know. The only family she had was her mother, and she lived in Minnesota with her new husband. Jess saw her only at Christmas. And she hadn't seen her biological father since he left her and her mother when she was ten, which was why her mother had insisted that Jess go to nursing school. She frequently told Jess, "You should have an education in case you need to support yourself." After Jess had gone to nursing school, found out that she didn't like it, and graduated from law school, she wondered why she hadn't realized earlier the limiting effects of her mother's point of view. Jess's mother clearly thought, whether she knew it or not, that the only "real" job for women was staying at home and having babies. Jess preferred being a lawyer.

It was later than her usual eight o'clock when Jess got to her office, and she was carrying much more baggage than her usual briefcase and purse. She had Reesa with her in a carrying case riding on top of a contraption similar to a baby buggy, which was also carrying Reesa's litter box and food. Jess decided she couldn't risk leaving Reesa home alone until she had a better idea about why her condo had been ransacked. Contrary to the police officer's conclusion, Jess thought that the break-in was more likely connected to the Peoples Hospital case.

She was still mulling over the situation when she stepped out of the elevator onto the forty-second floor. Attempting to maneuver Reesa's carriage, she almost ran into Drew. Looking at the baby buggy, he gave a big smile and said, "Now, this is news!"

Not wanting to try to explain in the hallway, Jess invited Drew into her office. As she was getting Reesa's litter box out, Drew went to the coffee room to put water in one of the Good Kitty dishes. If she hadn't known that Drew was a cat person, Jess would've been a little embarrassed by all the special cat paraphernalia she brought to the office with Reesa. When the litter box, food, and water were organized, Jess sat down in her office chair, and Drew took up the "client's seat" on the other side of the desk. Reesa—the ungrateful cat—walked over and rubbed against Drew's legs.

Once Jess had explained what had happened, Drew was more concerned about the break-in than Reesa's safety but decided not to express that opinion right away. It might come out wrong, considering the length of their relationship, so he made conversation about Reesa while he absorbed the information about the break-in.

Jess explained that Reesa was short for *res ipsa loquitur*, a Latin name for a legal theory, which of course Drew was familiar with. She told him that she had adopted Reesa from the humane society just after her first big case involving *res ipsa*. Drew smiled. "The old barrel case, huh?" he said, referring to the facts in the famous case that the theory came from.

Res ipsa loquitur literally means "the thing speaks for itself." The phrase was coined by the judge in an ancient case involving a person injured by a barrel rolling out of a warehouse. The defendant in the case acknowledged that it was his duty to keep the barrel under control, but no one could explain how the barrel happened to get away. As a result, the defendant claimed, the plaintiff couldn't prove that the defendant was negligent. It's ordinarily the plaintiff's duty to prove negligence, which generally involves proving the acts leading to an accident. The court thought that was unfair in this instance. Thus, the court determined that since the accident was caused by the barrel, which was under the control of the defendant, the barrel wouldn't be rolling around unguided if the defendant hadn't been negligent. The result allowed the plaintiff to prove his case, whereas he otherwise wouldn't have been able to do so.

Jess smiled. Despite her concern over her cat and the break-in, a little levity was nice. She hadn't found a lot of men who seemed to appreciate legal jokes. "And," Jess said, "I sure didn't realize at the time how well the name fit for Reesa. She really does speak for herself, and she lets you know when she isn't happy. Her vet calls her 'the mouth.'"

"My cat was the same way. I could always tell what she wanted, but she kept her instructions short. I think she felt she had to do that when talking to humans. I could almost hear her thoughts about how slow people are."

Jess laughed. "Right, I think Reesa has the same opinion."

"Well, tell me, what did the police say about the break-in?" Drew asked, steering the conversation to the more serious issue.

Jess explained that the police thought it must have been the work of a disgruntled boyfriend. She frowned as she spoke, adding that it might be a logical suggestion if she had a recent boyfriend but that she hadn't dated anyone seriously for a over a year.

Drew smiled again. "Ms. Jessica," he said, "that is hard for me to believe."

Jess felt that premature menopause reaction coming on again and decided to change the subject. Focusing back on the Thompson case, Jess explained, "I know that it seems hard to believe, but I think that the break-in might be related to the case that I have against Peoples Hospital."

"Peoples Hospital—isn't that the one that was taken over by a national hospital group a couple of years back?" Drew asked.

"Yes, it was. The parent corporation is Virginia-American Hospital Corporation. I get a real kick out of that name, since its initials are VAHC. Who in their right mind would insist on keeping 'Virginia' in that name after going nationwide?" Jess chuckled. "It's such a set up for jokes about a giant corporation vacuuming up hospitals. I guess their CEO is really proud of being from Virginia and won't let that part of the name go. I even got a call from their counsel, Will Baker, about that. He said that he needed an agreed order to confirm that I wouldn't mention anything about vacuum jokes in court, and if I didn't agree to an order he would make a motion for one. He is such a jerk, and this was one of the few times I have heard him sound sheepish." Jess chuckled again.

Both Jess and Drew grinned as they pictured Will Baker having to explain to the judge that she should enter an order prohibiting anyone from using the word "vacuum" in relation to his client. Of course, he could just ask Jess to agree that she wouldn't use the acronym for the hospital. The reason that Baker wanted a court order was so that if anyone made such statements the court could order punishment of the person, such as assessment of terms—a legal word for fines. Jess and Drew also both knew that the reason Baker had called Jess instead of just making the motion was that the court rules required him to. The rule was designed to limit the number of motions that judges have to deal with. They also knew that the judge would probably grant such an order if Jess wouldn't agree to it, so there wasn't much point in her resisting Baker's request.

Absent the rule requiring him to call, Baker probably would have just spit out one of his canned motions suggesting that Jess wouldn't agree to a reasonable request, and Jess would have been required to take the time to write a brief in response and possibly even attend a hearing on the subject if the two lawyers couldn't reach agreement on an order. This is a good way to make a plaintiff's lawyer spend time on a case, which works to the benefit of defense counsel, since plaintiff's lawyers are paid by the case and defense lawyers are paid by the hour.

Jess and Drew also got a chuckle out of the fact that the rule cramped Baker's style. Both knew him as a hard-charging, take-no-prisoners kind of attorney. "You called him a jerk," Drew said. "I generally call him an asshole."

"Well, I generally do too, especially just after I've talked to him," Jess grinned. "But I was using my clean language since I don't know you that well."

"Well, then you won't blush when I tell you about one of my clients, the Friends University of Central Kansas," Drew laughed.

Mouthing F-U-C-K Jess laughed and said, "You're kidding!" Jess also thought that she must have "blushed herself out" in the last twenty-four hours with Drew.

"You're right—just checking whether you were paying attention," Drew said. "But seriously," he continued, "you know I'm a business litigator so obviously I know nothing about medical malpractice theory. I'm a good listener though, and I do know a little about the law. Why don't you run by me whatever it is that's bothering you about the case. Maybe I can add something. I certainly don't have any attorney-client relationship with Peoples or VAHC, and I don't represent any doctors."

Jess knew that Drew had more than a little knowledge about the law. She wasn't the only one whose name had appeared in the bar journal. She also appreciated the opportunity to talk about the case. Like most attorneys, she generally found a new point of view helpful. But the fact that attorneys can't disclose client secrets to others means that the number of persons with whom an attorney can discuss the nitty-gritty of a case is limited, and under these circumstances, Drew would be required to keep any client secrets confidential. Jess launched into her story.

She had issued the usual interrogatories and requests for production—written questions and requests for records or other documents. The problem was that sometimes it's tough to ask the right questions. And the opponent surely wouldn't help. For example, if Jess asked for the number of patients at Peoples who died after cardiac arrest, she'd get a long rendition about protection of patient privacy and, since death by cardiac arrest can occur without negligence, a canned response about how the request is overly wide in scope, overly burdensome to obtain, and not reasonably calculated to lead to the discovery of admissible evidence—the "it's a fishing expedition" response.

In order to avoid this problem, Jess had honed down the request and thought about asking for the number of people who died of a stroke associated with a code. "Wrong!" she'd thought to herself. "That won't work. Stroke *after* a code is a known risk." Jess knew asking that question would be a setup for another response about patient privacy, onerous requests, and fishing expeditions.

She had tried to avoid all of this likely give-and-take by making her questions really narrow from the beginning and taking the risk that John Peterson's interpretation of the autopsy was right—that the stroke occurred early in the code and actually caused Brad's death. Either there were no deaths by strokes occurring at the beginning of codes, or the hospital wasn't telling about those episodes. The answer that Jess received to this interrogatory was a flat "none."

Knowing that one form of discovery or a particular question might not reveal the critical information, most lawyers—including Jess—ask a canned interrogatory about possible witnesses, requesting the names and contact information of people who would know about the issues in the case. This time Jess asked for the names and contact information of those working in the ER at the time of Brad's death. This was especially important because for some reason the person who recorded the events of the code hadn't signed the record, even though there was a place for a signature on the form.

Jess had received Baker's canned response about fishing expeditions and a grudging list of names, but this time Jess was thinking that there might be some information out there that she was getting close to. In particular, the head nurse in the ER who was there the afternoon of Brad's death was apparently no longer working at the hospital, and Jess had been trying to find her without success. With a name like Joyce Brown, she was pretty hard to trace without help from the hospital. Jess had a motion pending to require the hospital to produce Brown's employment records to help Jess locate her. In fact, that motion was set for the next day.

Since Jess wasn't able to locate Ms. Brown, she hadn't been able to dig out the information that she knew must be there to verify her hunch about the hospital. She needed that information now, and she also needed a doctor's opinion to verify her hunch. Time was getting short: the summary judgment was scheduled for hearing, and her response brief and affidavits were due next Monday. Jess either needed the information necessary to obtain a doctor's affidavit about the merits of the case, or the case would be dismissed.

Chapter Eleven

It wasn't just the presuit events that made the Peoples Hospital case different. Even though it had been six months ago, the event was so unusual that it really stood out in Jess's mind. She thought back on Dr. Haseem's deposition, as she summarized it for Drew. Jess had scheduled the deposition to occur in her conference room, as usual. She had planned on five people being present: Will Baker, Dr. Haseem, Jess, Mary Thompson, and a court reporter.

When the parties appeared at Jess's office, there was one additional person, who Will Baker introduced as Lars Hansen. "That's unusual since Dr. Haseem is the witness," Jess thought. "He's certainly allowed to attend under the rules, but it's amazing he's spending his time here. He is *really* hands-on." In this case, Dr. Haseem and Peoples Hospital were both parties. Hansen, of course, was appearing for the hospital.

Jess and Mary sat down on one side of the table, with Jess closest to the court reporter at the head of the table, and with Dr. Haseem on the other side. Baker sat down next to Haseem, and Hansen took a seat at the end of the table, directly opposite the court reporter.

Once the deposition started, it became clear why Hansen had come. Immediately after the witness was sworn in—affirming that he would tell the truth, the whole truth, and nothing but the truth—Dr. Haseem turned to look at Lars Hansen before he answered almost every question. "How odd," Jess thought. "Normally a witness looks to his attorney, if anyone, when concerned about answering a question."

Anytime Haseem hesitated before he answered, which was a lot since he was so tentative, Baker would throw in an objection. Some of the objections were designed to guide the witness's answer, such as "Objection, asked and answered. Dr. Haseem already said that he followed protocol." Some were just designed to interrupt the flow of questions. In any event, the end result was that all that contention caused the deposition to go on for hours, and Dr. Haseem was sweating so profusely that he had to take off his sport coat just thirty minutes after it started.

When the objections got so frequent that Jess commented on them, Baker became even more agitated and responded with the oft-used attack, "I am aware of the requirements of the rules, even if you aren't Ms. Lamm." As he said this, he pounded on the table to emphasize his point.

Jess interrupted her rendition of the deposition to say to Drew, "I always wonder when guys are pounding the table or shaking fists at women lawyers if they do that kind of macho shit to their wives." Drew smiled thinking of his younger days when he had tried the same tactics in depositions. He had long since decided that life was too short to play those games.

Jess proceeded with her discussion of the Haseem deposition. At the usual midmorning break to the deposition, Haseem, Baker, and Hansen met in the hallway to discuss the issues raised by the questioning. The extraordinary thing was that Baker and Hansen did all the talking. It was quite a scene—the tall sport-coated blond directing the conversation and the shorter, sweatered attorney looking up at him, totally ignoring the witness. "Very strange," thought Jess, viewing through the conference room window. "Does Hansen put all the words in Haseem's mouth?"

Since the defendants and court reporter were out of the room, Mary and Jess made conversation. "I didn't remember quite how tall Mr. Hansen was, but I do remember that sport coat—or maybe they all look alike. He looks like such a nice man, it's hard to believe that he wrote the letter you showed me. That was very different from the attitude he had after Brad's death."

Shortly, the "bad guys" and the court reporter came back into the conference room. The rest of the deposition proceeded as the first part: Jess asking questions; Dr. Haseem looking at Mr. Hansen, sometimes directly and sometimes out of the corner of his eye; and Baker frequently making objections.

In any event, Jess was able to find out that Dr. Omar Haseem had graduated from medical school in Baghdad, and he had been practicing medicine in Baghdad when the U.S. troops arrived. The chaos that ensued never subsided, and even got worse. He and other health care professionals began receiving death threats. He tried to ignore the threats because he felt that he owed it to his people to stay and treat them, but the threats grew worse and worse. Several doctors from his hospital were kidnapped by Shi'ite militia members, and they turned up dead later. His wife, Fatimeh, could no longer teach because her school had been closed. The student attendance had trickled to nothing because it was too dangerous to attend.

In 2004, Dr. Haseem and his wife fled Iraq. Though they weren't particularly religious and didn't even follow most tenets of the Muslim religion, their first names identified them as Sunni Muslims. In Iraq, that was enough to warrant a death threat from the opposing Shi'ites. The Haseems had settled in Jordan briefly and then moved to the U.S. with the help of Mr. Hansen, whom Dr. Haseem had met previously when he was in the U.S. completing his residency in emergency room medicine.

Dr. Haseem insisted that he had "followed code protocol" when treating Mr. Thompson. He was so eager to tell Jess this that he blurted it out in answer to a question about whether he remembered the day that Mr. Thompson came to the hospital. Jess was certain that Dr. Haseem had been thoroughly coached in his testimony.

When questioned about his care of Mr. Thompson, the deposition of Dr. Haseem's testimony sunk to a new low. Despite repeated questioning on the subject, Dr. Haseem insisted that he "did not recall" the details of the treatment in the ER the day that Mr. Thompson died. Yes, Mr. Thompson's heart had restarted, but Dr. Haseem "did not recall" when. The nurse who was recording the events of the code should have recorded when the heart restarted.

Dr. Haseem acknowledged that it was his common practice to run out EKG strips at critical points of the code, and he probably did during Brad Thompson's code. If they weren't in the record that Jess received, maybe they were separated from the file. The recorder is usually a nurse—in this instance probably the head nurse for that shift, Joyce Brown—but Dr. Haseem insisted that he couldn't remember for certain who it was and couldn't tell from the record. He admitted that he would have expected more detailed records.

Dr. Haseem also couldn't remember why he had waited until the very end of the code to give sodium bicarbonate again; that would depend on when the heart restarted. Dr. Haseem agreed that a doctor would not ordinarily give sodium bicarbonate once the heart restarted because there would be a danger that the blood pH would swing too far. He wouldn't have given the sodium bicarbonate at the end of the code under normal circumstances, if the heart was then beating normally, so the heart probably wasn't beating normally, but he couldn't recall what the rhythm was at that time.

In contrast to his lack of memory regarding the care of Mr. Thompson, Dr. Haseem was certain about what had occurred during his conversation with Mrs. Thompson. Dr. Haseem agreed that he might have said "resuscitated" or "sorry"—he often did try to show sympathy to the family members after the death of a loved one. When asked if he said to Mrs. Thompson, "This should not have happened," Dr. Haseem paused even longer than usual and, after looking at Hansen, insisted that he did not make that statement.

Aside from looking at Lars Hansen before answering each question, Dr. Haseem simply stared at the table. His voice was so low that he could hardly be heard, and the court reporter repeatedly asked Dr. Haseem to speak up.

Mary, who was listening to Dr. Haseem, alternately looked pale white and then mad red. Jess took a break from the deposition to talk to Mary in the hall. "How can he say those things! I know what I heard. How can he not remember about Brad's care! It was Brad's life!" Mary exploded. She and Jess decided Mary should leave the deposition; she had heard enough. Like Mary, Jess had the distinct impression that Dr. Haseem was lying.

Chapter Twelve

Eyeing the clock on the bookcase behind Drew, Jess noticed that it was now nine twenty in the morning. She decided she should wrap up this rendition of the case. She felt guilty about taking up so much of Drew's time. He didn't seem troubled about that, so she mentioned her concern. "I feel guilty about keeping you. You must have a dozen things sitting on your desk that you're worrying about."

"Not a problem," Drew said. "I just finished a two week trial, and I've decided that I owe myself a little R 'n R."

To himself, Drew thought, "That's something I should have made a practice of before—taking time off." Like Jess and Danni, Drew had also been with a large firm for the first several years of his practice. Focused on becoming a good trial lawyer, Drew worked sixty hours a week. He was especially driven to achieve because he had chosen the law business over his father's software business in California. Drew's father, of course, was extremely unhappy about his insistence on becoming lawyer. Every time they saw each other before his father's death some two years ago, his father would remind him that there was a place for him in the software business. It was not until his father's death, which was followed shortly by Drew's separation from his wife, Sherri, that Drew decided he had spent more than enough time concentrating on his law business and needed to pay a little more attention to the people around him. This wasn't so easy to do at that point, since he had lost the two most important people in his life—one was dead, and the other had tired of his neglect.

Drew had been more than successful making a name for himself in the law business. He had the kind of brain power that allowed him to do whatever he focused on, and he had been extremely focused. When his father died, that focus wavered to the point that he decided he needed a break from the constant running from one thing to another. He had taken a leave of absence from his law firm to go to Europe for three months. At first he thought he'd spend some of the money his father left him, but that got old fast. He didn't find Europe very satisfying all by himself. Not that he really lacked for lady friends, but Drew did feel alone. He was used to spending a lot of time alone since he had been so focused on his work, but none of the women he met filled the hole he was becoming aware of, and he began to wonder if there was a better way to live his life. Returning to Seattle, Drew had decided he needed to be somewhere that people weren't living the same dogged pursuit of success that he had been living. That was why he had left the old law firm and moved to the Columbia Tower.

He didn't talk about why he had made that transition, as he was sure that anyone he told would mimic playing the violin and call him a "poor little rich guy."

"Poor little rich guys need love too," he thought, but chose to avoid that conversation.

Drew was beginning to be glad that he had made the move. He had come up with the idea from thinking about his father's favorite saying: "The definition of insanity is continuing to do the same thing and expecting a different result." Drew wished he had paid more attention to his father's advice when he was alive.

"No, don't worry about the time," Drew said. "I'm enjoying this." A little surprised, but pleased, Jess continued.

Chapter Thirteen

Following up on instinct driven by events at the Haseem deposition, Jess noted the deposition of Lars Hansen. Ordinarily she wouldn't have thought People's CEO would have anything to offer in this lawsuit, but he seemed to inject himself at every turn. This time, only he and Baker appeared for the deposition. "Guess Haseem isn't running this lawsuit," Jess thought.

Mr. Hansen was extremely pleasant in his demeanor—so much so that Jess thought her diabetes would have been acting up if she had the disease. He testified that he had a master's degree in hospital administration with an emphasis in finance and that he had originally started with Virginia-American at a small Kentucky hospital seventeen years ago. After three years there, he had moved up within the company to Virginia where he became a billing liaison between VAHC and federal regulators. While with VAHC, he had met his wife Anika and risen in the organization until he reported directly to the CEO. He claimed that he had come to Seattle because he wanted a more hands-on position. He admitted that he had taken a significant cut in pay to make the move but insisted that it was worth it to be able to do what he loved. He also claimed he had been watching for an opening at a VAHC hospital and snatched up the Seattle position as soon as he saw that it was available.

"Right," Jess thought. She made a note that she needed to find out what really happened back in Virginia.

In answer to Jess's questions about why he appeared after the death of Mr. Thompson, Hansen reiterated his love of being a hands-on CEO. He liked dealing with people and helping those in need, which was why he had taken the job in Seattle in the first place. "He sure is consistent," she thought.

In answer to why he was so involved in this case, Hansen professed confusion as to why his involvement would be questioned. When pressed, he said that he had come to the deposition to help comfort Dr. Haseem because he wasn't familiar with the U.S. legal system. "He's very smooth," Jess thought. She could see why he had been a rising star with the company.

When Jess asked why Hansen had authored most of the letter his attorney sent in response to Jess's inquiry prior to starting the case, she noticed a flash of surprise cross Hansen's face, which dissolved as fast as it had come. At the same instant, Baker came up out of his seat and halfway across the table at Jess. "Objection. You cannot inquire into attorney-client discussions."

"On the contrary, Mr. Baker, my question was why Mr. Hansen authored the letter. I didn't ask him to discuss attorney-client communications," Jess retorted.

"You may answer the question, Mr. Hansen, but be careful not to discuss anything that you and I have talked about," Baker advised Hansen.

Having been given an opportunity to think about his answer during Baker's ranting objection, Hansen said, "I just feel very strongly about my hospital. We do a darn good job, and I don't want anyone impugning our reputation as an excellent health care facility."

"And what is Peoples' grade in the HealthGrades Patient Safety in American Hospitals Study?" Jess asked. Again she thought she saw a flash of surprise. After a brief pause, Hansen claimed he didn't have that information at his finger tips.

"Do you find it a reliable source of evaluation of health care at hospitals?" Jess asked.

"Well, it has some flaws," Hansen weaseled.

"Doesn't VAHC boast on its web site that eighty percent of its hospitals are rated in the top two tiers of that study?"

"Objection!" Baker interjected again. "Assumes facts not in evidence. There is no evidence that VAHC mentions HealthGrades on its web site."

Again Hansen responded to Baker's coaching. "Well, I don't know about that. I concentrate on my own hospital here in Seattle to make it the best I can," Hansen answered.

Jess was pretty sure that Hansen knew darn well about the rating of his own hospital and the boast on the VAHC web site. How could he not know about it, having spent twelve years at headquarters?

Turning to Baker, Jess asked if he would have his client check on the information about his hospital's rating. Baker gave the usual, "Ask an interrogatory on that," which was what Jess expected him to say. She also expected that he would object to such an interrogatory if and when she took the time to issue it. She would have to think about whether all that was worth the effort. It might be tough to get the information in at trial. She was sure that Baker would fight like hell to keep out any evidence about a bad rating.

Having heard the story of Baker's behavior at the depositions, Drew chuckled, "Yeah, I know that old table-pounding ploy. In fact, when I was a 'newbie' I attended a deposition in which the senior partner got so carried away that he grabbed the necktie of opposing counsel and almost choked him." Drew shook his head. "Life is just too short for all that."

"Isn't that true," Jess agreed. "Well what do you think? Do you think I have my neck hanging out on this one?" Jess asked.

Drew replied, "Absolutely you do, but I think that your instinct is right. I think there's something more going on at Peoples than meets the eye; you just have to find it. If I can help you do that, let me know. For right now, though, I guess I really should get some work done today." Despite Drew's decision that he was going to take some R 'n R, reality did require that he get back to his office and get a few things done. One of the problems of being a sole practitioner was that there was no one in the office to get things done when you're out in trial for days on end.

Drew petted Reesa on the head and picked her up off his lap, where she had settled shortly after he sat down. She seemed a little put out since she hadn't made the decision to get down, but Jess was sure Reesa would get over the trauma.

Chapter Fourteen

"They don't treat you fairly, Lars. I think you should go to work for someone who appreciates you. I can talk to my father. I'm sure he could find a place for you back home in Virginia." Anika's father was in the upper echelons of management for a drug manufacturer that was doing very well of late. Lars wasn't about to use that connection if he could help it, but he didn't want to discuss it with Anika. He was sure it would cause an unnecessary argument.

Lars and his wife Anika were sitting in the living room of their spacious residence in Broadmoor—an elite, gated section of Seattle. As always, Anika was tastefully dressed, this time in an aquamarine lounge dress that fit every inch of her cover-girl figure and accented her startlingly blue eyes and long blond hair. Lars had taken off his sport coat and tie upon arriving home and, rather than putting on his customary smoking jacket, simply rolled up his sleeves. He was picturing himself as corporate hero, having survived the deposition, and wanted to feel the part. Both sat with their customary martinis in hand. Actually, Lars had been feeling so exhilarated on his way home that he had called Anika to have the martinis ready when he arrived.

"It just isn't fair the way they treat you after you brought them from a few little Podunk hospital scows to a nationwide fleet of top-notch hospitals." Anika was repeating the description she had often heard from Lars in the past. These discussions had started when Lars was skapegoated during the federal investigation of VAHC. At least that was how Lars had told it to Anika.

Shortly before Lars and Anika had moved to Seattle, VAHC had been the subject of an investigation by the FBI for fraudulent billing practices. "Fraudulant billing!" Lars had protested, when he was pleading his case before the board to avoid being fired. "They make the paper work so complicated, you can't help but make a few mistakes! It's those guys in accounting. When they get a bonus for increasing revenue, sometimes they get carried away. I've increased our bottom line five percent as a result of reorganizing our billing practices alone." Lars also thought to himself but didn't say, "You sure liked the extra income from my work. If I weren't innovative, this company would still be just a Podunk convoy of ten hospitals. Then where would you stuffed-shirts be?" Lars liked boat analogies and fancied himself an admiral in his daydreams.

This was the explanation that Lars had often told Anika in their evening discussions back in Virginia. In the end, VAHC had agreed to a settlement with the government to repay $500 million of "erroneously billed" charges and signed an agreement to change their billing practices.

Anika missed the days back home in Virginia and wanted to go back. Lars had been a vice president at VAHC when they lived there, and he was integrally involved in helping the corporation rise to the position that it now held. They would go to the symphony at least twice a month, were members of the country club, and were even invited to the only inaugural ball for President Bush that counted when he was reelected. They were members of the Rangers club, an organization for top level fundraisers for his election.

For some reason, VAHC didn't seem to appreciate Lars's hard work, which included not only his reorganization of billing practices, but also his innovative use of bonuses to doctors for maximizing use of tests administered at the corporation's hospitals. Lars had satisfactorily explained the increased use of tests to federal auditors as a result of defensive medicine and had been careful not to make a paper trail of the relationship between the bonuses and the doctors' use of tests.

One of Lars's biggest contributions to the VAHC bottom line was the development of a subsidiary company to repackage pharmaceuticals for the corporation's hospitals. The subsidiary's name was Unit Dose Inc. With the formation of a subsidiary to take over unit-dose packaging—medicine packaged in single doses for administration to patients—Lars had been able to capture the income stream for VAHC that had formerly gone to expensive middlemen, thereby bringing the hospital's revenue sources into the twenty-first century. There was a lot of profit in buying drugs in bulk and reselling them in unit-dose size. Even with the government trouble, VAHC obtained its pharmaceuticals from Unit Dose to this day.

Sometimes, Unit Dose would even buy extra drugs that they knew they probably wouldn't need and would then sell them at a higher price. Theoretically, hospitals aren't allowed to do this since it might constitute price manipulation, but Unit Dose wasn't a hospital per se. Besides, so long as it's reasonably careful about what it buys and sells, a company can defend on the basis that it was just wrong in the amount it needed. There's really very little government oversight on the matter. Some state governments try to prevent this practice, but they're overwhelmed by the enormity of the problem. There are just too many drugs and too few regulators. Even the drug manufacturers can't always track their own drugs. Sometimes a retailer or wholesaler can even get a manufacturer to pay the rebate twice in this resale process.

The rebate is an especially important part of the profit in buying and selling drugs for VAHC and other institutions. VAHC, through its subsidiary Unit Dose, could realize the entire amount of the markup for drugs from manufacturer to the patient. The actual sales price for a drug is a closely guarded secret and is only known by the manufacturer, the purchaser, and maybe a few select others. Part of the price is reduced by the "rebate," which some would call a kick-back, that drug manufacturers give to hospitals and pharmacies for placing their pharmaceuticals on the company's list of available drugs. For certain, the drug manufacturers and the large purchasers don't like the idea of sharing these facts with government officials and have been fairly successful in keeping the information out of their hands. However, when working at VAHC, Lars had been pretty sure—and had been encouraged in that thought by his father-in-law—that the corporation was doing okay on its drug prices. Of course, VAHC hospitals, like most retailers, charged much more for drugs to uninsured patients than they charged to insured patients. Obviously, in the case of insurance- and government-reimbursed drug costs, the corporation had to comply with the guidelines, cutting into the profit a bit.

Drug companies are more than happy to give incentives to hospitals to use their drugs. When patients go home from the hospital, they usually continue taking the same drugs that they began taking in the hospital, so it's worth a few dollars a pill to make sure that a particular company's drugs are used at as many hospitals as possible.

Lars was proud of his handiwork at VAHC. Through his management, the corporation had benefited from the increased revenue of unit-dose packaging and had even been able to reduce the nurse-patient ratio as a result. It was great to be able to show that the unit-dose method reduced drug administration errors too. Lars had been a star for the corporation for twelve years and suddenly he had become no good to them anymore.

Chapter Fifteen

"Well, everyone suffers injustice in life," Lars thought to himself. Lars was proud that he had been able to bounce back from his crisis at VAHC. Despite the fact that he had been relegated to an insignificant hospital in Seattle, Lars was making a fine comeback, even though he had known nothing about the West Coast when he arrived. Hell, before he left Virginia some of his friends had even kidded him about whether they were still riding horses and using bows and arrows out there in the western territories.

When he came to Peoples Hospital, Lars had reduced the expense of hiring doctors and nurses by bringing in a number of them from foreign countries. In general, Lars found that Filipino nurses were well-trained and easier to deal with than their U.S. counterparts. Certain foreign doctors were also much easier to deal with, particularly when coming from war-torn or poorer areas. The latter immigrants in particular were very grateful to be in the U.S., if not also willing to work for less.

Lars first met Dr. Haseem when he was in the U.S. doing a residency in emergency room medicine. Omar Haseem had been rotating through one of VAHC's Virginia hospitals under a program to provide advanced training to foreign doctors. Hansen had been especially interested in the program having started out in rural Kentucky where they needed doctors from any source. Lars tried to make a connection with the training program even though he was in the higher echelons of VAHC's administration at the time. It was hard to get U.S. doctors in the less desirable areas, and the

U.S. policy to allow in foreign-born doctors to fill the gap seemed like a good plan.

When Iraq had become a quagmire of killing and the Haseems fled to Jordan, Haseem had contacted Hansen. Haseem was one of the lucky ones who had actually had U.S. training, so he could not be held up by the Iraqi government's refusal to release transcripts as a method of retaining its doctors. With Hansen's help and Washington connections, Haseem had been able to come to the U.S., and he was extremely grateful. "As he should be," Hansen mused arrogantly.

On the social front, the Hansens frequently attended Seattle Symphony performances at Benaroya Hall and were members of the "Founder's Circle." They were also known in the best social circles in Seattle, which to Anika's narrow-minded surprise included a lot of Asians and Jews. But because she considered the "injustice" Lars had experienced as well as her own trials and tribulations as the privileged wife of a wealthy businessman to be among those of the worst type, she decided that she fit right in with others who had been persecuted.

Lars also decided that Peoples should sponsor a junior soccer league, an activity he was very attentive to. This seemed to bother Anika. She had once said that she couldn't understand why Lars wanted to spend time with "those people," and she refused to go to most events. Lars wouldn't talk about why he paid so much attention to soccer, and after a few attempts to get him to, Anika decided not to bring it up anymore. Lars found that it was a good way to keep his ear to the ground about the availability of foreign-born staffing, since soccer is popular in most of Europe and parts of Asia and Latin America and since many professionals and semi-professionals often attended the soccer events with their children. It was a way for Lars to demonstrate his involvement in the community, thereby improving his image, and to learn valuable information.

In a convoluted way, Lars had actually met Ricardo Guzman, CEO of Drug Repackaging and Distribution, or DRD, through soccer. Through friends of friends of soccer acquaintances, Hansen had learned that Guzman was starting a new repackaging plant in Toppenish, Washington, a small, struggling town in the eastern part of the state. The Toppenish city leaders were thrilled to have Guzman open a plant that promised jobs for skilled and semi-skilled laborers. As compared to the jobs available in Toppenish—primarily farming and warehousing jobs—this new plant held the hope for a possible influx of higher paid employees and a better tax base. Apparently Guzman had been able to obtain significant tax concessions for his plant when he came to town.

Meeting Guzman allowed Lars to realize the goal in the back of his mind that he would take some of the profit in pharmaceuticals for himself. Lars figured that if his expertise wasn't good enough for the VAHC board of directors, he would use it for his own benefit.

As distinguished from the arrangement that Lars had set up for VAHC with Unit Dose, Lars decided that he would take advantage of the availability of this local repackager for himself. This had taken some doing because the corporation already had a good deal with Unit Dose, and Lars had to have a justification for not using the national repackager. Fortunately, DRD was small enough that Lars had been able to work out a better deal than the corporation's hospitals obtained from Unit Dose, but DRD wasn't big enough to supply the whole hospital system. "Maybe someday," Lars thought. If so, that could make Lars even richer.

The deal that Lars had put together with DRD was that Lars himself would receive the "rebate" for putting its drugs on People's list of available drugs. He had set up a bank account in Panama to receive the money. In case anything went wrong, Lars wanted to develop a nest egg. He didn't want to be in the same situation that he had found himself back in Virginia ever again, having to beg for a job from ungrateful stiffs.

Lars began thinking about developing this nest egg when he learned that he was going to Seattle. Contrary to his father-in-law's hints, he had discovered that the Virgin Islands were no longer a safe haven for protection of money. Once Britain became involved in the European Union, it had imposed EU tax requirements on its "dependant territories," including a withholding tax on savings. He not only wanted to be able to control his own tax payments, but he also didn't want a paper trail to steer the authorities to his bank account. Guzman had been pretty clear that he wasn't going to send out tax notifications to the IRS about the rebates he was providing to Lars, and Lars didn't want one from the bank where he put his money either.

So instead of the Virgin Islands, Lars had chosen Panama. With the U.S. interested in keeping Panama stable in order to protect the Panama Canal, life was so good that the Panamanian government had decided it didn't even need an army to protect itself. Because of political stability, the economy of Panama was developing generally, and the country had realized a boon to its banking industry. Law firms were advertising online that they would help you set up "protected" accounts and that they would maintain absolute "confidentiality." Preparing ahead, Lars had insisted that he and Anika move to Seattle by way of a cruise through the Panama Canal. He wasn't about to put his money in a place or deal with lawyers that he hadn't seen before.

Lars was rather proud of himself for the forethought he had exercised. When he left Virginia, he wasn't sure how he was going to develop his nest egg, but from his prior experience, he knew that such an opportunity would present itself. Really, the thing with Guzman had fallen in his lap. "Luck comes to those who are prepared," Lars thought.

Sitting in his house in Broadmoor, Lars patted himself on the back frequently for learning from his mistakes. Keeping the existence of this nest egg from Anika did bother him a little, but only a little. Certainly if she stuck with him, Anika would benefit from his forethought as well.

Chapter Sixteen

Omar Haseem's reaction to the deposition was quite different from Lars's. Afterward, he had gone back to the hospital to finish his shift, and by the time he got home, he was sure he was going to be sent back to Jordan, maybe even Iraq. The thought so distressed him that he could hardly speak.

When he opened the door to his home, he began to feel better. His wife Fatimeh was cooking a dinner of lamb and rice, and there would also be cucumbers and yogurt. Their four-year-old son, Osman, was playing on the floor with a coloring book he had received from daycare. Omar thought to himself that this country was not the Iraq that he loved, but neither was Iraq nowadays. This was certainly better than living as a refugee in Jordan, and he didn't want to go back under any circumstances.

Fatimeh looked up as Omar walked in and closed the door. His face was drawn, and his shoulders sagged. She walked over to him and took him in her arms. As he let her hug him, tears began to roll down his face. This was not the Omar that Fatimeh first met. He had been so strong and resilient, even when they had fled Iraq. But Fatimeh knew that things had been difficult at the hospital lately, and she also knew that Omar's deposition was scheduled for today. It was clear that it hadn't gone well. Fatimeh's hug gave Omar strength, and he returned the affection with his own hug. They stood and held each other for several seconds until Fatimeh remembered that the rice was cooking. Even though they enjoyed a crusty bottom on the rice, this dinner was going to be burned if she didn't attend to the cooking.

Seeing that his father was crying, Osman sensed that something was wrong and started to cry. "Daddy, Daddy," he cried and ran over to hug his father's leg. Omar sat down with his son on the couch and soothed him with a big hug. Omar didn't want to upset his son, so the tears also stopped.

"What did you do at daycare today?" Omar asked in English. He and Fatimeh wanted Osman to be American, so they insisted that he speak English, even at home. This wasn't difficult for Osman, since he had hardly begun speaking when they fled Iraq. The most difficult part of the plan was that Omar and Fatimeh always tried to speak English in front of Osman to set an example for him. Sometimes, like tonight, doing this was almost too much on top of everything else.

Omar missed the Iraq that he used to know, and he even missed the Iraq as he had known it when the Americans first arrived. Iraqis were full of hope that the Americans would bring a new era of freedom to the country. Omar and Fatima were especially open to the idea, as were many of the other educated people of Baghdad. However, in the countryside where many of the people were less educated, there was a yearning for return to the "good old days," even though almost no one could remember a good time. Even so, they were certain that those days must be better than what they had recently seen.

With all the fighting, the hospital where Omar worked was busy all of the time. He worked very long hours because there were so many who needed help. Even with the chaos and lack of medicine and equipment, Omar felt it was his duty to do the best he could to care for his countryman. If he didn't do it, who would? Eventually, though, he couldn't continue ignoring the threats and let his stubborn sense of responsibility to others cause his family to be at risk.

One day Omar, Fatimeh, and Osman left for the market in their car and never came back. They took nothing with them but a few changes of clothes and as much money as they could hide under Fatimeh's burqa, in case they were stopped. Fatimeh never wore a burqa, but that seemed to be the best way to take what they could out of the country. Besides, they had no idea who they might meet on the way who would take offense at Fatimeh wearing western dress.

In Jordan, Omar couldn't practice medicine, so he took a job as a cab driver in order to make ends meet. Fatimeh took in laundry since she couldn't get a teaching job in Jordan and because there was no one to take care of Osman if she left the house.

Immediately upon arriving in Jordan, Omar started planning to move on to Britain or the U.S. Since he had done a residency in the U.S., he was luckier than many of his colleagues. He also had a contact at VAHC hospitals, who was well-placed and might be able to help him cut through the red tape prohibiting most Iraqis from immigrating to the U.S. Omar had found it difficult to locate Lars Hansen but eventually found him in Seattle. Hansen had maintained some of his contacts and fortunately was able to help Omar and his family come to the U.S. Omar felt himself lucky beyond measure.

Chapter Seventeen

When the Haseems arrived in Seattle, Hansen's assistant at the hospital had helped them find a place to rent, and Omar started working right away. Fatimeh found a job as a teaching assistant at a school on Beacon Hill, where there were a number of refugees. Her ability to speak Arabic made her a valuable asset. She was intent on obtaining her teaching credentials and was taking classes at nights and on weekends.

Osman went to daycare at a nearby home where a woman, who had left Iraq years ago, cared for six children, including her own. Though she was Shi'ite, that didn't matter here in the U.S., and Fatimeh was happy to meet someone from home. All the children at Osman's daycare spoke English, which had been a prerequisite for Fatimeh when investigating daycare situations.

Omar was working twenty-four-hour shifts as an emergency room physician at Peoples, which was strenuous but nothing compared to what the situation had been in Baghdad. The hospital had all the medicine and equipment it needed. Omar hadn't seen some of the equipment before because it had been a few years since his residency, but it didn't take him long to become very familiar with the new machines. At first, Omar was in heaven with the largess of working at a well-equipped hospital.

After a while, however, Mr. Hansen started suggesting to Omar that he wasn't giving good care. People weren't recovering from code situations like they had before. Often they would regain normal sinus rhythm, only to fall back into their original arrhythmia, or irregular heartbeat. Omar had noticed this trend too. Mr. Hansen told him that Joyce Brown, the head nurse in the ER, had brought the problem to his attention.

At first Omar wondered if he was doing something wrong. He was afraid to ask because he felt isolated from most of the other doctors, but he kept his eyes and ears open, watching for clues. This was a difficult thing to get a handle on since ER staffing was cut to the bone, generally allowing only one doctor per code, and once the problem surfaced, Mr. Hansen set a rule against attending codes if you weren't involved in the care. He had been Omar's savior by getting him into the U.S. and giving him a job. How could he be wrongly accusing him now?

Shortly after this began happening, Mr. Hansen also required that he be called every time a code went bad, which suggested that Hansen was aware that this problem was happening with others. That helped a bit, but Omar also knew from his experience in Baghdad that those in power could assign blame, and the truth might not help. Omar's visa required that he be working in the U.S. If he lost his job at Peoples, would he be able to get another job? What would happen to him if he was blamed for these deaths? Omar wasn't sure, and he definitely didn't want to test the situation.

When Brad Thompson had come in, Omar couldn't believe that it was happening again, though it appeared a little different this time. He had been relieved when he saw normal sinus rhythm after the first shock. That was a very good sign—the patient had recovered. In fact, there was a fleeting second when he even appeared to regain consciousness.

Almost immediately, though, Brad appeared to have a seizure. After the seizure, he had remained unconscious, and the pupils of his eyes had been fixed and dilated, which indicated brain damage. Had he had a stroke? It was very unlikely, considering his age and the almost immediate resuscitation. He also had very labored breathing, which was really clear every time Haseem had the respiratory therapist stop bagging him to let him breathe on his own.

The patient's heart continued beating for about an hour. During this time, Haseem had to tend to others, but he had the respiratory therapist continue bagging Mr. Thompson and had the nurse monitor his vital signs and report to Haseem while he was out of the room. He checked back on Mr. Thompson frequently and had three blood gases drawn over the duration of the code because his body didn't seem to be correcting his blood pH like it should. At first Haseem had thought that the results were wrong because the pH didn't correct, but then he began to think that he had seen this happen before. In any event, the bicarb that he had given apparently didn't help enough. The patient had normal sinus rhythm for about forty-five minutes, but his pH teetered around 6.9—a point at which the body's organs couldn't live for long. Possibly the acidosis was causing this strange reaction.

The patient's heart was showing symptoms that could be due to continued acidosis—his heart rate was becoming more irregular and rapid, and his blood pressure was dropping as a result. Maybe he needed a little nudge to help correct the blood pH. Although Haseem knew it was risky, he decided to give the patient one more amp of bicarb. He knew that giving a patient more bicarb when his heart was beating could cause the pH to swing too far the other way, but leaving him in acidosis was risky too. Haseem took the chance and ordered administration of bicarb for the acidosis and epinephrine to raise the blood pressure. But the drugs didn't right the situation, and Brad died within minutes. How could that be!

Haseem had been so distressed that he could barely speak. He had tried to compose himself when he went to talk to the patient's wife. As soon as he started to talk, he realized that was a mistake. The overwhelming emotion overtook him again, and things he didn't intend to say involuntarily erupted from his mouth. He started to explain that Brad had been resuscitated, but the problem had happened again. "This should not be happening," he said, just as Hansen appeared. Seeing Omar upset and hearing the last of his uncontrolled rambling, Hansen shooed him back into the treatment area. He didn't want any further confessions spewing from Haseem's mouth. After Hansen spoke with Mrs. Thompson, Hansen located Haseem, and the two went to the conference room right off the admission area to discuss the matter.

Mr. Hansen closed the door, and the conversation that followed stood out in Omar's mind. He told Mr. Hansen what had occurred, which didn't take very long since he had been in hospitals long enough to understand the medical lingo of cardiac events. Mr. Hansen's response was, "Omar, I'm concerned that you're letting me down. I went to all the trouble to help you come to the U.S., and now strange things are happening in my hospital. I hope I'm not going to have to let you go."

"Mr. Hansen, I am very careful. I don't know what is happening. I have carefully reviewed each code in my mind. I have read and reread protocol. I have read and reread this EKG. I know that I am giving good care," Haseem said as he held up the EKG strips.

Hansen's response was to grab the strips and tear them up. Then he said, "Omar, I want to see the chart when you are done. I should run this by the quality control committee, but since we have known each other for so long, I'm going to make an exception this time. However, I suggest that you don't tell this preposterous story. I want to help you, but no one is going to believe you. I suggest that you keep this quiet, and I'll do what I can to help. I think what really happened here, Omar, was that Mr. Thompson never regained normal sinus rhythm, and you're trying to cover it up with this story. I think the chart should reflect the truth here. I will support you on that Omar, but you have to give me something to work with."

Just then there was shouting out in the waiting room area. The two men looked out and saw that it was Mrs. Thompson. Hansen went out, talked to her shortly, and came back into the conference room. He picked a few papers out of the file cabinet, put them in an envelope, and took them out to Mrs. Thompson.

By the time Hansen returned, Omar was sitting with his head in his hands.

"Mr. Hansen, am I the only one having this problem with codes?" he asked.

"You are, Omar, you are. You are my friend, but you have to work with me on this one," Mr. Hansen said *again* as he walked out of the room.

Omar could not believe what he was hearing. How could Mr. Hansen be saying this? He was telling him to lie about Brad Thompson's death, and Omar was pretty sure that Mr. Hansen was lying to him about who was having this "code problem." Omar didn't know for sure what was happening at the hospital, and he felt he had no choice but to comply with Mr. Hansen's direction to change the record. He couldn't tell his family that they were going back to Jordan, or even worse, Iraq.

Chapter Eighteen

"No drinks at McComick's tonight," Jess thought. She had a kitty to get home and some investigating to do. Drew had insisted that he help Jess get Reesa to her car. The ungrateful cat seemed to have adopted Drew. Reesa sat on Drew's lap the whole time that they were discussing the case. Jess was a little embarrassed but enjoyed it just the same. Drew seemed to be a cat-person—one more point for him—and his assistance getting Reesa's things to the car was really helpful. Taking Reesa to work was more trouble than she had expected, and it might not be something that she could do every day.

After Jess settled Reesa at home, she took the elevator down to the lobby to talk to the door man, Tommy. Ordinarily in Seattle a man of Tommy's age would not use the diminutive name, but Jess guessed that his jobs had always been the type that would justify the use of the familiar moniker. The job did present somewhat of an intellectual challenge for him. His silver gray hair and earnest but lined face suggested that he was at least sixty years old and didn't own another black suit like the one he wore on his job. He seemed to enjoy being a doorman and was friendly and helpful to the residents.

Jess asked Tommy if he had seen anyone come through the lobby the day before that he didn't recognize. He was immediately defensive, of course, because it was his job to keep people out of the building who shouldn't be there. He insisted that no one had gotten past him, but Jess was a little skeptical. She wasn't so sure that someone couldn't have distracted him while maybe even pilfering one of the spare keys for each condo that he had in his office.

Tommy was sure that if anyone got up to Jess's condo, they would have come through the elevator from the garage, not the front door. The elevator connected to the garage, one floor below the lobby. Though an automatic door opener was required to get through the garage door from the entry off the alley, there were no separate security measures to prevent someone from getting into the elevator from the garage. Once in the elevator, an intruder could go anywhere without being seen, except by the video camera.

Tommy reminded Jess of the closed circuit TV that the condominium had installed last year in the elevator. Jess, who didn't take the time to read the lengthy minutes of the monthly meetings of the condo board, had not been aware of the addition. Though she was interested in what was going on around her condo, the minutes were fifteen to twenty pages long and usually began with something like, "We would like to thank the Ms. Jones in unit 2104 for her contribution to the flower arrangement in the twenty-fourth floor vestibule." Jess didn't have time to pick her way through to the meaty portion of the minutes. Neither had she noticed a camera in the elevator, and she asked Tommy to show her where it was.

Tommy was proud of "his" closed circuit system. He took Jess to the elevator and pointed to the mirrors on the sides and ceiling of the elevator. "See there," Tommy said, pointing at nothing, in the upper-right, front corner of the elevator. "That's where it is. It's a one-way mirror."

"You mean a two way mirror?" Jess asked.

"Well, you can see through it, anyway," Tommy replied. "Seems like people don't know that—sometimes they do the darnedest things in the elevator."

Tommy said that he kept the discs from the camera system for a week. If Jess wanted to look at the one for yesterday, he would be happy to get it out, but he insisted that he could not let it out of his sight—those discs were his responsibility. If Jess wanted to watch the discs, she would have to look at them on his TV in his office.

Jess was not that keen on sitting in the stuffy little office, but she was even less eager to have another break-in, so she sat down on the chair that Tommy offered her in front of the viewer. The disc showed four camera locations: one just inside the entrance of the garage, one on the next floor up in the garage, one at the lobby door, and one in the elevator. They each played on a quarter split of the screen, included a timer showing the date and time of the scenes, and they appeared to be synchronized.

Jess and Tommy sat down to watch. It took about three seconds for Jess to figure out that the pictures weren't moving. She looked at the timer and noticed that it was running at actual time. Tommy hadn't put the viewer on fast forward, and at this rate, they would be there all night.

"Tommy, is there a fast-forward button for this TV?" Jess asked. He looked at Jess with a spark of surprise and said, "There is one. That's a smart idea, Ms. Lamm!" Jess grinned inside—she was now sure that it was possible to sneak past Tommy through the lobby.

They watched the time crawl by. Even on fast-forward the viewing was dull. During the middle of the day there was very little activity aside from a few women coming in with groceries and a couple of dogs taking their owners for a walk. Most of the residents of the building worked during this time.

Just when Jess was thinking that this was a waste of time, she looked up from the TV and saw Paul and Teresa walking through the lobby door. She put the TV on hold, asked Tommy to leave it "right there," and said that she would be back in a flash. She grabbed the elevator with Teresa and Paul.

On the way up the elevator, Jess told her neighbors about her lack of progress in determining who broke into her apartment. She also told them how worried she was about leaving Reesa alone in the apartment during the day. Before she could start the next sentence, Teresa gushed, "Leave her with us! We'll take good care of her until this gets sorted out. She is such a sweet cat."

Jess hoped Teresa wouldn't change her mind when she saw how demanding Reesa could be if she didn't get her dinner on time. "Oh, well, maybe Reesa can be on her good behavior for a few days. She can be sweet if she wants to, and she knows the difference," Jess thought to herself. She was relieved to have Reesa taken care of, even if it put a strain on the relationship with her neighbors. The three of them made arrangements to meet at seven thirty the next morning to transfer Reesa to Paul and Teresa's condo.

Jess took the elevator back to the lobby to finish the investigation of the intruder and found Tommy nervously looking at the TV. He was staring at it intently and practically jumped off his chair when Jess said, "Hello, Tommy."

"Ms. Lamm, I know you told me to leave it right there, but I thought I might be able to help. I know you have a lot to do, so I moved the tape along. You know, that fast-forward thing really helps!"

"Say, Tommy, I really meant it when I said that you should call me Jessica. It's really okay. In fact, I prefer it. So, what did you find?"

Tommy smiled, appreciating the camaraderie of the investigation, and finally agreed to call Jess by her first name. "Okay, Ms. Jessica, here is what I did. I decided I might be able to recognize someone different from the usual, so I pushed fast-forward. And there he was! I know I've never seen that person before. Do you see him? There he is!"

Tommy had stopped the monitor at 3:23 p.m. There was nothing on any view except a man in a tan suit and fedora hat in the elevator. The hat was tipped down low over his face, and the intruder never looked up. About the only thing that could be seen of him was a bit of short black hair below the hat in the back when he entered the elevator and his dark hand as it reached for the elevator buttons. The picture wasn't really clear enough to identify anyone, but it was a start. Jess noticed with an uncomfortable feeling that as far as she could tell the man was short and slight. His body looked the same size and shape as Dr. Haseem's. Jess told herself, "I don't believe it. I won't believe that he would try to stay in Iraq to help his people and then come here and become a break-in artist."

Jess and Tommy fast-forwarded again. There was one more dog taking his owner for a walk, and then the stranger in the tan suit and hat went down the elevator at 3:45 p.m. Again, he didn't look up at all; he just pressed the buttons and got out on the garage floor.

Jess and Tommy looked at the garage cameras to see how the intruder got out in and out of the garage. Doing a fast reverse to scan the period prior to the intruder entering the elevator, Jess and Tommy saw plenty of cars coming in and not waiting for the garage door to close behind them. It looked like it wasn't too difficult to get into the garage without the remote control, and there had been a few episodes where people's cars had been vandalized inside the garage. The condo board was always putting out warnings in the meeting minutes asking the residents to stop and watch the doors close to prevent entry by intruders.

Tommy wasn't sure he would recognize an intruder's car because there were so many residents. They were supposed to register their cars with management, but he knew that they weren't really good about reporting a change. Jess could imagine that registering a new car was not high on the to-do list of most residents.

But at least they had something. Jess was sure that this was no boyfriend difficulty. She didn't want to jump to conclusions, but she thought again about how Dr. Haseem from Peoples Hospital had the same skin tone and was roughly the same size as the intruder in the video. "Probably just a coincidence," she thought.

"Enough for tonight," Jess said as she yawned, said good night to Tommy, and took the elevator to her condo.

Back at home, Reesa told Jess in no uncertain terms what she thought of late night dinners. Thinking it was going to take only a few minutes talking to Tommy, Jess hadn't refilled Reesa's dishes when she brought her home. Reesa had pushed her dish into the entryway and was sitting and looking at it when Jess came in—no small feat since this required pushing the dish through the living room. "Yeow, yrrrrrh, yrrrrh! Squeak, yrrrh, yrrrh!" Reesa repeated over and over as Jess picked up her Good Kitty dish, went to the fridge, and filled the dish with the appropriate amount of food. As soon as Jess put the dish down, Reesa took a bite but then followed Jess into the bedroom. She continued "talking" as if to say, "I deserve better than this." Reesa had a good vocabulary and was making use of it. Jess knew the routine—Reesa wanted petting after a hard day at the office, and so did Jess. She kicked off her shoes and replaced her clothes with her bathrobe, and she and Reesa stretched out on the bed in front of the TV. It wasn't long before both were asleep.

Chapter Nineteen

On Wednesday morning, Jess woke up with a jolt. "There's something I'm supposed to remember today," she thought. "Uh, Reesa goes to Teresa and Paul's for the day." Looking at the clock, Jess saw that she had forgotten to allow extra time to get Reesa settled next door. It was seven o'clock, and it generally took Jess awhile to get moving in the morning. Jumping out of bed, she decided a strong cup of coffee was more important this morning than washing her hair. She started the coffee maker, replenished the food and water in Reesa's dishes, and jumped into the shower. Twenty-five minutes later, having slugged down a cup of coffee and swiped on some mascara, blush, and lipstick, she was beginning to wake up.

Jess called her neighbors, and Teresa picked up after one ring. "We're ready!" Teresa said, apparently looking at caller ID. "In fact, how about if Paul and I come over and pick her up? I know you're really busy right now. We'll be right over." Teresa put down the phone before Jess could even respond, and the door bell rang within seconds. There was Teresa, bright-faced and cheerful, her hair pulled back in a ponytail, with Paul standing behind her, not so bright-faced. The two of them swooped up Reesa, her Good Kitty dishes, her litter box, and the princess kitty herself. They were on their way out the door when Jess blurted out, "Uh, when should I pick her up?"

"No worry," Teresa said. "Just come over when you get home. We'll get along just fine!" Even from five feet away, Jess thought she heard Reesa purring, and she could see that she was already cuddling up to Teresa. "Well, not to worry about Reesa!" Jess told herself. She felt like the mother delivering her child to the first day of kindergarten, realizing that she was going to feel much more upset about the situation than Reesa would.

Chapter Twenty

Throwing on her "law suit," Jess was out the door in record time. Like most lawyers (and politicians for that matter) Jess understood that the definition of justice depends on what side you are on. There's a lot of chance in a judge's determination, depending on the particular issue, her world view, and sometimes even how many motions she has on her calendar that morning. Anything from a rabbit's foot to a lucky suit can help nudge things your way. Jess's favorite was her lucky brown suit with the tan blouse. She had worn this outfit several times to court, often with success.

Jess drove down Second Avenue, turned up the hill on Marion, south on Fifth, west onto Columbia, and into the Columbia Tower parking entrance. Her mind was in the courtroom, but fortunately her Camry knew the way to the office by itself.

Today, Jess was on her way to court to argue her motion to require Peoples Hospital to produce the personnel records of Joyce Brown. Jess had been battling Baker trying to get the records since it had become clear how important Brown was after the deposition of Dr. Haseem. Jess had requested the production of the personnel records at least four months ago after she received answers to her interrogatories that the woman no longer worked at Peoples and struck out trying to locate Nurse Brown on her own. The prospect that someone named Joyce Brown could be anywhere in the U.S.—or the world, for that matter—made it difficult to find her.

Arriving at floor F in the parking garage, Jess was glad to see that her usual parking space was empty. She was up the elevator to the office to pick up her brief case and back down in record time, rushing down Cherry to the King County Courthouse—the Superior Court in Seattle—on Third and James. She didn't want to use the Fourth Avenue entrance at this time of the day, because it would mean taking the elevator from the second floor. It was hard to get an elevator from there, since everything going up was packed from the first floor. Again, the gods seemed to be smiling on her. The crowd going through the metal detectors was smaller then normal, and even the slow moving elevators were better than usual. This was good because if she'd had to climb the stairs to the eighth floor, she would have been hot and sweaty by the time she arrived at the courtroom. The judge wouldn't be receptive to an excuse that the elevators were slow. Hopefully this was a good omen for the upcoming motion.

As Jess entered the courtroom, she saw her opponent Will Baker already sitting with the four other attorneys who had hearings on the calendar that day. This system of preassignment, of one judge being assigned to follow a case from beginning to end, had some good points. It was at least better than the "motions calendar" where all motions scheduled for the day are heard by one judge. Under the motions calendar system, a lawyer could sit all morning twiddling her thumbs, waiting for her motion to be heard, and even have to come back in the afternoon. Clients never seemed to understand why appearing for a motion took so long. On the other hand, the reason that this matter had not been decided before was that the assigned judge's calendar is often so busy that it's difficult to get a hearing scheduled.

The real positive about this case was that it was currently assigned to Judge Judith Pacer. She had been a plaintiff's lawyer when practicing law, and she knew about the games that defense counsel play in order to hide the facts. So her natural sympathy was on the side of the plaintiff's lawyer.

Despite the fact that Jess thought Judge Pacer was sympathetic to plaintiff's counsel, Jess was certain that the reason the judge had decided to hold a hearing on this discovery matter was her tendency to bend over backward to understand any possible legitimate arguments the defendants might have. Ordinarily, discovery matters like this one would be determined without oral argument in the preassignment system, and the judge would determine the matter solely from the pleadings filed. In this case, Baker claimed that Jess's effort to obtain Nurse Brown's personnel records was merely a fishing expedition and cited the old "right-to-privacy" argument. Jess was sure that Judge Pacer wanted to be certain she really understood the motion.

As Jess was mulling the situation over, the bailiff called out, "All rise." After allowing counsel to be seated, Judge Pacer said, "The first case is *Thompson v. Peoples and Haseem*. Are counsel ready?"

"Yes, Your Honor," Jess and Baker said simultaneously, as they walked to the counsel tables. Though not always the case, these counsel tables were the typical separate tables situated between the pews for court spectators and the judge's desk—the "bench."

Judge Pacer looked at Jess and said, "Ms. Lamm, your affidavit shows that you have made several attempts to locate Nurse Brown."

"Yes, Your Honor, we have," Jess said as she launched into a description of the several online attempts to locate Nurse Brown that her assistant Lorraine had made. She ended with the fact that they had even hired a private investigator to attempt to locate her. Even though Jess was pretty sure that Judge Pacer had already read the information in her affidavit, that was not always the case, depending on the judge. And, she also knew that sometimes just hearing it again can reinforce the impact of the written material. Jess also threw in a final retort to the argument that she knew Baker would make. She was entitled to a reply to what Baker argued, but sometimes a little preargument inoculation helps. "Mr. Baker has called this a 'fishing expedition,' Your Honor. If it is, then the premature death of a forty-year-old husband and father gives me a valid fishing license."

The sides of the judge's mouth gave an ever-so-slight twitch. She liked the anticipatory response to Baker's canned speech but wanted to maintain her judicial demeanor. Then she looked at Baker and said, "Mr. Baker, wasn't Nurse Brown very likely one of the people in the room when Mr. Thompson died? How could providing this information to Ms. Lamm possibly be a fishing expedition? Isn't Ms. Brown an essential witness in this case?"

"Judge, we have, of course, turned over Mr. Thompson's medical records, every hospital procedure remotely related to a code situation, and even the staffing records for the day of the death. Ms. Lamm has taken the deposition of Dr. Haseem and even Lars Hansen, the CEO of Peoples. We have been very cooperative, but there has to be a limit. Ms. Brown has the right to her privacy. At best this is a fishing expedition, and at worst this is unadulterated harassment!"

"Well, Mr. Baker, the limit is beyond the point at which we are now. You will produce complete copies of Ms. Brown's records of employment with Peoples by four o'clock this afternoon. If you believe that there is anything that should be withheld for privacy reasons, I will give you an opportunity to take up that issue with me by notifying my bailiff and Ms. Lamm by noon today. Furthermore, you will inform Ms. Lamm of the last known contact information regarding Ms. Brown and the names and contact information of any relatives that Ms. Brown is known to have in the state of Washington. This information will be provided with Ms. Brown's personnel records. Ms. Lamm, you are aware, of course, that Ms. Brown's personnel records are to be kept confidential and used only for the purpose of locating her and prosecuting your case in this matter. Mr. Baker, I had better not hear of any further delay tactics, or you and your client will be sanctioned. You are protective of your clients as you should be, but the Thompsons have a right to prosecute their case as well. Ms. Lamm, I will sign your order after you have added the additional terms. Perhaps you and Mr. Baker can step out into the hall and agree on the supplementary language."

As Jess and Baker followed the judge's instructions, Jess was attempting to restrain herself from smiling, though she couldn't prevent the flush of victory from flooding her face. Baker had been over-working the judicial system in this case and throwing up every roadblock possible. While this wasn't unusual in a medical malpractice case, Jess had the impression that Baker was working overtime on this one. She was pleased to see that Judge Pacer was not going to allow the delay tactics to continue. She hoped the judge would retain the case for trial so that she would appreciate the background of the discovery roadblocks Baker had thrown up. It's often the case that once a judge gets the flavor of the conduct of the suit, her evaluation of the lawyer's activities figures into future rulings.

Under the old motions calendar system, when a judge was assigned at random to hear case motions, Jess often found that lawyers would adopt positions they would never take if the judge knew the history of the case—sometimes in direct contradiction of their last argument on the same subject. On those occasions, Jess would walk out of the courtroom rolling her eyes and thinking, "No wonder people think lawyers are snakes."

Jess and Baker worked out the wording of Judge Pacer's order. Custom, and sometimes the court rules, require that each attorney provide a proposed order with a motion and a response to the motion—judges rarely, if ever, write their own orders. Jess presented the proposed order that she and Baker worked out, made a copy of it, and left the original with the clerk. She wasn't totally sure she wouldn't need the actual wording of the order later on today and wanted to have it easily available. She had no confidence that Baker was going to comply without more of a fight. The original order would be winding its way through to the file in the bowels of the courthouse and would be unavailable for days, if not weeks.

Jess was also glad that a few months ago she had requested and received from Baker an agreement to continuance, or rescheduling, of the trial date. In King County, as in many courts in Washington, the trial date is set when the case is filed in order to keep cases moving through the system. The rule evolved when the King County judges determined that long periods between case filing and trial were a result of the lawyers not paying sufficient attention to their cases. Maybe this was true, or maybe not, but it worked out well for insurers by stretching the deadline for compensation of victims.

Jess easily obtained a continuance when she requested it, because Baker and his clients had no interest in speeding the case to trial at that time. A few months ago, Jess had been looking at the calendar. She determined that if she didn't obtain a six-month continuance, Baker's delay tactics and delayed hearing on her motion could prevent her from obtaining the information that she needed in time for use at trial. She was really glad that she'd had the foresight to obtain the continuance then. Baker might not have agreed to it at this point if he thought that he could spring the trap that he had set by delaying. "Lawyers can work any system," Jess thought.

Chapter Twenty-One

Jess left the King County Courthouse by the Fourth Avenue entrance and walked the block back to Columbia Tower. She was still smiling to herself when she got to the office and listened to her phone messages.

"Speak of the devil!" There was a phone message from Joyce Brown. The message said that Joyce had heard from Mr. Hansen that Jess wanted to contact her. "W-h-h-h-a-a-a-t!" thought Jess. "Hansen knew where she was all along!"

She immediately called Ms. Brown back, but got her voice mail. Within minutes, however, Ms. Brown returned the call. She wanted to meet Jess away from her office. Jess didn't know why Joyce would want that, but getting her information was important enough to meet her practically anywhere.

Before setting up the meeting, Jess confirmed that Ms. Brown was no longer employed at Peoples. Even though it wasn't clear that Ms. Brown would have been a "speaking agent" for the hospital if she were still employed there, Jess didn't want to have an issue about whether she ought to be talking with her outside Baker's presence. The ethical rules for lawyers—some insist that this is an oxymoron—prohibit counsel from talking to opposing parties outside the presence of the party's lawyer. Since corporations don't speak for themselves, they have to speak through people—speaking agents are people in authority who, because of their position, "speak for the corporation." Baker had not *yet* raised that issue with relation to Joyce Brown, but Jess just wanted to determine whether it might be raised later. Since Joyce wasn't currently employed by Peoples, she couldn't possibly be a speaking agent. Jess didn't have time to fool with yet another motion from Baker—this time alleging unethical practice.

Jess set up an appointment with Ms. Brown at Anthony's Bell Street Diner, a water-front restaurant, for lunch. It was away from the office but still downtown, and they were to meet there at eleven thirty, to beat the lunch crowd, and make sure that they would be seated at one of the booths. Jess wanted as private a situation as possible to make Ms. Brown feel more comfortable. She used her speed dial to call for reservations just to confirm a table.

Jess also decided that she would take a subpoena with her for a possible deposition of Joyce Brown. It had been so difficult to find Joyce, and if this was because she was hostile, a subpoena might be necessary to require her to appear for a deposition. Jess opened up her computer and tapped out some changes in her subpoena form, just in case.

Jess forwarded her phone to Lorraine and explained that there was a remote possibility that Baker would call before noon. Jess assumed that contact from Joyce Brown was Baker's method of complying with the court's ruling and that she would hear nothing more on this subject today. Even though Jess didn't have Nurse Brown's records, she apparently was going to be able to talk to her, and that was the current purpose for obtaining the records. Arguing to get the records at this point would be time-consuming and likely unsuccessful.

Jess took a cab down the hill to Western Avenue and then north to Anthony's. Anthony's did have a parking lot a block or two north of the restaurant that's open for lunch and used for valet parking in the evening. This is really helpful since finding parking in downtown Seattle is extremely difficult. But if Jess took her car out of the Columbia Tower at lunch, she'd have to search for a new parking spot when she returned. She didn't want to have to make that search for such a small trip. Of course, another alternative is walking, but unless you're an Olympic athlete with hairspray like Jimmy Johnson, you wouldn't want to do that either. The weather can be very windy, the air is humid, and the streets have a steep uphill and downhill slant. These factors play havoc with your hair, and if you're walking very far, you can expect to arrive more than a little disheveled.

Jess reached the Bell Street Diner just before eleven thirty and asked for a booth. Waiting for Ms. Brown to arrive, she glanced out the window at the spectacular view. The sun created little dancing lights on the top of the clear blue water, which faded back to the blue-purple mountains in the distance. Immediately outside the window of the diner were outside tables, then lines of yachts and working ships tethered at the marina.

Looking toward the door, Jess was pretty sure she saw Ms. Brown enter—Joyce had said that her hair was light brown, shoulder length, and that she would be wearing a blazer and jeans. She was about 5 feet 5 inches tall with a thin build, was wearing minimal makeup, and her hair was disheveled from walking the Seattle sidewalks. The general impression was that of an efficient, business-like woman in her late thirties or early forties. Jess raised her hand and waived. Ms. Brown walked down the aisle, stopped in front of Jess's booth, and said, "Jessica Lamm?"

"Yes, and I assume that you are Ms. Brown, right?"

"I am."

"Please do sit down! I have really been trying to find you!" Jess said. To herself, she added, "And where the heck have you been?" She decided not to voice that question yet because she didn't want to scare Joyce away. Then Jess said, "Do you mind if I call you Joyce?"

"Please do. Nurses aren't used to being addressed so formally."

The waitress appeared and asked, "Can I tell you about our specials for today?"

Both being in a hurry, Joyce and Jess ordered the fish special and a glass of iced tea. Joyce said that she was on her way to work that afternoon, and Jess wanted to get back to the office too.

As soon as the waitress left, the two women resumed their conversation. Jess smiled at Joyce and said again, "I've been trying to get a hold of you. How was it that you decided to call me?

Joyce smiled back. "I've been living with my sister, and I have a new job in Renton. I don't have a landline phone in my name. I just use my cell phone. Mr. Hansen told me that you changed your mind and decided that you did want to see me."

"So that's why I've had such a hard time finding her! Hansen has been hiding a witness and has been lying under oath! That's perjury!" Jess thought to herself. She could hardly retain her composure but decided not to get into Mr. Hansen's white lie just yet since she didn't want to lose the opportunity find out what Joyce could tell her.

"I wanted to talk to you because you were one of the nurses in the room with my client Mr. Thompson during the code."

"Yes, I was. In fact, as the head nurse on duty in the ER, it was my job to observe and take notes on the code," said Joyce. "Somebody has to do that—the others at the code are all absorbed in what they're doing and don't have time to record."

"I used to be a nurse too but it's been years since I've seen a code. Tell me what happened during this one," Jess prodded. She'd been in such a hurry to meet Joyce after receiving the phone call that she didn't have time to think about bringing the record. Silently, she wondered, "Why the hell didn't I notice that Joyce was the scribe on the ER record? Wait, there wasn't a signature, was there? But Haseem said she might have been the scribe. Damn!" Jess scolded herself.

"I didn't know you're a nurse," Joyce said. "Once a nurse, always a nurse, I say." Joyce paused as if she was trying to recall the situation and then began again. "Well, the patient regained normal sinus rhythm the first time we shocked him, but he never came out of the coma. The respiratory therapists had to continue bagging him. Every time we stopped the bagging to check, he had very labored breathing. We thought about putting him on the ventilator, but he never really stabilized enough to do that. I'm assuming you know what an Ambu bag is, right?" Joyce asked.

"Right. As I understand it, the respiratory therapist puts an airway in the patient in a code and then attaches the Ambu bag. It's been a while since I practiced nursing, but I guess it's the same old hand pump."

"Still is. I guess that technology hasn't changed a lot," Joyce said.

"Isn't it strange that a patient would have trouble breathing after regaining normal sinus rhythm?" Jess asked.

"Sometimes yes, sometimes no, but we had been having that problem at Peoples for a while. We seemed to be having a problem with codes. More frequent than usual patients would die, some even after they regained normal sinus rhythm. Often they seemed to develop a breathing problem."

"Really! Do you have any idea why that would be?" Jess asked. To herself, she thought, "I can see why Hansen wanted to keep Joyce under wraps. This is dynamite!"

"I don't, but it happened more often than I would like—I tell you. I mentioned it to the nursing supervisor once, and Mr. Hansen got wind of the problem. He started requiring us to call him whenever a code went bad. That guy is a workaholic; he's always on duty."

"Was there a written policy on that?" Jess asked.

"Well, not that I know of. We were just following up on what seemed to be a problem. I guess he was concerned."

"Did this breathing problem happen only with a particular doctor?" Jess asked.

"Well, I'm not sure. I mostly worked with Dr. Haseem, and sometimes patients do have labored breathing anyway. I'd have to think about that," she replied.

"So, what happens when a patient has a breathing problem?" Jess asked.

"Well, you have to figure out why it's happening or at least deal with the result of the problem. We also seemed to have many cases of acidosis. I even wondered if the lab tests were right, we had it so often. Generally you give bicarb. It comes in preloaded 50 cc syringes because you have to be able to give it fast. Once the patient is back in normal sinus rhythm, or NSR, you have to be careful about administering it. With the heart beating, it's easy to overmedicate the patient and have him swing too far the other way so that his blood becomes too alkaline. So it's kind of a problem to know what to do."

"So what did Dr. Haseem do in Mr. Thompson's case?" Jess asked.

"Well, Mr. Thompson was worse off than most. He not only had labored breathing, but his pupils were fixed and dilated almost from the very beginning," Joyce said.

"Really? I didn't see that in the chart," Jess said.

"I'm sure it was there. I'm pretty good at recording. I have a lot of experience doing it, and I understand how important it is," Joyce said.

Wishing more and more that she had brought the ER record, Jess asked, "That is kind of odd, isn't it? I thought that pupils not reacting meant brain damage. You wouldn't expect that in a code when you have immediate resuscitation, would you?"

"True, but you don't expect the patient to have a seizure right out of the box either. Mr. Thompson had a seizure a few seconds after he regained NSR, which was pretty strange."

"I didn't see that in the record either," said Jess.

"What record are you looking at? Are you sure that you have the right patient?" Joyce asked.

"Well, I think so. I'll have to check that," Jess said. Still beating herself up for not bringing the ER record, she made a mental note to check the record she had received. She knew that the copy she had said it was Mr. Thompson's record—that was the first thing she had checked—but it was just a copy. She wondered if close scrutiny would indicate that it had been doctored.

"So Mr. Thompson regained NSR almost immediately, right? Don't you usually save an EKG strip when there's a change in heart rhythm?" Jess asked.

"Of course we do! You must not have the right chart," Joyce said, sounding a little aggravated at Jess's apparent failure to find what Joyce knew was in the chart.

"Well, like I said, I'll check that," Jess said, "but what did Dr. Haseem do for all of these problems?" Again Jess thought about the trouble she'd had contacting Joyce Brown and told herself to keep going with the questioning.

"Well, it's kind of tough to know what to do in a situation like that. There was a time there when we thought we had a success—when NSR returned. Then the patient had a seizure and never came around after that. As soon as we established the IV lines, we gave Mr. Thompson two amps of bicarb and also some epinephrine to prepare the heart for shocking. Then we shocked him, and he regained NSR.

"At first we thought we had saved him, but then he seized and continued to be comatose even though his heart restarted. Obviously there was something going on. It looked like he had a lung problem too since his breathing was so labored. Of course we were giving him oxygen, but that didn't help much, probably because of the lung problem, whatever it was.

"Dr. Haseem told me to watch him, and the respiratory therapist continued bagging him. We kept taking blood gasses, and he kept hovering around 6.9—it's supposed to be 7.35, you know. Even though his heart was beating, his pH didn't correct. His heart also started showing rhythm changes, and of course his blood pressure dropped as a result. I'm not an expert in reading EKGs, so I really don't know what the rhythm was. Dr. Haseem ordered one more amp of bicarb and epinephrine—to bring up the blood pressure, I assume. Dr. Haseem probably thought the labored breathing was the reason the pH didn't come up. Mr. Thompson wasn't regaining consciousness, and his heart was going downhill. It was really a last ditch effort to save him."

"Let me see if I follow you. You're saying that Mr. Thompson's breathing difficulty was preventing him from breathing off enough carbon dioxide and therefore caused his blood to remain acidotic even though his heart was beating? Dr. Haseem thought the acidosis might have caused Mr. Thompson to remain unconscious and to continue having heart rhythm problems."

"Well, possibly, but I don't know for sure. I think it's more like the idea that breathing problems can cause the buildup of lactic acid in the cells if the lungs can't take in enough oxygen to supply the body's needs. It could have been both, too. Doctors don't really discuss their thinking with us in a code. They just give the orders on what to give, and I just assumed that was what he was thinking.

"The brain is pretty delicate, and Dr. Haseem probably thought the acidosis might be causing Mr. Thompson to remain unconscious. And you can't just leave someone in acidosis forever either because the body organs start shutting down. I figured Dr. Haseem thought the acidosis was getting to Mr. Thompson's heart too. Like I say, the third amp of bicarb was sort of a last ditch effort. Unfortunately, it didn't work. Shortly after that Mr. Thompson went into ventricular fib again and that was it."

"Then what happened?" Jess prompted.

"Well, that was it for the code. Dr. Haseem called it off after we had really tried everything we could think of. We couldn't get Mr. Thompson back into normal sinus rhythm. Mr. Hansen came for his report, and I wrote up the record."

"Wasn't this a Sunday afternoon?" Jess asked. "Does Mr. Hansen ever leave the hospital?"

"Well, I haven't seen it done other places, but Mr. Hansen is really hands-on. He comes to every code situation where there's a problem."

"Really, why does he do that?"

"Well, I don't know. He didn't at first…but like I said, he started doing it after we had code problems. He also made a rule that no one could attend a code who wasn't giving care—he probably thought people were getting in the way. You know, you have plenty of people on a code anyway, especially at the beginning—one or two respiratory therapists, two nurses, the doctor, one or two pharmacists, and the scribe…sometimes we order X-rays, so there are X-ray techs. It can get pretty crowded and confusing with gawkers too."

"When did he make this rule?" Jess asked.

"Maybe early to mid-2006, close as I can remember," Joyce said.

"Hmm, about the time of Brad Thompson's death or the lawsuit," Jess thought.

Jess considered whether she ought to serve the subpoena she had brought but decided just to gowith an affidavit for the summary judgment. She took a guess that Joyce wasn't really hostile because it looked like her absence was Hansen's doing, not her own. If the case went to trial, Jess would need at least a deposition, and probably in-court testimony. "One thing at a time," Jess decided. She'd have to type the affidavit and get Joyce to come to the office to sign it.

"You said you have a new job. When did you leave Peoples?"

"It was about a little less than a year ago. We were just too busy at Peoples. I got tired of always running hard and trying to juggle the schedules of the nurses. I talked to one of my friends who worked at Renton Hospital, and she said that they weren't so busy. So I applied there and put in my notice at Peoples. Boy, that got attention! Mr. Hansen stopped by the ER and saw me the very next day—said he was sorry to see me go and that I should keep in touch just in case they needed me on this case."

"So you've been keeping in touch with Mr. Hansen since then?"

"I have—he wanted to make sure he could contact me, just in case. He said that up until now they haven't needed me."

Yet again, Jess marveled at how smooth Hansen had been, but decided not to get into that with Joyce until she had her testimony in black-and-white. "You know, I would really like to get an affidavit from you. It's a written statement that we can file with the court. Could you come to the office and sign it? I'll have it typed up and ready for you to sign when it's convenient."

Joyce looked surprised. She hadn't expected that anyone would care about what she had to say. Mr. Hansen had asked her to report about her conversation with Jess, and she felt a twinge of concern.

Jess, seeing a frown on Joyce's face, sensed her hesitancy. "Do you think that would be a problem?"

"Well, I don't think so. Mr. Hansen just said that I should call him after I talked to you. He said there was nothing I had to say that you would care about. I didn't know I was going to have to sign a statement."

"Well, often it's not necessary. It's just that we have a motion coming up, and I'm sure you don't want to come in for a deposition. That is a big deal and takes up a lot of your time. And the court won't just accept my rendition of what you say—that's hearsay. The court wants the facts straight from the witness."

"Well, I guess I can do that. Where and when would you want me to come?"

"I'll have the statement typed up and ready for you tomorrow morning. You can review it for accuracy, and I'll make any necessary changes if I get anything wrong. How about tomorrow morning about nine thirty?"

"That will work. Can you tell me how to get there? I know that driving in downtown Seattle is tough!"

The waitress appeared with lunch and Jess decided that small talk was in order. She didn't want to risk making Joyce more uncomfortable, and it looked like she was going to cooperate. Jess made the final decision not to serve the subpoena since sometimes it causes witnesses wavering between hostile and cooperative to clam up or "forget" like Dr. Haseem.

The two finished their lunch, and Jess paid the bill and hailed a cab. She asked for Joyce's cell phone number and then delivered her to the bus stop to catch her bus to Renton.

Chapter Twenty-Two

Arriving at the office, Jess no longer had to suppress her anger. Outraged thoughts looped through her mind, one after another and back again: "Hansen had Joyce on tap all the time! He testified in his deposition that he didn't know where she was! How could he be so cavalier about perjury? This really puts a different light on the case." Needing to talk this over with someone so she wouldn't explode with anger, she checked Danni's office and found that she was out. Well, maybe Drew was in.

She walked down the hall and looked into Drew's office. He was just putting down the phone. His sleeves were rolled up and his hair disheveled from repeated brushing with his hands. It wasn't that there were long locks to brush back—sometimes brushing the outside of the head works to clear the cobwebs inside, or at least it feels that way. It was amazing how good he looked, even knee-deep in work. "Do you have a minute?"

"Sure, come on in. You're all dressed up, Ms. Jessica. Looks like you've been to court."

"I have, actually. I had a motion in the Peoples case this morning. Judge Pacer read Baker out for being so obstreperous. It was a real pleasure." Jessica paused shortly and then changed the subject to the real reason she had stopped by. "You will never believe what I just found out!"

She continued without hesitation, not really expecting Drew to guess. "The reason I was in court was to get the personnel records of the head nurse the day Brad Thompson died. She attended Brad's code and even made the record on it. I haven't been able to locate her because her name is Brown, and there are a few dozen Browns in the Seattle area alone, as you might expect. So as soon as I get back to the office from the hearing, I get a phone call—from Joyce Brown! She has been in touch with Hansen, the Peoples CEO, since the case started. The arrogant son-of-bitch testified at his deposition that he didn't know where she was!"

Drew was surprised. "Really! I count on witnesses stretching the truth, but that's off the radar scope! How did you find this out?"

"I just talked to her. I didn't want to question her too much on being so hard to find, since I didn't want to spook her, of course. She said she's been in touch with Hansen all the time and that he just told her I wanted to talk with her."

"Well, he has more chutzpa than I do," said Drew.

"Me too," Jess agreed. "But that's not all. I just had lunch with her. She says she left Peoples because their staffing was just cut to the bone. She got tired of being overworked and, being head nurse in the ER, trying to schedule staffing. But nurses are used to being overworked, so it must have been pretty bad. The reason she's been missing is that before she left Peoples, they had a rash of episodes in which patients had relapses with codes. Patients would recover normal heartbeat and then develop trouble breathing and sometimes lapse back into a cardiac problem and die. She even confirmed that Brad had a stroke-like event in his code."

Jess suddenly realized something else. "This gives new meaning to what Haseem had to say, or rather didn't say at his deposition. She had just recognized what Haseem *really* had said to Mary that day in the ER. "Right, that's it! Remember that I told you Mary Thompson remembered Haseem saying, 'This should not be happening.' Well, I have always assumed that Haseem said 'happening' instead of 'happened,' because he was so upset or because he's not a native English speaker. What if he didn't make a mistake? What if mention of an *ongoing* problem that he was worried about just slipped out of his mouth?"

"That *is* interesting. Geez, Jess, I think you're right!" Drew agreed.

"That's why he did the head snap when I asked him the question at his deposition—he was coached on that. I asked him whether he said that Brad shouldn't have died but that wasn't what he was talking about—he was talking about the ongoing problem. I need to order the deposition and see if my recollection is right. Too bad I won't be able to get it before Monday

"Hmmm…anyway…after that, Hansen laid down a couple of rules at the hospital that are mighty suspicious in light of this case. Around the time that Brad came to the hospital, Hansen handed down a rule that he had to be called every time there was a code gone bad—if a person dies after a code, he's supposed to be called. Brad died on a Sunday afternoon, and Hansen even came in then. Everybody says he's hands-on, but this is crazy. First he shows up to talk with Mrs. Thompson after Brad's death, and then he comes unglued when I write a letter inquiring about it. Now, I find out that he's coming to every code death. What's going on here?

"And that's not all!" continued Jess. "He also limits the number of people that can come to codes. Now, I understand that having too many people around can be a problem, but why make it a standing rule? Joyce says she's never seen that done anywhere else, and neither did I when I was a nurse. Is that to cut down the number of witnesses? You know that everyone involved in a code is really busy with his own little area of care. Gawkers wouldn't be so busy and would have a better opportunity to get a look at an overall trend if they came to several codes. He'll probably say that it's just to make sure no one gets in the way—but why doesn't anyone else do that? That makes me wonder about People's answer to our interrogatories on whether or not they've had any other events where the people seemed to suffer a stroke. I think I need to talk to my expert about this."

"I think you've stumbled onto something there, especially since the hospital claims that Brad died of cardiac arrest rather than a stroke. It sounds to me that there may be something going on at Peoples," Drew agreed.

"Even a blind hog finds an acorn once in a while," quipped Jess.

Drew smiled—he didn't picture Jess as a hog. "I think that we should discuss this over a glass of wine and celebrate."

Jess smiled. She thought that sounded like a good idea, but she needed to make sure she had the statement ready for Joyce to sign the next morning. Once more Jess thought about how tough it had been to get in touch with her, and her anger at Hansen bubbled up again.

"How about if I meet you at McCormick's at four thirty," Jess said. "I have a couple of things I've got to do this afternoon, and I sure want to have Joyce's affidavit ready for her. She's coming in tomorrow...I hope."

"See you then," Drew said as Jess got up to leave. Drew's eyes followed her out. "Fine figure," Drew thought to himself—again—as Jess left his office.

Jess went back to her office and began typing the Brown statement. The days when lawyers dictated documents for secretarial typing are gone. Every attorney types nowadays—it's often easier to think when you are writing than when talking—and you can see the result. Then she called John Peterson.

"Hi, John, I have something to run by you. Do you have some time to fit me in tomorrow? The People's summary judgment is coming up in the Thompson case soon, and I think I just found out some serious information." Jess thought about how handy it was to have a medical contact who actually answers her phone calls. "The availability makes all the difference in cases like these," she thought.

Having made an appointment with John Peterson for one o'clock the next day, Jess looked at her watch—it was four twenty in the afternoon. "Hmm," she thought. "Interesting that I haven't heard from Baker about Joyce's personnel records. I wonder how much of Joyce's fake disappearance Baker has been involved in. It's one thing to have your client pulling these stunts. It's another to have the attorney involved. That's witness tampering, which is grounds for bar discipline.

"And why did they have her call me instead of giving me the records? Is there something in her records that they don't want to show?

"Anyway," she thought, "it's time to get down to McCormick's and meet Drew. Taking the elevators and then the escalators down to the Fourth Avenue exit can sometimes take all of ten minutes. What a pleasant thought—meeting Drew for drinks again! Well, it's better than pleasant!"

Chapter Twenty-Three

On the way down the elevator Jess thought through the case schedule for the next couple of weeks. It was going to be make-or-break time, and Jess really wanted to do right by Mary Thompson. She felt a little pride in having uncovered at least the tip of something—the "it" that she was looking for. Thinking of Joyce and the impact that her unavailability could have on her case caused Jess's anger to rise again. It was hard to let it go when the impact was so significant. "Hansen is off the charts!" she thought again.

Jess walked out the Fourth Avenue entrance of the Columbia Tower and hurried along the sidewalk close to the building. "Raining as always," she thought, "and I forgot my umbrella again." Jess's umbrellas—she had several—were always in the wrong place at the right time. "Fortunately, McCormick's is not very far."

Slipping in through the main entrance, Jess turned left and crossed the hallway to the bar. She was early, but Drew was earlier. He was sitting at the corner table sipping a merlot and reading, and he had ordered for her. How nice!

Brushing her hair in place with her fingers, she walked over to Drew. The sound of her heels on a non-carpeted floor announced her arrival, and Drew looked up and smiled.

"Well, any problems with your statement for Ms. Brown?" he asked.

"Huh" was the really articulate response that came to Jess's mind. He really seemed to be paying attention. She had only mentioned Joyce Brown one or two times. The name was important to Jess, but Drew had no reason to care about it much. And all that wrapped up in a wonderful looking body—almost too good to be true!

"Hi to you too, and thanks for asking! Well, no problem with the statement. My only problem is how to work it into the legal theory. I know that there is something there, and I know there should be some way to show that it's actionable. I just have to give it some thought…I'll work on that tomorrow."

"Say, you see this picture of Nixon up here on the wall?" Drew asked, pointing to the black-and-white picture behind him.

"Actually, I have noticed that before. I kind of wondered why anyone would think that a picture of Nixon is decorative," Jess said.

"Well it's history," Drew said. "Ehrlichman, you know the guy that went to jail in Watergate?"

"One of the many," responded Jess.

"Well, he was from Seattle. In fact, his old law firm was in this very building before it became part of the Columbia Tower."

"You are just a wealth of information." Jess smiled.

"Stick around. There's more where that came from," Drew said as he smiled back.

Jess thought, "Even this is fun…talking about nothing."

Chapter Twenty-Four

At seven thirty on Thursday morning, Jess was driving down Second Avenue on her way to work. Not only had she and Drew discussed "important" things, like why the picture of Nixon was on the wall, they had also discussed a few more practical things, like the case law and factual basis to respond to the summary judgment coming up in the Peoples case. Jess had a lot to do to get the pleadings ready for filing on Monday, and it started with Joyce Brown's statement. The final thing was to check what she needed to prove her case under the *res ipsa loquitur* theory. That would take a little research.

She had torn herself away from the bar, despite the urge to stay. Drew was one hell of a guy—a body and brains all rolled into one. "I wonder why his wife let him get away. Maybe her loss is my gain," she thought. "We'll see."

"Back to work," Jess did a soft mental face-slap to bring herself back to reality. She needed to get into the office and look at the statement she had typed for Joyce to confirm it was as near perfect as she remembered.

In the office, Jess first checked her voice mail. "Bad news," she thought, when she heard Joyce's voice.

"Hi, this is Joyce Brown. I know I said I'd come in and sign a statement today. I…I can't come in—someone trashed my car. The windows are bashed in. The seats are slashed," Joyce said, clearly agitated. "I can't figure it out—my car was in the garage. I have to get it fixed…I'll have to give you a call."

"Damn," Jess thought as she tried Joyce's cell number. As she expected, there was no response. She beat herself over the head wondering if she should have served the subpoena. Would that have made a difference? Sometimes danger causes even the most responsible people to ignore legal "compulsion."

Jess would try again, but she felt concern growing in the back of her mind. "This is quite a coincidence, both of us victims of vandalism. It's one thing to have a random act from someone passing by. Breaking into a garage to get to a car looks as intentional as the break-in of my condo," she thought to herself. She was sure after her last contact with the police that they wouldn't see this as anything more than a coincidence. Then another suspicion rose again. "I wonder if Dr. Haseem was on duty last night. Can't be—I can't believe he'd do this."

"Well, to the books, anyway," she thought. "We need to see what the court thinks about *res ipsa loquitur*."

Jess spent the next four hours on the computer checking the application of *res ipsa loquitur* in a medical malpractice setting. She had originally thought she might be able to use the legal theory, and the information that Joyce had provided made it clear that the theory could apply in this case. There really had been a stroke during the code. Without Joyce's information, it had been an uphill battle because of the sparse record and vague information that Jess had from Dr. Haseem's deposition. She was glad to see from her research that the *res ipsa* theory was well developed for this factual setting.

What the case law also showed is that plenty of doctors and hospitals protested the application of the theory to their cases. The courts had generally agreed with them, but not in every case. At first the theory was applied to prove malpractice when a sponge was left in a patient. In that situation, the court decided a doctor's affidavit wasn't necessary to prove malpractice. That looked pretty reasonable to Jess.

Later, the theory was expanded into other situations, but unfortunately the court didn't think a victim could get along without a doctor's affidavit in these cases. In 1972 in *Zebarth v. Swedish Hospital Medical Center*, the court had applied the theory to a case similar to this. In that case the patient had suffered from radiation burns in treatment of cancer. A doctor testified that this result wouldn't have occurred absent negligent care—the treatment recorded in the hospital's record couldn't have produced the result. Jess chuckled at the text of the case. It wasn't the factual situation she was chuckling at—it was the legal jargon set out in the case for application of the theory. "Why do they always have to make legal theory look so onerous?" Jess thought, and then she read:

The plaintiff must provide evidence of:

1. The defendant's exclusive control of the instrumentality producing the injury;

2. The lack of voluntary participation or contribution by the plaintiff to produce the injury; and

3. One of the following…

The legal requirements for application of *res ipsa* continued down the page an additional paragraph. Reading elements for most legal theories cause peoples' eyes to glaze over. Sometimes there's no way around it since theories must be well defined, but sometimes they just grow like a snake over time, with the court adding a few new ideas as the case law develops.

Well, at least it was clear that the Thompson case fit the legal theory, but contrary to her wishful thinking, Jess saw that she was going to need the affidavit of a medical expert to prove her case even under *res ipsa*. It would be hard to convince a judge that a nonmedical person would know a stroke wouldn't have occurred in Brad Thompson's case absent negligence. Would John Peterson be able to give her an affidavit on that? This would be a little outside the scope of his specialized training as a vascular surgeon. She needed the opinion by Monday, and it would be hard to get if John couldn't do it.

"Damn that unethical asshole!" Jess thought again about the effect of withholding Joyce's location. "I wonder how much Baker knows about this."

She thought about whether she should have bitten the bullet early on in this case and paid the flat fee retainer of $7,500 to $10,000 that any expert other than John Peterson probably would have required to review the file and give an opinion. The problem was, at that time and even now, she wasn't even sure what kind of expert she should approach—an ER doc, a pathologist, one of each? Without having the information that Joyce gave her, she would really have been making a wild-ass guess, and it wasn't totally clear now what kind of expert would be necessary.

Jess hated the thought of running this by an expert taking a guess on the right specialty. More than once she'd had an expert charge her a big retainer for review and then tell her, "Sorry, this is outside my scope of expertise." But they never seemed to want to give the retainer back. On at least one of those occasions, Jess was sure that the doctor had just had second thoughts about testifying, but even he didn't want to give her the retainer back.

"Oops, its lunch time," Jess noticed looking at the clock on the bookcase. She had an appointment with John Peterson at one o'clock. She decided she could walk up to "pill hill," one of the seven hills in Seattle—officially named First Hill—where there's a concentration of hospitals and high-rise buildings that housed doctors' offices. She decided to grab lunch on the way and hoped her head would clear in the meantime. She felt like *res ipsa* was coming out her ears, and the anger at Baker wasn't helping either.

Jess redialed Joyce's cell one more time. No answer.

Chapter Twenty-Five

Finishing her sandwich in John's waiting room, Jess was hoping she could cool down before she met with him. The trek up the hill had brought on "the glow" of exertion.

But her worry about having time to cool down was short-lived. John's assistant said he was delayed at the hospital in surgery and that he'd be about an hour late. "Damn, I don't have time for this," she thought. "Too much to do and no time to do it." Fortunately, Jess always carried her blackberry with her. She took care of some e-mails while waiting.

At a quarter after two, John walked through the waiting room on his way to the office. He waived Jess in. "Really sorry," he said as he took off his sport coat and put on his lab jacket. "The patient just wasn't cooperating with my schedule. This is one of the reasons I keep telling you we should meet after work." John grinned. "Now what's this new information you have?"

Sitting down in the patient's chair, Jess took out her notes and the autopsy report. John's suggestion and his change of coats brought to mind the reason that she always tried to see John during office hours. She had always found him to be a handsome man, and watching him change coats reminded her that he was well-built.

Ignoring the standing invitation, Jess responded to the business portion of their meeting. "The new information came from the nurse who was in the emergency room."

After she finished explaining what she had learned from Joyce, John responded with a grin, "You attorneys are looking for a conspiracy around every corner."

"When you deal with slime bags you start looking for slime," Jess thought. "No use discussing that with John, though. He lives in a different world."

Jess continued, "The rules Lars Hansen instituted around codes in the hospital require that he be called on every code gone bad, and he even limits the number of persons that can come to a code. When you put that together, it suggests he knows there's a problem and is hoping to cover it up."

The grin left John's face. "Well, let me step back. An unusual number of bad codes can be a problem. Usually nurses are able to tell that kind of thing. I've actually never heard of a CEO being called to codes gone bad. That is really a medical, not a business, kind of thing. I've often thought that the gawkers at codes ought to be kept out, but I've never heard of a CEO ordering it. Do you have proof that Hansen did that?"

"There he goes again, trying to take care of the legal end of my case," Jess thought. In Jess's experience, experts, especially male experts, are so used to dealing with women in the role of the assistant that they can't seem to drop the habit of assuming they need to be guided.

"You let me worry about that. What I need from you is to tell me why a CEO would think that he should be called for every code gone bad?"

"I have to agree with you. That's extremely abnormal. Offhand, I can't think of a reason for it unless the guy is a workaholic. The other issues that you raise…inadequate staffing is always a problem. Limiting responders to codes is…though it is unusual, it's not a bad idea. Sometimes gawkers can get in the way. As I said, I've never heard of that being a hospital policy."

"What do you think about the trend of relapses after regaining normal sinus rhythm?"

John paused. "You may have something there, even though I kidded you about conspiracies. If a young guy like this patient, who had no appreciable atherosclerosis, recovers on the first shock, his chances of living are pretty good. I'd say the statistics about poor recovery from cardiac arrest don't really apply here, but it still does depend on the underlying cause of the arrhythmia. If the trend is enough that it stands out to a nurse, I think there may be more there. Did she say how often it happened and if it happened to more than one doctor? It's hard to say what's going on without more information."

"Unfortunately, she didn't have those facts. And it's *really* unfortunate because I have to get out a response to the hospital's summary judgment motion this coming Monday. They've been keeping Nurse Brown under wraps until now. Now I understand why."

"Well, I have to admit that her information is tantalizing. But there you go again! You lawyers are a suspicious lot," Peterson kidded Jess.

"It comes from experience, John. It comes from experience," Jess retorted.

Jess was glad to hear John confirm her suspicion about what Joyce said. She was disappointed to see that his expertise didn't add the critical conclusion—what caused the death. She was hoping for some revelation but didn't get one this time. She was going to have to dig some more.

Jess had to settle for leaving a copy of the autopsy report with John. He said he'd take the report with him and give it some thought over the weekend.

Chapter Twenty-Six

Jess decided to walk back to the office. Her frustration on not being able to get the facts on Brad Thompson's death was frying her brain.

Back at the office, she decided to talk to Danni, who knew something about the case. Maybe she would have a bright idea. Unfortunately, Danni wasn't in the office. Jess checked with Lorraine and learned that Danni had just settled the case that was going to trial in a matter of days and had decided to spend a little time on vacation with her husband to make up for the sixty-hour weeks she had been putting in. Danni told Lorraine about her plans and left a message for Jess to be sure to get in touch if she needed help.

Jess didn't even need to ask where Danni was on vacation this time of year. Danni and her husband, Dave, had a condo on Lake Chelan that Danni had inherited from her family. The condo had a view looking over the lake at the mountains of yellow-and-green patchwork and the crystal-clear, blue waters. You could easily see the bottom of the lake where it was as much as thirty feet deep. The condo had four hundred feet of beach, a huge lawn, and an Olympic-size pool. There is plenty of space to sunbathe, plenty of nearby restaurants to have a bite to eat, and overall, it's just a wonderful place to vacation.

Chelan is about four hours from Seattle, except on holidays when the whole state is on the road. Being on the east side of the Cascade Mountains, the climate is almost the polar opposite of Seattle. The sun is out almost every day in the summer in Chelan even though the natives might not describe it as such. "They just don't have the weather on the west side of the state to compare it with," Jess thought.

Danni let Jess use the condominium on occasion, and she understood why Danni would take off to the lake whenever possible.

Lorraine delivered the message about Danni's whereabouts in her usual, professional manner. Jess could tell from her tone, however, that Lorraine was thinking that Danni really needed the time off. Lorraine was especially protective of her right now since she and her husband were trying to have a baby.

Lorraine was the traditional sort. She always came to work in a skirt, practical heels, and perfectly coiffed hair. Her idea of "professional" was being a secretary. She wouldn't accept the title of legal assistant, even though her performance was way above the normal secretary and even beyond the next step up in training, the paralegal. Though Lorraine had never told Jess this, Jess was sure Lorraine thought that if women worked sixty hours a week, it should be in the home. She constantly reminded Danni and Jess that they should take better care of themselves. Women weren't meant to drive themselves to the grave, at least not while doing "men's work."

Well, right now Jess had more pressing things on her mind than worrying about Lorraine's disapproval of her lifestyle. And since Danni wasn't there to talk, Jess decided to check on whether Drew was in. Not an unwelcome opportunity!

Chapter Twenty-Seven

Drew was in his office, his head buried in a newspaper. Jess popped her head around the door jam and said, "Hi, got a minute?

"For you? Absolutely! But I have more than time for you." Seeing the red begin to rise in Jess's face, Drew quickly surmised that statement had come out wrong and added, "I just got around to reading this morning's paper. Look what I found…a glowing report about your favorite person, Lars Hansen, CEO."

Drew folded the paper to show Jess the full-page spread in the *Seattle Times* about Lars Hansen. It looked like the story had started out as a feature on Peoples Hospital but morphed into a celebration of the life of its CEO. There was a photo montage of Hansen at the office, Hansen with his beautiful bombshell wife, and Hansen with the junior soccer team that the hospital sponsored.

The story started with a rendition of Hansen's tenure at Peoples and VAHC. Hansen had been with the company for seventeen years. The story praised his performance at Peoples, touting that he had taken the hospital from a failing institution about to close to a profitable, well-honed health care facility. "Hmm, whoever wrote this got all his facts from the horse's mouth. I've always wondered why someone who's been with the company as long as he has would want to come to Seattle to run an individual facility," said Jess.

"My thoughts exactly…but look at what he says. He's made a practice of bringing in doctors from war-torn or impoverished countries 'to remedy the medical shortage plaguing the U.S.' And also to get staff that's beholden to him, I bet," Drew added wryly.

"I didn't know Seattle had a shortage of doctors. He says he has tapped into a stream of Near East and Asian immigrants. I bet they're so glad to be here they can hardly believe their luck. He has also maximized the use of Filipino nurses. He touts the benefit of globalization. I bet he likes the gratitude that he gets as well."

"So Dr. Haseem isn't an aberration," Jess noted.

"Hansen also talks about use of drug repackaging to 'save time and prevent mistakes.' He says that VAHC hospitals have their own repackaging facilities to assure quality control," Drew read from the article.

Looking up from the paper, he added, "I actually had a suit involving a dispute over drug profits. I learned enough to know that repackaging of drugs can be a big money-maker for a hospital. The difference between the cost of drugs in bulk and repackaged can be huge. The question is how much money is it and who gets it. Generally, I think, the amount of profits on drugs is a closely guarded secret. Sometimes the normal profits aren't enough for repackagers. They're always trying to get more and pay less, which can result in some pretty shoddy controls or even counterfeit drugs."

"Really!" Jess exclaimed. "That is a bit of interesting information. Well, I applaud Hansen for being so 'open-minded,' but I don't agree with the 'well-honed' machine idea. Brad Thompson's death was not just an 'act of God.'"

"Maybe I ought to be looking into how Peoples' repackager measures up." She and Drew discussed what Peterson had to say and what she had found on *res ipsa*. They agreed that she needed a lot more information.

Chapter Twenty-Eight

On the way home from work that night, Jess stopped in the lobby to pick up her mail. Tommy virtually tackled her as soon as she got out of the elevator. He had obviously been waiting to talk with her and was bubbling over with news.

"Ms. Jessica, you'll never guess what I found out," Tommy said.

Jess knew he *really* wanted her to guess, but she had too many things on her mind to play that game. The best she could get out was, "What, Tommy? What have you found out?"

"I found out how he got in!"

Jess assumed that Tommy was talking about the intruder, and she was immediately more interested.

"It has really bothered me that we couldn't see him come in the garage. I just know he didn't come through the lobby when I was on duty. So I practiced walking through the garage so the cameras wouldn't see me. And I did it! I made it all the way through the garage without being seen. Do you want to look?"

Tommy looked so proud of himself that Jess knew she should look at the video, but she really needed to get up stairs and pick up Reesa.

"Tommy, that's great! Thanks for checking that out."

Tommy beamed and said again, "Let me show you!"

"I have to pick up Reesa and get dinner, Tommy, but if you save it I can watch it another time."

"I am going to save it, Ms. Jessica. I'm going to show it to the manager. We need to fix those cameras."

"Thanks, Tommy. You did good work." He really did have a good heart.

Chapter Twenty-Nine

Jess was lying in bed scrunching her eyes closed as tightly as possible. The sun was starting to stream in through the window, and Jess wasn't ready to wake up yet. She wanted to extend her daydream about Drew a little longer. Drew sitting at his desk...Drew sitting across from her at McCormick's...Drew in bed? "Geez, Jess, get a grip!" she scolded herself. Then, she thought, "Amazing! That sounded like my mother."

Jess knew that if she opened her eyes, she would see Reesa's nose about an inch from her right eye, waiting for Jess to show signs of being awake. As soon as Reesa saw the eye open, she would climb on top of Jess and start purring up a storm. This was Reesa's way of showing her love, but also her way of pushing Jess to get out of bed to get her breakfast.

It was Saturday, and Jess had a big weekend of doing research planned. Jess just knew there had to be something in the autopsy report that would confirm her theory about Peoples. And maybe she could find out something about Peoples' repackager. Were there any quality control issues? Jess kept thinking about the last time she had seen Mary. She had looked so worn out from her efforts on the case.

The phone rang, jolting Jess's mind out of her daydreaming and back to reality.

She picked up the phone and answered, "Hello?"

"Good morning, Ms. Jessica." It was Drew. "I thought that you might like to go for a bike ride with me today, if you're into that sort of thing."

"Well, good morning to you! And yes, sometimes I am into that sort of thing, especially on days like this." The sun streaming in the window in Seattle is a rare event even in July, and that made it even harder to turn down Drew's invitation. "But, unfortunately, I have another self-imposed date today—research. I have a response to a summary judgment motion due Monday in the Peoples case. I don't want to lose that motion, and with what I have right now, there's a good chance I will. I just don't want to let Mary Thompson down."

Drew, of course, didn't have to be told about the significance of a summary judgment motion. Even with the help of the *res ipsa* legal theory, there was much more to do. From their discussion Thursday afternoon, Drew knew that if Jess could give some information to explain why there might be a rash of code relapses, it might help convince the judge to give her more time to respond to the summary judgment motion—especially considering Joyce's short appearance and subsequent disappearance.

"Well, I say never suffer alone. If you won't go bike riding with me, how about if I help you with your research. I happen to be an attorney, you know. I know about that kind of thing," Drew volunteered.

"You're kidding! You would pass up one of the ten sunny days of the Seattle summer to help me do research? You're on! I think I should hang up before you change your mind!"

"No problem. I know what I'm in for. What time and where?"

"My office at nine o'clock?"

"See you then."

"And thanks!" Jess said as she hung up the phone.

Jess and Reesa arrived at the office just minutes before Drew. If you have to do research on a beautiful summer day, it is *a lot* better not to be doing it alone. Reesa often helped Jess with research on weekends when there weren't too many people in the office. Her major assistance was sitting on Jess's lap and purring. That was Reesa's method of typing, and she was really good at it. She insisted on sitting on the keyboard on occasion when she thought Jess needed a break. That was usually helpful too.

Just as they were getting set up, Drew looked in the door. "Well, I see you two are already hard at work. My cat used to come to work with me on occasion."

"Really! Well, if you set your laptop down in this office, you're likely to have a furry friend right away. I'll get you a more comfortable chair." Jess went next door to Danni's office and pulled her chair in. "Have a seat. Danni has back trouble, so this is a really comfortable chair—only the best for my research assistant."

"This is working out to be a fun Saturday, after all," Jess thought. For the umpteenth time, she also thought, "Drew is more than just a pretty face and sumptuous body." She almost heard her mother's voice again, but she was having such a good time that she was able to suppress it.

"Well, what are we looking for, Ms. Jessica?"

"I'd like you to see what you can find out about Peoples or VAHC. I can't believe it's totally innocent that Hansen shows up after all bad codes. I'm wondering if we can find anything online that would suggest that Peoples has a problem with code deaths or just deaths. I'm going to read this autopsy report again."

About an hour and a half later, Drew, Jess, and Reesa were silently working away. Well, Reesa wasn't so silent. She was purring on Drew's lap as he surfed the Internet.

"Drew, you don't happen to have any biology in your background, do you?" Jess asked.

"Well, not much. At one point, I thought about going to med school. But the time in the labs got in my way. I had too much partying to do as an undergrad. I did take anatomy and physiology, though."

"Well, do you know what a patent foramen ovale is?"

Drew paused and then said, "I think I do remember that a patent foramen ovale is a hole in the heart. It's a defect that can linger if the heart structure doesn't change like it's supposed to at birth. You medical people call it a 'PFO,' don't you?"

"Hey, a man of many talents!" Jess said. "The reason I ask is that Brad Thompson had a PFO. I hadn't thought it was important until now. I keep thinking about what Joyce said—that there was a pattern of bad codes." Jess paused. "John Peterson, my expert, has looked over the Thompson code records with a fine-tooth comb. He says that as far as he can tell, he can't really say there's anything wrong with the care, although the record is pretty sparse. I wonder if I've been so focused on the fact that I thought the records were doctored that I missed another possible cause. If there were other code relapses, they might have looked different because Brad had a patent foramen ovale. That could be where I went wrong—if I did go wrong—on formulating my interrogatories about other bad codes. I'm not sure that Hansen or Baker didn't just lie in the answer they gave me, especially since I know that Hansen was in touch with Joyce Brown all along. But I wonder if the other patients with bad codes died of complications that looked different. They might not have had strokes because they didn't have a hole in the heart that funneled blood to the head."

"What difference would that make?"

"I'm thinking that other codes had complications that were even harder to find. For example, if there's a bad medication given in a code, it would ordinarily go to the lungs in someone who didn't have a patent foramen ovale. The medication would come up from the vein, to the heart, then to the lungs."

"Okay, I'm following you," Drew agreed.

"Well, if the medication that Brad received went to the head, instead of the lungs—because of the patent foramen ovale—it might be a little clearer in him that something was going wrong. The medication goes from the vein, then to the heart, and more to the head because of the PFO. Then it kills part of the brain during the beginning of the code. The brain is pretty sensitive and, if it gets a dose of the wrong thing, would be more harmed than if the bad drug was sent to the whole body. Even if someone else had a PFO—if you didn't push to find out what happened, like Mary Thompson did—you might never know that there was a predeath stroke. The rest of the brain dies anyway at the end of a code. You have to be looking at the brain pretty closely to see if it all died at once. I bet it's so rare, that no one would normally look for it. It would explain why there was a rash of bad code results and why Hansen appears to be thinking that all the doctors might be having a problem. I think it's the medication.

"That also explains why Hansen tried to keep Joyce Brown out of the way. He probably thinks she might be picking up on something, like the fact that the problem doesn't just occur with Dr. Haseem."

"And, if that's true, the hospital could have a much larger problem—with bad drugs," Drew added.

"True," Jess agreed. "This is something like a medication error—giving the wrong medication. Medication errors aren't all that rare but often they don't kill the patient. As long as the wrong drug goes to the lungs, not the head, and is sent out to the whole body, it becomes so dilute that unless it's a really potent kind of drug or a drug that is really wrong for the patient, it probably won't make a difference.

"I should run this by John Peterson," Jess said as she picked up the phone and called him on his cell. He didn't answer, so she left a message. John called back shortly. Seeing the caller ID, Jess picked up the phone and started right out with her question.

"John, I think the clue we've been missing here is the patent foramen ovale. Remember, the coroner mentioned that Brad Thompson had one."

"Well good Saturday morning to you too, Ms. Lamm. Don't you ever lighten up...even on the weekends? You lawyers are too intense."

"Sorry, John. I know. I tend to get that way when I know there's something out there that I just can't put my finger on. So, good Saturday morning to you too. How are you today?" Jess paused. "Okay, so now let me tell you about my theory..."

When Jess finished explaining, John paused a minute and then said, "Well, I'm making rounds, but I don't plan to spend the whole day in the hospital. Why don't we meet for lunch? I'll bring the autopsy report, and we can look over the information about the PFO."

Jess turned slightly red. She knew John had more in mind. "Sure, I can do that. However, I have a friend with me who's helping me do research. I'd like him to come too. I'll buy."

Jess could almost hear the smile dissolving from John's face on the other end of the line.

"Sure, no problem. Where shall we meet?"

"How about the Bell Street Diner at one o'clock."

"See you then." The phone went dead.

Jess and Drew sat in silence for another hour, continuing their research. Jess worked on her brief about *res ipsa*. That ugly thought appeared again—the brief was due by four o'clock Monday afternoon. She was used to pressure, but this was more than the usual amount. Not getting in a response on time can be catastrophic—it might not even be considered, and the case could be dismissed, permanently.

"Does *res ipsa* apply to bad drugs," she wondered. "Probably not, I'll have to check, but it's a good alternative basis anyway."

Jess's mind began wandering. She wondered what Drew could tell from her side of the conversation with John. She wondered if he had noticed her red face when John suggested lunch.

Breaking the silence, Drew said, "Well looky here! VAHC has a relationship with a suspect drug repackager. It says here that VAHC, through its subsidiary repackager, is a leader in developing unit-dose repackaging. This repackager is under investigation by the FDA."

Jess and Drew stared at each other, allowing the information to percolate. Could this explain why Hansen was so rabid about his defense? If bad drugs were the problem, Peoples would be in a world of hurt. Every patient would be wondering if a bad result was because of bad drugs, and justifiably so. Lawsuits would be coming out of the woodwork.

Of course, just finding this information doesn't make it admissible in court. Somebody has to verify under oath that Peoples really is working with the suspect repackager. That information should be verified by someone from Peoples, but there was no time to get that testimony from Hansen or anyone else at Peoples between now and Monday.

Chalk up another advantage gained by Baker's delay. It was becoming clearer that Jess was going to be seeking a continuance on Monday so she would have more time to get the information. She'd have to build a good argument as to why she deserved one. Clearly Baker wasn't going to cave in on that request.

Still mulling over the situation, Jess and Drew decided to walk down the hill to the Bell Street Diner. The sun was shining, and the air was warm. No Seattleite could let this kind of a day go without taking some time to enjoy the outdoors. Walking down Cherry, Drew and Jess were lost in thought, but not too lost to notice the twinkles of sun dancing off the blue water of Puget Sound and the mountains in the background. Looking down at the water from up the hill caused the view to be framed between the buildings, making it look like a giant big-screen TV displaying a startlingly beautiful scene. "I love this town! Seattle is really one of the prettiest cities that I know," thought Jess.

Chapter Thirty

Jess and Drew arrived before Peterson, so they took a seat and ordered a glass of wine. Shortly, John Peterson entered, located Jess and Drew, and strode over in his usual unhurried, dignified style. He wore a brown leather bomber jacket and slacks. "The bomber jacket is especially appropriate since he flies his own plane," Jess thought.

John had once told Jess that he really loved flying—escaping the hustle of life to peace and quiet. Jess could understand that. There was surely a lot of hustle in John's life. He had asked Jess if she wanted to go for a flight over Mt. St. Helens one time. "It would have been tempting if there weren't strings attached," she thought.

John was pulling the autopsy report out of his jacket pocket as he walked. As he sat down, Jess said, "John Peterson, I'd like you to meet Drew Stewart. Drew, John is the guy who helps me scope out cases to see if there's anything there. He's a surgeon with a specialty in vascular surgery, but he hasn't forgotten the basics from medical school. He's been a big help at times."

"Nice to meet you, John," Drew said, in a not-so-convincing voice.

Turning back to Jess, John said, "Well, one of the reasons I was late is that I stopped by the hospital morgue and ran the autopsy report by the pathologist. He agrees with me that the evidence of brain damage could mean the coroner got the cause of death wrong. It may well be that Brad Thompson died of a stroke rather than cardiac arrest. You just couldn't tell at the time because his heart kept beating for a while."

"So he agrees with my theory?" Jess interrupted.

"Give me a second here," John continued. "Not only was he just forty years old, but the autopsy shows no evidences of atherosclerosis, making it extremely unlikely that he would have a stroke. So why did he have one?"

John paused, and Jess said, "Go ahead. We're dying to hear." Actually John knew that, but he wanted to deliver the information with his usual flare.

"Well, if Brad Thompson did die of a stroke, it's possible that what killed him came from the drugs that he received in the code—as you theorized. Ordinarily you wouldn't see the result in the brain, but Brad had a PFO, as you mentioned."

"But wouldn't the coroner have noticed if there was a lot of drug in the brain or the lungs?" Jess asked.

"Not necessarily. You have to know what to look at and test for. Most drugs wouldn't cause such a massive effect on the brain even if they got there in concentrated form. So you have to determine what would make this different. One thing that you usually give in a code in large amounts is sodium bicarbonate. I talked to the pathologist about that. The thing is, if that were the culprit, you might not even find anything...even if you looked. Bicarb breaks down to things that naturally occur in the body—water, carbon dioxide, and salt. Heck, some carbon dioxide might even be removed from the body through the lungs before the patient died, since he continued to breathe. The problem with that theory is that we give bicarb all the time in codes, and we don't get a result like this."

"John, we've discovered that Peoples may be getting bad drugs," Drew interjected. John turned to him as though he hadn't remembered that Drew was there. The whole time that he was discussing his theory, John had been looking at Jess. Drew was beginning to wonder if he were invisible.

"Really, what do you know about that?" John asked.

"Apparently a drug repackager that the parent company of Peoples deals with is under investigation by the FDA. One of their facilities has been repeatedly cited for safety violations for the past eleven years. They've had seven citations in this year alone, and they're serious enough that the feds suspended operations at the facility. The company is also being investigated for receiving counterfeit drugs from China. That's a tough one—as long as they look right, it's difficult to tell whether you're getting the genuine thing. Nobody stamps "counterfeit" on the label," Drew said wryly. "You can't test every one, and usually they don't test any."

John looked at Drew with renewed interest. "Maybe he isn't just a pretty face," John thought to himself. "How did you find this out?" he asked.

"Well, I have a little information from a prior case, and I did more research on the Internet this morning. Unfortunately, I haven't yet found out what drugs the violations involved. But you have to think that there may be stuff out there that the feds didn't catch as well. So even if we're able to tell what was recalled, the actual culprit might be something else."

John followed up on Drew's thought. "You know, if there was bad bicarb, it's possible that it could form bubbles because of the wrong combination of ingredients. Bubbles can cause a stroke, just like a blood clot. If the bubbles were so voluminous that they couldn't make it through the small vessels of the brain, they could stop the blood flow. We might not even see them since byproducts of bicarb occur naturally."

"Well, as someone famous once said, 'Even a blind hog finds an acorn once in once in a while,'" Drew interjected.

Jess smiled at Drew and turned to John. "Inside joke," she said. Turning back to Drew, Jess said, "And you don't know how right you are. I first heard that from a labor lawyer friend of mine who is famous, or at least more famous than I am. I just adopted it."

"Hmm, this guy is competition," John thought.

Jess continued, "What about the other part of my theory… about the other codes, John. Would this explain why we didn't get the information about other bad codes, assuming that Peoples was being honest in their answers to my interrogatories. I asked about other evidence of strokes during codes. But some strokes might be missed because they didn't do an autopsy. The other patients might have died as a result of some other manifestation of the problem—a respiratory manifestation."

"Right," John said. "Too much gas or bubbling in the system might act like a pulmonary embolus—a blood clot in the lungs—and stop blood flow. That would sure make it harder to resuscitate. You might not even see it as a relapse, because depending on when the bad bicarb was given, you'd never see a recovery. The patient would just die, and everyone would think it was from the heart problem initiating the code situation. In any case, it would be hard to nail down. You'd probably just have to look at the overall rate of success in code resuscitations.

"In fact, there was probably a little respiratory impact in this code too. It's probably an over-statement to conclude that the stroke actually caused the death itself, at least without a follow-up autopsy. Something equivalent to a pulmonary embolus was probably helping the patient toward death in this case too. Not all of the bad drug would necessarily go to the brain.

"Well," John said, "now that I solved your case for you, Jess, you promised me lunch. You two have been slopping down wine and haven't even offered me any. I want to collect on your promise."

"Miss, we're ready to order," said Jess, waiving over the waitress. She knew the case was far from solved, but at least it was moving in that direction.

Chapter Thirty-One

It was really difficult to go back to the office. The sun outside, a glass of wine, and wonderful company made it almost impossible. Despite that, Jess and Drew did take a cab back to the office for more research. No one but a fitness freak would walk up the hill from the waterfront to the Columbia Tower—not if there's a choice.

"The only reason I'm doing this is for Mary and Madaline," thought Jess. "It's hard to believe Drew is willing to waste such a great afternoon inside."

"That may tell you something." Jess heard her mother's voice again, but didn't pay attention.

Back at the office, they discussed how to split up the work. Drew would continue with the research regarding drug information, and Reesa decided to help him by sitting on his lap again.

Jess started drafting the brief and affidavits to present the information they had uncovered to the court. The trouble was that they had nothing concrete. She could hear John Baker's argument already—heck, she could almost write it for him! "Mere speculation! There has to be some end to the fishing expedition!" Jess hoped the fact that Hansen appeared to have lied about knowing the whereabouts of Joyce Brown would buy her more time, but it was really her word against Hansen's on this one.

Her success on obtaining a continuance would boil down to whether Judge Pacer believed Jess's rendition of what Joyce had told her, which Jess would offer by affidavit. It's not uncommon that lawyers offer their own versions of the facts to buy time to respond to motions, so judges can be skeptical about reasons for requested continuances. Jess thought she had a good reputation for veracity with the judge, and you'd really have to be stretching things to make *this* up.

A couple of hours later, Drew turned around his chair and said, "Look at this! I think we've hit pay dirt."

"What? Tell me what you've got!" said Jess, glad to hear some good news.

"Well, I've been looking for what was recalled from Unit Dose, Inc., the drug repackager. Original name, huh?" Giving Jess no time to respond—because she looked so intense—he proceeded. "One of the recalled drugs was sodium bicarbonate. Actually, they discovered a problem because some of the syringes had white residue in them. That's a no-no for bicarb."

"That is good news," Jess laughed, "just not for the patients."

"Right! Well…then they traced the drug back to a manufacturer in Hangzhou, China, which takes a long time. When you're a foreign entity investigating problems in China, the Chinese government can work really slowly, like when the FDA was trying to investigate the poison cough syrup production. It took a year for the investigators to get into the plant, and by the time they got there the plant was closed and its records destroyed, according to the *New York Times*."

"That's a shocker," Jess interjected wryly.

Drew continued, "It turns out that making sodium bicarbonate is a pretty intricate process because sterilization destroys some of the carbon dioxide in the mixture, but you definitely want it to be sterilized. So you have to add additional carbon dioxide to the original, presterilized mixture to come out with the correct end result. Well, the Chinese drug manufacturer contracted out that part of the manufacturing process. The sub decided that all the fuss of adding carbon dioxide and checking the pH was unnecessary. In order to make a bigger profit, he used sodium bicarbonate off the shelf, like you buy in the grocery store here. He also didn't want to waste extra money to pay highly qualified workers or to clean up the water he was using before he mixed up the solution. As a result, what was ending up in the syringe wasn't of the highest quality.

"No one would have known, except that a couple of the syringes had so much sodium bicarbonate in them that it came out of solution leaving minute portions of white stuff in the syringe that the sub's 'quality control' missed. Unit Dose's quality control thought there might be a problem and investigated. It turns out that the first response to the inquiry was to use something that dissolved better—baking powder instead of baking soda. Anyway, by the time Unit Dose was able to get to the bottom of the situation, the manufacturer said he wouldn't use that sub again and everything was taken care of.

"In the course of its investigation, Unit Dose's quality control found out that the sub was taking his water from the Grand Canal, which is a tenth century waterway that connects Beijing with Hangzhou. The problem is that most waterways in China's urban areas are polluted—seventy-five percent according to the government-run Xinhua News Agency. In fact, the *New York Times* reported that a World Bank study concluded the pollution is causing about 760,000 premature deaths per year in China. The Chinese government response to this was to have the information taken out of the report, citing possible impact on social stability. You can probably assume that the Grand Canal has a problem too, whether or not the government admits it. In fact, the Xinhua News Agency admitted there was a spill of two hundred tons of sulfuric acid around the Yuhang district of Hangzhou in 2006. Their method of fixing the problem was to dump seven hundred tons of liquid alkali to bring the pH back to a reasonable level, at least temporarily. Who knows what else is in the canal. It's not unlikely that there's still sulfuric acid, since China is one of the top producers of sulfuric acid in the world. Sulfuric acid is used to make everything from metals to pharmaceuticals.

"In any event, when you put the sulfuric acid together with sodium bicarbonate you get bubbles, sometimes lots of bubbles. Unit Dose's investigation revealed that the sub's workers just shot the resulting air out of the syringe when that happened in their own version of bicarb and then filled up the syringe again. Think of those bubbles circulating through the body up to the brain!"

"But they're taking out the bubbles," Jess interjected. I mean, it's gross to think about the manufacturing process, but the end result may not have been so far off."

"True, but I haven't finished yet. What if…what if other pharmaceutical manufacturers make their medicine the same way—using polluted water? Apparently the Hangzhou area is a big drug manufacturing area. If we assume they're using the same polluted water—only you mix the bicarb with the sulfuric acid water in the patient rather than the syringe by giving the drugs in quick succession or even at the same time. It sounds far out, but so is the fact that someone actually substituted dyethylene glycol, the prime ingredient in antifreeze, for sweetener in cough syrup. The end result was several deaths starting with kidney failure. This substitution was *intentional* according to the *International Herald Tribune*. Hey, it's cheaper!"

"Actually, they do dump a lot of drugs into the patient in a code—it's a really critical situation…" Jess paused. "But how could they allow people to do that kind of thing? Isn't there some kind of government oversight?" Jess asked.

"Well there is, but the oversight isn't what you would hope, to say the least. You heard recently about the ex–drug regulator who was put to death? He put together a new central group to regulate the manufacture of drugs in China. The problem was that he was too close with the companies he was regulating and apparently didn't regulate. This takes awhile to come out in China. The whistleblower—the one in the case leading to the death of the crooked regulator—was jailed originally. His name is Zhang. Now that he's out, he can't get a job because he's blacklisted. According to the *Washington Post* online, blowing the whistle is a bigger sin in China than making counterfeit drugs, because of the emphasis on the 'good of the community' over the individual. It's more important protect the jobs of the company's workers than stop making bad drugs, even if they kill people.

Supposedly punishment is only applied to people who are wrong when they blow the whistle. I bet Zhang wouldn't agree with that, if he could talk, and the *Washington Post* reported that he's been told not to," Drew finished.

"My god—let me see that! Jess walked over to Drew and read over his shoulder. There it was in the highlighted portion of the pages that Drew had printed from the web. "How can that happen? Somehow you think that the Chinese government newspaper is going to put the best face on a problem. And I tend to believe the *Washington Post* over the Chinese government when it comes to what Zhang has to say. "Drew, you're a genius!"

Bending over Drew—who was sitting on the super chair—Jess put her arms around him from the back and gave him a kiss on the cheek. Neither she nor Drew even flinched. It just seemed right. And his body felt really warm and comfortable against her chest. The warmth took on a tingling of anticipation as it radiated throughout her body.

"Like I said, Jess, only with you."

"Well, I think you deserve dinner for finding all this information...how about if I take you to dinner—my treat," Jess offered.

"Can't pass that up, and wouldn't even try," Drew said.

"Hey, bring the info that you have there, too, would you? I want to look at it a little more."

"No problem. I'm way ahead of you. Got a file folder?"

Chapter Thirty-Two

"How about McCormick's?" asked Jess. "It's close and I'm starved."

"Do you think Reesa will mind if we leave her here again?" Drew quipped.

"She doesn't get a vote. Let's go," said Jess. Locking Reesa in the office, they took the elevator and escalators down to the Fourth Avenue entrance of the Columbia Tower and walked the short distance to McCormick's.

They were seated in one of the small booths just inside the door. The booths are fine if you don't mind sitting close to your eating companion, and neither Jess nor Drew minded at all.

After looking over the menu to see that her favorite salad was still there, Jess looked up and said to Drew, "I can't believe you spent this whole glorious day indoors with me. You are really a hell of a guy. I really appreciate it. And *then* you even find the winning ticket for my case! Can I look at that information again for a minute? I just can't believe that they really do that kind of stuff." Jess spent a little time rereading the highlighted portions of the information that Drew had found online. She was so amazed that she had to reread it to believe it actually said what she thought.

While she was doing that, Drew thought back on all the time he'd spent working evenings and over weekends on the big case of the day when it was going to trial and how his wife had simply gotten tired of being home alone. That's what had happened. He had felt that he owed it to his job, and she slowly developed a hatred of him for leaving her alone. It was wonderful to meet someone you could share the time with doing what you liked.

Like most men, Drew didn't say all of this to Jess. What he did say was: "Ms. Jessica, I can't think of anything I'd rather do than spend the day with you!"

Dinner was McCormick's usual great presentation of seafood, but Jess and Drew hardly noticed it. They were more focused on sitting and talking to each other about the challenge of the day and how to overcome the remaining obstacles to avoiding dismissal of the Thompson case.

As they were finishing the meal, Drew said, "Ms. Jessica, can I help you get Reesa home?"

Jess knew that there could be more involved than simply delivering Reesa to her condo. "Let's do," Jessica agreed, replying to the unspoken question.

Chapter Thirty-Three

Drew followed Jessica out of the Columbia Tower garage and to her condo on First Avenue. He found a place to park on Blanchard just off First, and Reesa and Jess met him at the lobby door. He petted Reesa on the way up the elevator. Jess handed him the keys to open the door while she held Reesa.

As soon as Drew shut the door, Reesa jumped out of Jess's arms. Jess turned to him, put her arms around his waist and pulled him close. God, he felt good! His face, his lips, his chest, and all the way down his body.

Jess moved Drew into the entrance to the bedroom where they kicked off their shoes and tore off their clothes. Reesa respectfully sat in the entrance to the bedroom and discreetly looked out.

"My god, he's gentle!" thought Jessica.

"Oh, Ms. Jessica," was all that Drew said.

Half an hour later, they were laying together contemplating the scene outside Jess's bedroom window. The condo was actually one big fishbowl of windows around a central core where the bathroom and entry were located. The two outside walls, which were mostly glass, afforded a view of the city east, south, and west as far as Elliot Bay. The view out the bedroom was east—distant skyscrapers. They were far enough away that Jess made the assumption you didn't have to worry about "Peeping Toms," and she often left the vertical blinds partly ajar so she could enjoy the view. It was especially beautiful that night, as the twilight began to cover the city and the city lights and stars came out.

"This feels so good. Not just the lovemaking, but the whole thing. I haven't ever met anyone like Drew," thought Jess. Then she said, "All I can say is that was wonderful. Words don't describe."

"You're wonderful, Jess. You're wonderful."

A few minutes later, Jess said, "We should take a shower. I have a great shower that the prior owner put in. You won't believe it." Jumping out of bed, she led Drew into the small but richly equipped bathroom.

The showerhead hung from the ceiling in the middle of the shower and sprinkled water down like gentle rain. Jess and Drew stood and held each other while the rain sprinkled down. They barely got through washing each other before they were back in bed making love again.

The evening turned to night, and Jess and Drew covered up a bit and moved to the living room to enjoy the view over Elliot Bay with a glass of wine.

The word "wonderful" kept buzzing through Jess's head. It didn't seem quite adequate but that was all she could come up with. "Maybe there is no word for it because it's so rare," she thought.

Chapter Thirty-Four

Sunday morning started as sunny as Saturday had been. "Two days in a row!" thought Jess. As usual she was lying with her eyes closed in order to keep Reesa quiet. She wasn't ready to get up—she'd had a great dream last night about making love with Drew and didn't want to give it up just yet.

But Drew's warm body *was* there. Jess felt down his leg with hers. Yes, it wasn't a dream. Jess rolled over and started kissing Drew on the chest and stomach. His body was as firm and the skin as soft as she had dreamed. They made love again.

After a discreet moment, Reesa jumped up on the bed. She was purring, purring, purring. Jess and Drew were lying in bed embracing, and Reesa placed herself on top of them both as if to say, "I am part of this family too! And, by the way, I need some food!"

Jess felt a little guilty since she had forgotten to feed Reesa the night before. "Amazing that Reesa isn't more insistent. She usually would have been. It must be Drew," Jess thought. She jumped out of bed, fed Reesa, and was back in bed in a flash.

But wheels were turning in Jess's brain. She began thinking of what she needed to do today to get ready to file her summary judgment response. Finally, she said, "Lets get up, and I'll make some coffee. I have a lot to think about and do today," said Jess.

"What is this 'I' stuff. I make love to you, and I'm no good anymore?" Drew asked with a smile on his face that showed he didn't really believe what he said.

"Really, you want to waste the only other sunny day this year in the office?"

"I wouldn't call it a waste, Ms. Jessica. Besides, I have an investment in this case now. And like I said, I like spending my time with you."

Jess smiled and flushed a little. "What a nice thing to say, and I think you mean it. That means we do have a little time." Drew had raised his upper body on his elbow. Jess shoved him back down and started kissing him on the chest again.

Thirty minutes later Jess and Drew were standing in the kitchen while Jess made coffee. "Well, look at that!" she said. She was looking at the bottle of coffee pot cleaner that she kept in her cupboard by the coffee filters she was pulling out. This has sulfuric acid in it. I have sodium bicarbonate too. Let's do a little test."

Jess mixed up a solution of sodium bicarbonate in water and dropped in some coffee cleaner. The mixture bubbled.

"Hmm. Interesting. Let's make this more like what we're dealing with, Drew. I want to see what this really looks like. Do you have that info on sodium bicarbonate syringes from yesterday?"

Drew pulled out the information again, and Jess gathered the equipment for her test, reading the information as she did. "The proportion of sodium bicarbonate to water is 4.2 grams to 50 cc's. That's 50 milliliters—I know from my nursing days," Jess said.

She riffled through her medicine cupboard and pulled out an old bottle of eye drops. "I think this is the closest thing to a syringe that I have. I have some tubing too, left over from my aquarium days. After I adopted Reesa, those fish kept jumping out of the tank. I thought that was kind of cruel and decided I wouldn't feed Reesa's habit."

Jess gathered the makeshift equipment, emptied out the old eye-drop solution, rinsed out the bottle, and refilled it with coffee pot cleaner. She and Drew measured out the water and bicarb. The amount of water was easy, since Jess's measuring cup included measurement in milliliters.

It was a little more difficult to figure the amount of sodium bicarbonate. Drew and Jess finally decided to measure the total amount in the box and divide that down to 4.2 grams. The box said that it contained 454 grams. Pouring it into a measuring cup, the box turned out to be about two cups. "Let's see, sixteen tablespoons per cup—that's thirty-two tablespoons total or ninety-six teaspoons. I always knew there was some good that would come out of my junior high home economics class. By the way, I'll have you know that I won the Betty Crocker Award in my eighth-grade year!"

"Well, I *am* impressed," Drew said, "but I've said that all along."

Working out the math, they decided that 4.2 grams of sodium bicarbonate was about 0.8 of a teaspoon. After all that math calculation, they eyeballed the measurement. "But, hey, the Chinese sub was just adding bicarb as he went too," Jess rationalized. "We have no real idea how much was in each syringe."

Just for good measure, Jess pulled out some baking powder too. They mixed that in the same proportions. It really did dissolve a lot better than the sodium bicarbonate.

"Here," Jess said, handing Drew the tubing. "How about if you squeeze the end of the tubing to keep the solution from running out. I'll pour in the bicarb," Jess said as Drew doubled over and squeezed the end of the tube. Jess commenced filling the tube through a funnel.

"Now for the final test. I would do a drum roll if I had an extra hand," Jess said as she inserted the eye dropper nozzle into the tube and squirted. The bubbles filled the tube and welled up and over the top. "My god, I wasn't even able to get the whole 50 cc's in the tube. Can you imagine how much bubbling there would be if I had put the whole thing in? I can't believe this. Let's do the baking powder."

Rerunning the test in their makeshift laboratory, Jess and Drew found that the baking powder produced at least as much gas and maybe more. "My god! I'm dumbfounded. I can't believe this!" Jess kept exclaiming to herself, as she was observing the bubbles produced.

"Well, now we need to figure out what the drug is that has the sulfuric acid in it. Let's get cleaned up and go to the office."

"Great idea! I'll help you shower," Drew said.

"Right," Jess smiled. "We do have to get to the office sometime today."

On the other end of the phone-mic, a slight, dark-haired man listened intently. He had been amazed at the input from the night before. He was thinking that Ms. Jessica Lamm was one tough broad. She seemed to live like a nun. But even aside from listening to the love making, he had struck pay dirt. The boss was going to want to know about this.

Chapter Thirty-Five

Drew, Reesa, and Jess arrived at the office at ten thirty in the morning. As Jess had mentioned, the sun was out and the sky was a rich blue. You had to see the almost perpetual drizzle interspersed with driving downpours from October to April to fully appreciate the effect of a clear sky in Seattle. Jess knew that if she looked long at the big-screen TV view of the water as they arrived at the office, it would be even harder to go inside. "Best not to look at that and make life difficult," she thought.

On the way to the office, Jess and Drew discussed the case. With the summary judgment response due on Monday, they had a problem with not having the necessary signed affidavits to respond yet. "I'm worried about getting a continuance on the summary judgment motion. Obviously, we don't have enough yet to prove that the bad drug was the cause. Baker is going to say that it's just speculation, and he would be right."

"I think the evidence of Lars Hansen lying is real killer for them. Like I said, I've rarely seen any witness have the audacity to lie about something so easily contradicted. I think…well, hope…that this information, along with the bad drug trouble that VAHC has had, will be good enough to get a continuance. And I don't think that you should let the *res ipsa* theory go yet either. You never know what the judge is going to hang her hat on. Let's give her all you've got."

"Well, I think that should buy us more time, at least. This really puts the case in a whole new position, though. I always wondered why Lars Hansen was so involved. Now it's beginning to make sense. He needed to direct the defense to make sure no one found out about the bad drugs. Assuming we're right, it appears that Hansen set up Dr. Haseem to take the fall on this. I guess this reinforces my general suspicion about the morality of mankind." Jess finished the last sentence with a note of sarcasm.

"Hey, watch who you're including in that!" Drew said.

"Yeah, I know. I guess when you see the bad side long enough you forget about the others like you," Jess smiled.

They parked in the garage of the Columbia Tower building, which was remarkably bare this Sunday morning. Reesa, at least, didn't seem to care that it was sunny outside. As soon as they settled in at the office, Reesa set right to work on Drew's lap. Jess and Drew split up the work; Drew took the affidavit for Peterson, and Jess finished the brief on the legal theories of *res ipsa* and product liability and drafted her own affidavit.

The objective was to give Judge Pacer enough to prevent immediate dismissal of their case. In any normal circumstance, the judge might not give Jess more time, and she didn't have to do it this time. This case had been pending for more than a year, and Jess hadn't been able to get at the "bad facts" until she talked to Joyce Brown. She hoped again that the proof that Hansen seemed to be hiding the location of the Joyce Brown would be enough to obtain a continuance. It probably would be; it should be, but it becomes tougher to judge when the stakes are so high. Jess and Danni knew when they took the Thompson case that they were taking a risk. With crunch time coming on the summary judgment motion, Jess was feeling the pressure.

Jess's affidavit retold her conversation with Joyce Brown. She also added the information that Drew had located on the web. Looking at the record, Jess and Drew decided that the culprit medicine, in addition to the bicarb, must be the epinephrine. They seemed to be given at about the same time. That was a guess, but really only a guess because they had no time to prove it.

Drew handled the affidavit for Peterson's medical information to help the court understand why the suspected cause of death was so hard to detect.

At about two o'clock, Jess and Drew finished the affidavits and briefs. Jess said, "I think that we deserve the rest of the day on the waterfront. It's my treat."

They delivered Reesa back to Jess's condo. Reesa was plenty talkative by now. She had been patient, working steadily with them throughout the day, sitting and purring on Drew's lap. But she was hungry now, and she had waited long enough for lunch. As she buried her face in her Good Kitty dish, her talking slowed to a few grunts between bites.

Chapter Thirty-Six

As she and Drew walked down to the waterfront from Jess's condo, Jess finally allowed herself to look at the sunlight dancing on the waters of Puget Sound. "Seattle is a beautiful city," she thought again, and it seemed especially beautiful today. She wondered how much her thoughts about Seattle were influenced by her relationship with Drew.

They stopped at the Pike Place Market on the way. As usual on a sunny weekend, it was packed with tourists gawking at the produce and stopping to stare at the fish vendors throwing around the fresh salmon, a big attraction in the Pike Place Market. The fish lie in iced casings forming an outward-facing square. The scales, cash register, and wrapping paper are in the open space in the middle of the square. When a customer picked a fish, the man—and they were all men in jeans and white aprons—picked up the fish by the head and tail and threw it to the vendor in the middle of the square. Though she had been there many times, Jess had never seen them drop a fish. This seemed like an incredible feat considering the slimy nature of the fish skins. "I wonder if they get points off for the day if they drop those," Jess said.

Drew laughed. "That's a skill really worth having," he said.

Jess took Drew's arm as they walked along. "I would chalk this day up as an eleven on a scale of one to ten," she mused to herself.

When they arrived at the waterfront, Drew said, "I think we should go to Anthony's upstairs, Anthony's Pier 66. I know you said you'd pay, but I'm having such a good time, I insist that it be my treat. "Anthony's is one of my favorite places to go."

"Mine, too," Jess agreed.

The main entrance to Anthony's dining room was the same as the street level entrance to the Bell Street Diner, featuring the fish made of baseballs that the owner purchased to support Mariner baseball in their 2001 heyday. The dining room upstairs replaced the moderate elegance of the Bell Street Diner with a more refined décor of copper, marble, and frosted glass contrasted with the same blond woodwork found below in the diner. In the women's rest room there was a glass sink with light coming up from below, giving a finishing touch to the elegance. Jess occasionally wondered what the men's restroom had.

"Hello, Mr. Stewart," the maitre d' greeted them. "Would you like a table by the window?"

"Oh, I see that you don't come here often," said Jess.

"Actually, Budd Gould is a client of mine—by the way, there are two D's in Budd—he owns the Anthony's restaurants. He's one of the few restaurateurs that I know who has a masters degree from Harvard. He's been quite successful by keeping his restaurants up with the latest and greatest, and he usually tries to locate them on the water. He's a real believer in the old adage: location, location, *and* location."

Drew and Jess started with the elegantly served hors d'oeuvres of sushi and sashimi and finished with the alder planked salmon and a bottle and a half of Anthony's house chardonnay. Per the usual standard at Anthony's restaurants, the "house" chardonnay was well above the norm.

Then Jess and Drew walked up the hill to Jess's condo and stopped on the fifth-floor balcony to watch the sun set over Puget Sound and finish the bottle of wine.

"I think I've pretty much maxed out on the wine," Jess said. "Since I have to get the response out tomorrow in the Peoples case, I had better get to bed."

"I'd be happy to help you do that," Drew said. "It would be a great way to finish up a wonderful weekend."

Jess grinned, "Only an attorney would say *that* after spending two days in the office on a weekend like *this*."

"Keep that in mind!" said Drew. "Besides, there was a lot more to it than that."

Drew and Jess were lying together asleep when Jess heard someone fiddling with the lock on the door. She waited a few seconds to see if the noise continued. When it did, she nudged Drew's leg with hers. His mouth was next to her ear. He whispered, "You heard it too. I wasn't sure if you were expecting someone."

Drew jumped out of bed in his shorts making as much noise as possible. By this time the intruder seemed to be coming in the door. "Who's there?" Drew said in a loud voice. There was a pause and then a shuffling of feet. The door closed, and Drew quickly reached the door and threw the dead bolt. Jess and Drew had been a little careless when coming in that night and forgot to throw the second lock. "Might have had something to do with the wine," Jess thought.

"Do you think that could have been a mistake," Jess said, though she couldn't see how. Her heart was beating at warp speed, and she was so breathless she could hardly get the words out. She was hoping Drew would come up with an explanation. "Not a chance," he said. "You had better make sure the deadbolt is on when you're here."

Despite Drew's joking in the bedroom and calm demeanor after locking the door, he was as alarmed as Jess. She could hear his rapid breathing, and when back in bed, the rapid beat of his heart.

On the other end of a nearby cell phone the intruder made a report. "I didn't get in far…a John was there…no, they didn't see me."

Chapter Thirty-Seven

Over that weekend, Jess had tried repeatedly to reach Joyce Brown. It wasn't until Monday morning as Jess was leaving for work that she was able to reach her, and then she didn't reach her directly but got a return call just after she made one of her many redials.

Joyce said, "I'm sorry, I'm not going to help you. I left town for a vacation, and I'm not sure when I'll come back. The evening after I talked with you, my car was destroyed. I don't think *that* is normal."

"Joyce, I had nothing to do with that. You know that, don't you? I need to get a statement from you. Your testimony would be very helpful for our case."

"I don't know what to think."

"Joyce, did you talk with Mr. Hansen about our conversation?"

"Well, of course I did—he asked me to—he has always been so helpful. I took a leave of absence from my job in Renton. He said that he would be happy to give me a job when I return if Renton doesn't rehire me."

"Did you talk to Mr. Hansen before or after your car was vandalized?"

"Well, I don't know what you are implying, but yes, I talked to him before and after. I told him about my car. He was very concerned. We discussed the situation and decided that just in case there was any danger to me, maybe I should take a vacation. I don't want to talk to you about this anymore. I know Mr. Hansen. I'll not listen to you suggest any more bad things about him."

After delivering the outraged torrent to Jess, Joyce hung up. Jess immediately tried to call her back, but there was no answer.

Chapter Thirty-Eight

Jess was at the office early to meet with John Peterson about his affidavit. She hoped her conversation with John would go better than the one with Joyce. The deadline for filing the affidavit was this afternoon, and she wanted to be sure that if John needed any changes she could make them on the spot. There would be no time for sending statements back and forth, even by e-mail.

John arrived on time, for a change. "Must be because this is his first appointment," thought Jess. Unlike his usual flirty self, John was all business. Jess handed him the affidavit, and he sat down to read.

The affidavit started out with the usual background information about John's credentials, training, experience, and publications. The critical language for the affidavit was that he was familiar with the standard of practice for medical care in Washington. Since Jess had worked with him before, this was old hat to both of them.

John did agree that Thompson should have been treated immediately when he arrived at the hospital, but without the EKG strips, he couldn't say what would have happened if he had received earlier treatment. It might even have been hard to say if the strips were available, since John wasn't a cardiologist. Joyce's information that Thompson had actually regained normal sinus rhythm suggested that he would have recovered were it not for his apparent stroke—the problem was that there was no diagnosis of a stroke.

Jess had been hoping against hope that John would feel comfortable offering an opinion that there had been a stroke, but she wasn't to be so lucky. "It says here that I'm offering an opinion that Brad died of a stroke and that more likely than not it wouldn't have happened but for administration of counterfeit drugs or negligent care. Sorry, Jess, I think that is a good possibility, but I can't testify to it. The law can't require that here—when this case is so hard to figure out. It's a big leap, Jess. I do believe that there's something very strange going on here, but I can't say that."

Jess wondered why John was so sure what the law should require, but she wasn't really disappointed. She knew him to be careful in his opinions, but she had hoped that with the information she and Drew had found on counterfeit drugs associated with VAHC hospitals that he could make the leap, especially since he had talked with his pathologist friend about the autopsy report on Saturday. No such luck.

Jess decided to backtrack to find out what John could support. "You do think that Brad had a stroke, right?"

"I do, Jess. I'm virtually certain in my own mind that he did, but this is a little out of my field. I know I've given opinions in the past that weren't directly in the surgical field, but those were in situations that were pretty clear. Those dealt with basic information, like Medical School 101. Here I would be offering an opinion that contradicts the cause of death given by the pathologist. I'm not sure I feel comfortable making that contradiction in court. If the other side had a pathologist who said differently—hell, the coroner already said differently—I could have a lot of trouble justifying that opinion. I'd like to help you, Jess, but I can't stick my neck out that far."

"You believe that the opinion of the cause of death is impacted by the reported circumstances of the death, don't you?" Jess nudged.

"Sure, I can say that. That's beyond question."

"You do believe that a forty-year-old man with no atherosclerosis shouldn't be having a stroke, don't you?"

"I do. My concern is that there isn't even a diagnosis of stroke here. I also know that there's nothing given in a code situation that should cause a stroke. I can say that. I just don't want to go making allegations against my fellow doctors on conditions that are outside my area of expertise, even if their care is not on trial. You know I get nothing but crap on these cases when I testify that the hospital or doctor screwed up. I don't feel comfortable about saying everything that's in this affidavit when I'm not sure that I can back up such an opinion. I'd be happy to help you get a pathologist. I think that I can get Maggie Smith to help you. She's pretty independent."

In the end, it turned out that Dr. Smith was on vacation until next week, so Jess had no hope of getting in touch with her to even schedule an appointment before the response was due. Jess revised the affidavit to make it as strong as possible to show what John thought had happened. She hoped for the twentieth time that it was going to be strong enough to convince the court to give her more time, and she thought again how hard it is to predict an outcome when the stakes are so high. She wondered if her blood pressure would confirm the strain she felt about this motion.

Chapter Thirty-Nine

Jess's brief and the two affidavits had hardly had time to reach Baker before he called. Apparently he had been waiting for the documents.

Jess picked up the phone after looking at the caller ID. Knowing who the caller was, she prepared herself. She had hardly said hello before he started attacking.

"You've gone over the line this time, Jess. I'm going to ask for terms! What the hell is this about Joyce Brown? You can't just accuse a guy like Hansen of lying when you feel like it. Did you think that you had to throw mud to justify your failure to make a case? I'm going to sue you personally for terms! I have $55,000 in fees on this case and $21,500 in costs, and I'm going to get reimbursement of every last dime of that from you personally."

Having finished his tirade, Baker hung up, giving Jess no opportunity to respond. Jess thought about calling him back but figured that this was not the time. Ordinarily she would have at least tried to reason with defense counsel that she needed more time to get the necessary medical opinion affidavit. But it was pretty clear that Baker was not going to cooperate.

Despite the fact that she knew Baker's threat was a lawyer-crap defense tactic, she began to wonder whether she could pay terms if the judge ordered them. Just because the ploy is lawyer crap doesn't mean the judge won't agree with the request. She and Danni had a cushion of some savings and a line of credit with the bank that they relied on to tide them over on the long periods when money wasn't coming in. That was necessary in a contingent fee practice, but $76,000 was going to take a good chunk out that the firm might need for other things. That, of course, was Baker's hope— to scare the shit out of her for pursuing her case. Ordinarily, the requirement for a medical opinion on malpractice is warranted, and Jess appreciated that. After what she and Drew had found this weekend, she was sure the hospital was hiding something. She just hoped the judge could recognize that too.

One of the ways to contest an award of terms would be to claim that the amount requested was unreasonably high. Jess thought about the time she had spent on this case. She easily had $45,000 dollars worth of time in, and she didn't keep careful track of her time on her cases since her fee was determined by her recovery, if any. So she wasn't going to be able to make a good argument that Baker's claim of $55,000 was too much. Jess had $12,000 in out-of-pocket costs that she had advanced, and she hadn't had to pay significant expert witness fees yet because she hadn't been able to pull the facts out of Baker. There wasn't much hope of convincing the judge that $21,500 in costs was unreasonable either.

Danni needed to know about the claim for terms, since a chunk of their financial cushion was at stake. Jess hated to call her to tell her about this problem. It would be a hell of a way to interrupt a vacation. Jess decided to think about it for a while. Maybe she could come up with something before Danni got back to the office.

Chapter Forty

As soon as he got off the phone with Jess, Baker called Hansen. Baker's tone changed substantially when talking with his client. Hansen wasn't immediately available, so Baker left a message, "I need to talk to you ASAP. A possible problem has come up with relation to our summary judgment motion that I need to talk to you about."

Less than half an hour later, Hansen called back. "You said there was a problem?" he asked.

"In response to our summary judgment motion, the Thompsons' lawyer wasn't able to get an adequate medical opinion, and we may have a shot at getting the case dismissed. That's the good news. The bad news is that they claim you've known all along where Joyce Brown was and that you've been hiding her. They also claim that Peoples is using bad drugs. If either of those is true we could have a real problem on this case," said Baker.

He also thought to himself, "And I could have a real problem, too. Why the hell didn't you tell me about this? This could be a conflict. I can't represent Haseem and the hospital if each is pointing the finger of blame at the other. What am I supposed to do, put on one hat and argue that Haseem caused Thompson's death, and then put on the other hat and argue it was People's fault? That won't be very convincing to the jury. If a conflict develops, I and my firm are going to have to withdraw and probably forfeit a lot of our fee on this case, since the work that generated those fees may have to be repeated. My firm isn't going to be happy, and neither am I."

"Don't worry, there's no problem," Hansen assured. "Joyce Brown is a druggy. She'll say anything; that's why I encouraged her to leave Peoples. I didn't want to ruin someone's career, but if she's going to make trouble, I guess it will have to come out. As for bad drugs, what are they claiming? I can vouch for Peoples' drugs too."

"Well they claim that VAHC has its own drug repackager, Unit Dose, Inc., and that Unit Dose has been cited for several quality control issues—in particular bad drugs used in code situations. They even say that you have taken actions that suggest you're aware of this, such as requiring that you be called for every code that goes bad and limiting the number of people who can come to code situations so that you have fewer witnesses."

"Well don't worry about that. At Peoples, we don't even get our drugs from Unit Dose, Inc. I worked out a deal with a local company so that I could have more control of the situation. You know I'm a hands-on kind of person. I want to know what's going on in my hospital, which is why I want to be called after bad codes. I want to make sure that we're doing things right. How do you know unless you check out what goes wrong? As for limiting the number of people who come to codes, that is absolutely true. But do you have any idea how many people come to codes? When a code is called you can get so many people standing around that you can hardly get in the room. They can actually get in the way of the treatment; forget the fact that they aren't doing their own work! We don't have a problem here."

"Well, we will need to get that information before the court. I'll need an affidavit from you on that. I'll write it up and e-mail it over. Call me about any changes you need. I need it back in the next day or two."

"No problem."

Chapter Forty-One

Jess couldn't get the conversation with Baker out of her mind. Much as she believed in her case, there was always the practical aspect of having to pay out $76,000. "Making the risk personal is a ploy," Jess reminded herself. She also heard the other voice in her head respond, "But it's a really effective one, isn't it?"

The toughest thing about the situation was that Jess couldn't actually control what happened in this case. She just had to do her best and hope for a little luck. She needed conversation to put this into perspective. Danni was on vacation and Lorraine wasn't going to be helpful. She would only take this opportunity to sigh and remind Jess that being an attorney was man's work anyway.

Walking down the hall to Drew's office, Jess was pleased to see through the office window that he was in and not on the phone. "Hi, got a minute?" asked Jess, looking around the door jam.

"Well, absolutely, for you." Drew smiled a big grin. Jess thought about the last few nights and wished she didn't have the weight on her shoulders that made them seem far away.

"I just got off the phone with Baker. John backed off on what he would verify in an affidavit, so we had to go with a pretty watered-down version. I haven't been able to get a supplemental affidavit since the likely prospect is out of town on vacation. Of course Baker is threatening terms. I know it's a ploy, but this case has gone on long enough and is so tough to make, the fees and costs are big—well nothing like if the case went to trial, but still big. I just can't focus on anything but the danger of losing $76,000. I know that's the point—distraction from the real issues—but it's working; especially on this case since it's been pending over a year, and I don't have an expert because I couldn't get the facts. Seventy-six thousand would be no small chunk to me."

Drew's face softened. He had heard about the way medical malpractice defense is carried on, but he was seeing it first hand— the scorched earth policy. Baker seemed to be especially good at it. Drew knew that was why insurers liked to hire him. "Jess, you know there's more to this than appears on the surface. You know what Joyce told you, what we found out online, and what John told you. You are onto something. Just hang in there. This is going to develop into something. You can do it. I know you."

Jess had hoped he would say that. Despite the fact that she had heard these threats of terms before, this time felt more real, and having someone sympathize with her caused her to choke up. Her eyes filled up almost to the brim with tears. "Thanks!" she said.

"Have you told Mary Thompson yet?"

"No, I just got off the phone with Baker. I need to get my act together before I call Mary. I don't want to make this more than it really is, or at least more than I *hope* it really is."

"Good plan. How about McCormick's after work?"

"Thanks! Sounds great! And I really mean thanks!"

That afternoon, Jess met Drew at McCormick's. She hadn't gotten herself put together for the talk with Mary Thompson. She needed time to let the emotion die down so that she didn't say the wrong thing or, even worse, make any bad decisions. "It's great to talk with someone who can help put this in perspective," Jess thought.

Much as she wanted to believe Judge Pacer was going to be on her side, there had been a few infamous cases around Seattle in which terms had been assessed. The courts had hit the culprit law firms for hundreds of thousands of dollars. Jess hoped the court wouldn't hit her for even the smaller amount.

Chapter Forty-Two

It wasn't until the next afternoon, when Jess thought that Mary would be home from school, that she called her client. "Hi, Mary, this is Jess Lamm. Something has developed in the case that I need to talk to you about."

"Oh, what is it?" Jess could hear the anxiety in Mary's voice—that reinforced her courage. Jess silently told herself to toughen up. "Mary deserves help, and she isn't going to get it anywhere else. That's why you went into this business, remember!"

"Well, you know that Peoples brought a summary judgment motion, and we have to win that or this is the end of the case."

"Right," Mary said, even more tentatively than before.

"Well, we were able to find out a few things about Peoples over the weekend after we found the nurse that we were looking for. The problem is that this opens up a whole new theory of the case. We're working with a really convoluted situation here, and it's tough to put together all the necessary evidence to make a legal case."

"Right," Mary said again. Her tone indicated ever-growing anxiety.

"Well, here's the deal. I think we can get enough to make the case. What we need is an affidavit from a pathologist to confirm that the cause of death on the autopsy report was probably skewed by the report of predeath care from the hospital—to confirm that Brad probably died as a result of a stroke."

"What? A stroke?" Mary's voice was much louder than before. This was the first time that Mary and Jess had discussed the information that Drew and Jess had dug up over the weekend. "I knew there was something there!"

"Well, we think that's the case, but we need a qualified opinion to confirm it."

"I knew there was something wrong," Mary said again. "They were so patronizing and pushy. How did you figure this out?"

"Well, as you know, the autopsy report made a comment about the cerebral damage. We talked about that but couldn't figure out why one side of the brain seemed to die before the other. It also mentions that Brad had a hole in his heart."

"What? I don't understand. He didn't have a hole in his heart. When did that happen?" Mary interjected. "What are they talking about? Is this another lie?"

"No, this is something that you and Brad wouldn't even have necessarily known about. The coroner mentioned it in the autopsy…the patent foramen ovale. It's a defect that can form at birth, and sometimes you wouldn't even know about it. I know it's easy to be suspicious about medical reports once you think they're lying to you, but that isn't the case here. Brad really did have a hole in his heart. You just didn't know about it. Trust me."

"I'm sorry, Jessica. This case is making me distrust everyone… okay, so what does this all mean?" Mary asked.

"Well, what it means is this—because Brad had a hole in his heart, he probably had a problem from counterfeit drugs that showed up in a different way than it did in other patients. Like I said, after we found the missing nurse, we were able to follow up on the information she gave us. We found out that People's source of pharmaceuticals has been cited for receiving counterfeit drugs. Because Brad had a hole in his heart, the gas from a drug that they used in the cardiac resuscitation went directly to his head and caused him to have a stroke. He actually did recover from the cardiac arrest but eventually relapsed because of damage to the brain and probably the lungs that happened early in the code. So you *were* right.

"But here's the problem." Jess explained about the time crunch and Dr. Smith's unavailability, finishing with, "So we think we can get the affidavit but we're not sure."

"So what does that mean?"

"Timing is everything now. You know how we've had so much trouble getting information from Peoples. Their whole approach to this case is to delay, delay, delay and then claim that there's nothing there because we haven't been able to put the information together. You know that, right?"

"Right. We discussed it, and I can see it too."

"Well, there is a question about whether the court will give us more time to get the affidavit that we need. If the court doesn't give us more time, our case is done. So the reason I'm calling you today is to let you know that not only is the hospital going to resist our effort to get more time, they are also claiming that because we don't have a doctor's affidavit, we should pay them their fees and costs. They're making this threat to get us to back off our case."

"Well, how much is it? I don't know if I can pay that. You know I've used almost all of Brad's insurance to try to keep things normal for Madaline."

"Right, I know, and there is only a remote possibility that they would seek the money from you. They're claiming over $76,000, and they're threatening me in order to make me drop the case," Jess said softly.

There was a long silence on the other end, followed by gasping. Jess thought to herself, "I should have told Mary in person. Jess, you coward!"

"Mary," she said out loud, "I know it's unlikely that you would have the money, and I don't think that it's going to come to this, but I have to tell you so that you are prepared in case it happens. The court would probably order me to pay it instead of you. I hope the court won't do anything like either of those, but you need to know that it's a possibility. I'm doing my darnedest to prevent that from happening."

"Jess, are you going to drop the case?" Mary asked in a voice so tight Jess could hardly hear her.

"If we did that we might be able to work out a deal with the hospital not to pursue this. But I don't want to, and I'm not sure whether that would work anyway. I think we should push forward."

"Thank you, Jess. I appreciate that." After a pause, Mary said, "Can you get an affidavit from someone else?"

"You can't imagine how much I would like to do that, Mary. The problem is that you can't go out and get just any doctor to testify. They don't want to do it. It makes enemies of the people that they work with. So we won't be able to just call someone up out of the phone book. We think the doctor we have in mind will be our best bet."

Jess thought that she heard Mary say, "Oh." It was so soft that she couldn't be sure.

"Mary, I am really sorry to have to tell you this, and I really hope that it doesn't come to this. I just have to let you know."

"I know, Jess. Sorry I'm being such a baby. I just can't believe that the world is so unfair as to take Brad from me and then punish me for fighting back."

"I know, Mary. I know. And I am sorry."

Chapter Forty-Three

Mary and Jess walked to the courthouse together on the day of the summary judgment hearing. Mary had taken the day off work in order to come, though she was hoping to make it back to school for the afternoon. Even though their discussion about the threat of terms had occurred nine days ago, the issue was front and center in the minds of both women. There was virtually no discussion; there was nothing more to say than what they had already said. This was not one of those days when either of them felt like chit-chatting.

Mary and Jess met Baker and Hansen outside the courtroom. The bailiff hadn't unlocked the courtroom door yet. Since the clients already knew each other, there was no need for introductions. Each side sat down, picking separate pews from the many lining the hallway outside the courtrooms—Hansen and Baker on one and Jess and Mary on another. Very shortly the bailiff unlocked and opened the courtroom doors. The parties filed in with their respective attorneys. Each side sat down at a separate counsel table.

Jess was more worried than she wanted to let on to Mary. In response to her information about what Joyce Brown had to say, Baker had put in an affidavit from Hansen that Joyce Brown was fired for drug use. Jess couldn't believe the affidavit when she got it. Obviously it made what Joyce had to say less credible, and Jess was wondering if the hospital's failure to turn over her records was a set-up. The disclosure of the alleged problem after Joyce became unavailable again made it impossible to ask her about it. And, of course, Baker was claiming that the information from Joyce should be thrown out as hearsay. Jess had tried to reach Joyce but still hadn't been able to do so. "Sometimes the rules of evidence just seem downright stupid," she thought.

To make matters worse, Hansen's affidavit also said that Peoples didn't buy its pharmaceuticals from Unit Dose Inc., making the information that Drew had dug up on the company's quality control problems potentially useless. Hansen testified in his affidavit that Peoples had a separate source of pharmaceuticals, called Drug Repackaging and Distribution. Jess was sure that it just killed Baker to make such a disclosure without delay, but under the cloud of suspicion that he or his client had withheld the location of Joyce Brown, even Baker didn't have the chutzpa to drag it out.

Obviously Jess would argue that this was but another reason they needed more time to investigate the source of drugs. Hopefully Judge Pacer wouldn't take the position that Jess should have asked earlier about Peoples' source of pharmaceuticals. Jess obviously didn't know the source was an issue in the case earlier, and she was really sure that if she had asked a question about it in her first set of interrogatories, Baker would have been crying "fishing expedition."

The problem was that Baker's reply brief criticized Jess for not finding out about the source of drugs earlier. According to court rules, she wasn't allowed another brief to point out the obvious—delay pays. If Baker's client had disclosed Joyce Brown's contact information earlier, she would have learned that the source of drugs was important early enough to allow time for investigation. It's easy for a judge to lose track of the chronology on issue development, especially if the case bounces from one judge to another as it did in the "bad old days" of the motions calendar system. The whole thing is confusing enough that even a judge familiar with the case—if in a hurry or predisposed to favor one side—might make up her mind after reading the last filing, Baker's reply brief. People often tend to stick with the opinion they originally develop, even when faced with good counter-arguments—especially if the situation is complex—and attorneys count on that sometimes. More than once Jess had encountered judges who made a decision based on a portion of the written record that overshadowed the rest in his or her mind and stuck to that decision no matter what. She hoped Judge Pacer wouldn't do that this time or if she did, that it wouldn't cause the judge to rule against her.

Jess was stirred out of her musing about the situation by the bailiff calling out, "All rise. The court of the Honorable Judith Pacer is now in session."

Judge Pacer sat down and said, "You may be seated." Looking over her notes taken from reading the pleadings filed, Judge Pacer said, "Are counsel ready?"

"Plaintiff is ready, Your Honor," said Jess.

"Defense is ready," said Baker.

"Counsel, please approach the bench," Judge Pacer said. Jess and Baker walked up to the chest-high wall separating the judge's desk from the rest of the courtroom.

"Counsel, I have read the briefs. Have you anything to add?" Judge Pacer asked.

It being Baker's motion, he was entitled to speak first. He introduced himself for the record. In the past, the court reporter recorded the hearing. Now it's a microphone that begins recording when anyone speaks. "William Baker, counsel for defendants Peoples and Dr. Haseem, Your Honor. I would ask that the court strike the affidavit of Ms. Lamm, Your Honor. It is clearly hearsay and should not be considered."

"Counsel, I asked you to step forward so that there would be no question that you hear me. I agree with you, Mr. Baker, that if I were to consider Ms. Lamm's affidavit for the truth of the facts as stated by Ms. Brown, it would be hearsay. However, I am considering it as a basis for Ms. Lamm's request for a continuance of this motion and as an offer of proof as to what Ms. Brown would say if she were here," Judge Pacer began. "It is proper to consider the affidavit."

"Well, as to the heart of the matter, Your Honor, the defendants' summary judgment motion should be considered at this time. Ms. Lamm has had over a year to make her case. The court should not allow further time for this fishing expedition that Ms. Lamm is undertaking. Peoples Hospital and Dr. Haseem have impeccable reputations. It is time that the cloud of suspicion created by this lawsuit be lifted."

Judge Pacer raised her hand, signaling Baker to stop. "Mr. Baker, I am not ready to hear the summary judgment motion at this time. I am well aware of the strain placed upon defendants as a result of a lawsuit. I am also well aware of the fact that we are dealing with the possible wrongful death of a young man in the prime of his life, leaving a widow and young child. In my mind, that justifies Ms. Lamm being given adequate time to obtain the facts, which as far as I can tell have been only grudgingly supplied in this case, if not hidden. If the claim proves true about Mr. Hansen being aware of the location of Ms. Brown and not disclosing it, I shall at the very least consider award of terms against the hospital."

Judge Pacer continued, "Moreover, Mr. Baker, if it also proves to be the case that there is an issue of the nature of the drugs that Mr. Thompson received, you and your firm would appear to have a true conflict of interest. You are well-qualified counsel, and I am certain that you have discussed this with your clients. Let me caution you to be sure that you have done an adequate job of that discussion in this matter. In particular, if you are concerned about the reputation of your client Dr. Haseem, you should be clear with him what the effect will be if he is erroneously adjudged to have committed malpractice when the real culprit is bad drugs.

"I am going to continue this summary judgment motion for six weeks to September 14. Please make a note of it. There will be no notice from this court. Ms. Lamm, any supplemental pleadings will be due from you by August 31, and Mr. Baker, your response is due no later than September 7. I will consider not only the summary judgment motion but also the defendants' request for terms at that time. If your client has *any*, and let me emphasize *any*, knowledge of the whereabouts of Ms. Brown, that information must be shared with Ms. Lamm immediately.

"Ms. Lamm, I do sympathize with the difficulty of your efforts in this case. However, I am constrained by the law to dismiss this matter if you do not produce adequate medical testimony regarding product liability or adequate expert foundation for application of *res ipsa loquitur*…and in view of the fact that this case has been pending for over a year, I will have to seriously consider the issue of assessment of terms."

Despite the warning, Jess was so relieved that Judge Pacer didn't dismiss the case, it was tougher than usual to maintain her courtroom demeanor.

Baker was obviously incensed, and he started to argue with the court's ruling. Dismissal had seemed within his grasp and seeing it fly away clouded his judgment. "Judge Pacer, this case has been pending for over a year. At some point there must be an end to the harassment that my clients are being put through. I respectfully ask the court to reconsider the decision to continue this motion."

Argument with the court's ruling rarely has any impact except to make the judge angry, but on occasion Jess had seen it turn a judge around. Before Jess could respond, Judge Pacer replied, "Counsel, I have made my ruling. This court is adjourned." The judge rose, and the bailiff stood and quickly called out, "All rise." The courtroom occupants stood, and the judge walked to the side door to her chambers.

Jess thought to herself, "Shit! Cheated death again!" She gathered her notes, walked back, and took Mary by the arm. They picked up their coats to exit the courtroom with decorum but as quickly as possible. The judge was out of the courtroom, but Jess did not want to leave any chance for Baker to try to reopen argument again. As long as one side wasn't in the courtroom to argue, nothing like that would happen.

Baker and Hansen followed Jess and Mary shortly. Jess stopped them for a moment in the hallway. "You don't know where Ms. Brown is, do you?" Jess asked, directing the question to Hansen. He hesitated and Baker jumped in. "I'll consult with my client in private and let you know, counsel. See you on September 14."

Considering what she had previously received from Baker in this case, Jess had little hope of hearing from him on this, despite Judge Pacer's instruction to disclose the information. It's pretty easy to just not answer the phone or claim ignorance when you want to withhold helpful information, and Baker was a master.

Jess parted company with Mary in the lobby of the Columbia Tower. Mary had hoped to get back for the afternoon at school and, if she left now, would just about make it.

Mary hadn't said much on the way back to the office except a quiet thank you, but there were tears of relief in her eyes. This was one of those times that Jess was glad she was on the plaintiff's side.

Chapter Forty-Four

Back at the office, Jess checked Danni's office and, seeing it empty, checked with Lorraine about when Danni was going to be back. "In about two minutes," answered Lorraine. "She just went down to Starbucks to get a latte."

Just then Danni appeared, sipping her latte. "Hey, what's up?"

"I want to talk to you about the Peoples case. Shall we go into your office?"

Reading the implication from Jess's invitation that the topic was serious, Danni said, "Let's do."

Danni sat down in her "super back" chair. Jess closed the door for privacy and took the client's chair. "I just got back from court on the Peoples case. The short version is that we have some interesting information on the hospital, but we haven't been able to get the expert testimony to back it up. We had a summary judgment motion today and got a six-week continuance. The problem is that there's a claim for terms because we don't have an expert affidavit. We have until August 31 to get it."

"Well, this isn't the first time that some defense counsel has claimed terms," said Danni. "That seems to be the second thing that they learn when they go to baby-defense-counsel school. The first is: 'Don't give 'em nothin'.'"

"Right, but the problem here is that we don't have an expert's affidavit, and this case has been pending for over a year. That really does line us up for a possible problem. Judge Pacer indicated that she was sympathetic but that she really was going to have to consider the terms request if we don't get an affidavit. Baker claims he has $76,000 in the case, and I don't doubt that."

"Hmm," Danni said, raising her eyebrows. "That *is* a chunk o' change...but look Jess, when we started out we knew this was going to come up. We both believe that we're doing the right thing here. We just have to do the best that we can. You think you can get an affidavit, right?"

"Right, in fact I have an appointment with the pathologist Peterson suggested on Monday."

"Well, what are you worried about, girl? You have it under control," Danni said.

Jess smiled. "Thanks, Danni. I'm so glad you're my partner."

Had she not been so relieved by the judge's ruling, tears might have welled up in Jess's eyes. The tightness in her throat was invisible.

Chapter Forty-Five

Baker and Hansen walked half of the six blocks to Baker's firm at the Washington Mutual Tower in silence. Finally Baker spoke. "You know, Lars, if there is anything to this claim about bad drugs, my firm is going to have to withdraw."

"What do you mean? You can't withdraw! You've put so much time into this case. When you signed up, you said that there was no conflict in your representing Dr. Haseem and the hospital."

"I said that when we thought the claim was about Haseem's malpractice. As his employer, Peoples would be liable for the mistakes that Haseem made on the job. But if the true cause is bad drugs, then I have a conflict. I can't claim that it was Haseem's mistake and then change my story in same trial and say that it was a bad drug. That isn't very convincing."

"There is no drug issue! It's just a figment of that woman's imagination."

"Well, I am going to have to sit down with you and Haseem and go over this with both of you. I can't continue to represent both Peoples and Haseem without doing that."

"Well, Haseem is out of town on vacation, so it can't be right away," Hansen said. "Or at least he will be," Hansen thought. Then, realizing that his immediate knowledge of Haseem's whereabouts would sound suspicious, he continued, "I just stopped by to talk to him about the case yesterday. I'll find out when he's going to be back."

"Well, let me know," Baker responded. Thinking to himself, Baker wondered if he had let himself be fooled by depending on Hansen for his facts.

They arrived in the lobby of the Washington Mutual Tower and parted company. Baker went left toward the elevators to his office, and Hansen headed right to the elevators to the garage to pick up his car. Baker was just about to step into his elevator when he remembered that he needed to check on whether Hansen knew how to reach Joyce Brown. He stepped out of the elevator and walked swiftly around the corner to the bank of garage elevators. Not seeing Hansen in the hallway, Baker surmised that he must have already caught his elevator. "Damn, he's gone," Baker thought. "I'll have to make a note to call him…but I'm not sure that I'll break my neck doing it."

Chapter Forty-Six

Back in her office, Jess thought about how to reach Joyce Brown. She considered calling Baker but decided to use that as a last resort. She had a thought percolating in the back of her mind that might work. She had been shocked to receive Hansen's affidavit that Joyce was dismissed for drug use, but until this morning's ruling, any time she gave Joyce a thought, the threat of terms seemed to overtake her attention. At first the allegation of drug use had shaken her belief in what Joyce had told her. Now being able to focus on something other than assessment of terms, Jess wondered if Hansen's affidavit was true.

Jess had limited experience with drug addicts in her life. It just wasn't the sort of thing that she ran into in her line of work. Maybe she had been fooled, but she had gotten the impression that Joyce was a very responsible person. She found it hard to believe that Joyce was a "druggy."

Jess decided that she would try one more time to reach her. She, of course, still had Joyce's cell number. Jess called and, as expected, did not receive an answer. She left a message. "Joyce, this is Jessica Lamm. I still really need to reach you—more now than ever. I wanted to let you know that Lars Hansen filed an affidavit with the court that says you were fired from Peoples because of drug use. I don't believe that's true, and I would like to talk to you about it. You could give me a call at the office or on my cell." Jess left the numbers and hung up.

Chapter Forty-Seven

Monday morning Jess had an appointment with Dr. Maggie Smith, the pathologist that John Peterson had referred her to. It would have been impossible to get the appointment without John's intervention. Jess never would have gotten past Dr. Smith's receptionist to even hope to explain her story. With John's help, Dr. Smith had received the autopsy report and emergency room record and learned a little about what was going on in the case. When Jess had called her office last week, she was at least ready to talk.

Jess arrived at University Hospital ten minutes early. She wanted time to navigate the maze to Dr. Smith's office. The information desk gave her directions. Like most hospitals, this one was a mass of hallways connected to each other in a plan that randomly developed as the institution expanded.

When she entered hospitals, Jess was always impressed with how amazingly insecure they were. You could get virtually anywhere with a white coat on. The system had been developed when you could trust people to adhere to the honor system. "Sort of like what we expect of the pharmaceutical industry," thought Jess.

Descending two floors down, Jess wound her way down a linoleum-covered hallway until she saw the door marked "Pathology." Pushing it open, Jess expected to see a long line of office doors. She was surprised to see that there was a receptionist at a desk and a small reception area. She told the receptionist that she was there to see Dr. Smith.

The receptionist made a call and hung up. Jess surmised that she had left a message on Dr. Smith's pager. A few minutes later, the phone rang. After a short conversation, the receptionist told Jess that Dr. Smith "would be out shortly." Jess took a seat on one of the two vinyl-cushioned chairs stationed beside a small metal-and-glass table, which was topped by a heap of magazines.

In a few minutes, Dr. Smith appeared. She walked over to Jess and held out her hand. "Hello, I'm Dr. Maggie Smith. I assume that you are Jess Lamm." Jess stood and shook Dr. Smith's hand. "I am. I appreciate your taking the time to see me."

"John is very persuasive. I haven't ever done this before." Jess assumed that Dr. Smith was talking about reviewing records for a plaintiff in a medical malpractice suit. That made Jess doubly appreciative that John had been able to line up Dr. Smith.

"Let's go to my office." Dr. Smith started down a hallway within the pathology department that led past several small, cubical-sized offices without windows.

"Must be in the basement," Jess thought.

Each office was poorly furnished with a metal desk and the same vinyl-cushioned chairs found in the waiting room, except that the offices also had desk chairs out of some better looking vinyl, maybe even leather. Most of the offices were rather dark, lit only by a small desk light, adding to the impression that you were walking into the bowels of a dungeon. Jess was constantly amazed at the way hospitals "decorated" the offices for their doctors. She had noticed in the last few years that some institutions were breaking that trend, at least in the areas open to patients. The lobby of University Hospital was quite pleasing, but the improvement hadn't spread to the lower floor. Jess thought the upgrade in the public areas must have a really positive effect on patients as they walked in the entrance. It sure did on her.

Dr. Smith walked into her office and invited Jess to sit down on one of the vinyl chairs. As they walked in, Dr. Smith made a point of turning on the lights. "We like to keep the lights low to make it easier to use the microscope," Dr. Smith said.

"John told me a little about what's going on here," she continued. "I have reviewed the autopsy report, and I must tell you that I'm not sure I can help you."

Not allowing herself to be deterred by the initial statement, Jess began her normal spiel. She knew that even though John had taken the time to explain a little about the case that he, like most doctors, was in such a rush most of the time that he hadn't covered all of the facts, and they weren't in the autopsy report. "Let me fill you in on a little background here that you may not be aware of," Jess began. "I know that mere death at a hospital does not mean malpractice. I would never have taken this case were it not for what I consider strange additional facts about the ER visit."

Jess continued without pause, knowing that Dr. Smith was only going to listen a very short while. As she spoke, she fast-forwarded through her mind about the details of the case that concerned her. "After the code, the doctor—Dr. Haseem—talked to Mrs. Thompson in the waiting room and said something about a relapse and how 'this should not be happening.' He's Iraqi and does have quite an accent, but Mrs. Thompson is certain about what she heard. Before Dr. Haseem could say much, the CEO of Peoples arrived. Apparently, the CEO is called in on every code-gone-bad at Peoples. This code occurred on a Sunday afternoon, and the CEO showed up. He claims that he is just a hands-on kind of guy, but I was a nurse before going to law school and I've never seen such a practice. All this might not be so significant were it not for the fact that the nurse recording the code insists that Mr. Thompson had a seizure at the early part of the code and his pupils were fixed and dialated after that."

Jess paused to let the information sink in. Dr. Smith had started rereading the report. She looked up and said, "Go on."

Jess continued, summarizing the medical information that she had learned from Joyce Brown and her observation about lack of success with code situations. She paused again. After a long silence, Dr. Smith looked up and said, "What did Dr. Haseem say about this?"

"Well, at his deposition he claimed that there was nothing wrong with the code, but when he said it, he looked like someone was beating him with a stick. He looked very uncomfortable with the whole thing."

"It is rather odd. I can't imagine a CEO showing up on unsuccessful codes. I don't know of any CEO that wants to be that hands-on," said Dr. Smith. "That means being at the hospital almost as much as the doctors. They don't pay CEOs for that."

"John and I have studied the autopsy report," Jess continued, as she discussed the difference in brain texture listed there.

"That did catch my eye," admitted Dr. Smith. "What did you and John surmise caused this?"

"Our information is that Peoples may be getting counterfeit drugs. We found information online that at least one of their drug repackagers has been suspended for receiving counterfeit drugs. Specifically, one of the drugs was the sodium bicarbonate syringes used in codes. Of course, VAHC denies it, but it's one of the facts that we have to investigate."

John agrees that excess carbon dioxide gas circulating in the body could cause pulmonary emboli, and in Brad's case, because he has a patent foramen ovale, cerebral emboli."

"Well, that is quite a theory," said Dr. Smith. "And frankly, I think you might be right."

Jess's shoulders squared up from the reduction of the load they were carrying. Had she heard wrong? Was Dr. Smith agreeing?

"*But*, and this is a big 'but,' I have talked to some of my colleagues about what it's like to testify in medical malpractice cases. You get the cold shoulder from your brethren who don't like it that you have 'crossed the line.' If I weren't in this ivory tower where I don't have to worry about referrals, I wouldn't even consider helping you. Life is too short to cut your professional throat like that. But seeing as how I *am* in this ivory tower, and John says that you are an honest lawyer, which in my opinion is an oxymoron, I will do it for you. However, I'm not willing to do this for free. I've heard these things can involve a significant amount of time. I'm willing to work with you on this, but I am going to need $7,500 up front. I don't want to find out five months down the line that I won't be getting paid."

Being familiar with the dilemma that doctors face in this kind of matter, Jess was prepared for the demand. "No problem. I absolutely understand. I can get you a check right away. I also need an affidavit confirming what we have talked about. We have a pending summary judgment, and I need the affidavit of an expert to verify our theory."

"No problem. Send it over, and I'll take a look at it," said Dr. Smith.

"Do you have a CV?" Jess asked, referring to a curriculum vitae, a document similar to a resume. "We need to list your credentials in any affidavit that we submit to the court to verify that you are truly an expert."

"No problem. I think I have one right here," Dr. Smith said, turning to the metal file cabinet behind her. After pulling open a drawer and riffling through several files, she pulled out a CV and handed it to Jess.

After making an arrangement to deliver a check with the affidavit for Dr. Smith's review, Jess left her office. As she walked down the corridor, Jess smiled. John had "done good" by her again. God, she was grateful! John was entitled to a bottle of Dom Perrier.

Chapter Forty-Eight

Despite his assurances to Baker, Lars Hansen was disturbed about what he read in Peterson's affidavit. As usual, Baker had sent him a copy of the pending pleadings, but Hansen hadn't had a chance to read them until a couple of days after the hearing in which the Lamm woman had obtained a continuance. After mulling over Peterson's theory, Hansen became more and more concerned. He thought he had covered himself by demanding that Guzman sign a contract guaranteeing that he would deliver genuine drugs on behalf of DRD. Peterson's theory might have uncovered the cause of problems in his hospital's codes. And it might be the result of counterfeit drugs, even though Peoples didn't get their drugs from Unit Dose. Knowing counterfeiting was becoming a bigger and bigger problem, Hansen had tried to put the responsibility for confirming drug quality on DRD. He was aware from his experience that the estimate he had seen a couple of years ago—that ten to twenty percent of U.S. drugs were counterfeit—was probably low now considering the trend toward global trade.

Hansen decided that he needed to check into this possibility. He would start by calling Guzman. Seeing the caller ID, Guzman picked up the phone and said, "Hello Mr. Hansen, how are you today?"

"Well, I'm concerned. You and I have gone over and over the code problem and this Lamm woman's lawsuit. All I get from you is assurances that there isn't a problem. But I'm beginning to believe what the woman has to say."

"Yes, Senior Hansen, and as I recall, I advised you that you ought to check your staff."

Hansen ignored Guzman's statement. At first he had been swayed by Guzman's assurances and suggestions that the real culprit was not Guzman's drugs, possibly because he himself wanted to believe that there wasn't a problem. "Our contract requires genuine drugs from licensed manufacturers. The bitch lawyer is now tying the code problem to possible counterfeit drugs. If she's right, my reputation and career are on the line. I need more than empty assurances this time. It looks to me that they may have figured out something here."

There was a long pause before Guzman spoke in a low but unequivocal tone. "Oye, gringo, who do you think you are dealing with here? I have taken about as much of your crap as I am going to. If I go down, I'll see that you do too. What do you think you are getting for the price!" There was another long pause as Guzman allowed the threat to sink in. "But that does not have to happen to either of us, *amigo*." Guzman emphasized the last word. "What does she have?"

This time there was a long pause on the other side of the conversation. "Who *is* this guy!" Hansen thought. "This is business, not the mafia." Out loud Hansen said, "I have an affidavit from her expert. She's working on a theory that it's the sodium bicarbonate that's causing the problem."

"Why don't you send me what you have? I can run it by my chemists. We can take care of this, I assure you."

"Well, I need more than assurances this time."

"No problem, *amigo*," said Guzman, emphasizing again. "You will continue to receive your 'value' out of our relationship."

Before Hansen could say more, Guzman hung up. Hansen faxed Peterson's affidavit to Guzman. He didn't want to think about this anymore today.

Guzman was still thinking. In fact, he was fuming. "These Americans are so coddled! A little lawsuit and they fall apart. *Jesus Christo*, how the hell did he think he could get drugs at such a low price?"

This was not the first time that Guzman had heard from Hansen—sometimes he felt like a babysitter. Hansen called about a problem with codes; he called about a lawsuit being filed. It seemed like he called at the drop of a hat. None of his Mexican customers had been so jumpy. Sometimes he wondered if doing business in the U.S. was worth the hassle, but he didn't wonder very long. "There certainly is more profit in the U.S. The babysitting is worth it," he told himself.

Hansen thought he was being so clever about demanding drugs from licensed manufacturers. Well, Guzman had taken care of that. The Chinese were that smart. Actually they were very smart, and Guzman had learned a thing or two from them. The Chinese knew how to copy virtually anything. What they didn't do right, he and his local "quality control" people did.

Guzman was proud of his "lab." It was essentially a sophisticated printing set up, which he used to correct any errors found on the packaging of the pharmaceuticals received from China via his "repackaging plant" in Mexico. No one around the town of Toppenish even knew what repackaging was. Certainly his Spanish-speaking workers weren't going to go to the authorities even if they could understand. Most of them were undocumented.

In fact, Guzman preferred to think of himself as an "undocumented pharmacist." When he had been forced to close down his warehouse in Mexico, he had moved and reopened it. It wasn't hard to do in Mexico. He wasn't licensed in the U.S., though, and after having had a problem in Mexico, it could have been difficult to open a plant in the U.S. He wasn't sure he could and didn't want to find out, which is why he had picked Toppenish to set up his operation. Hansen hadn't seen his "lab," since Guzman had told him they were just in the process of setting up their facility in Toppenish when they started working together. Hansen represented a potential good chunk of business and Guzman didn't want to let him know about his plans until he was dependant on the benefits that Guzman offered.

"¡Americanos! ¡Son estupidos!" Guzman thought to himself. "Americans act on the honor system. Who else in the world is so naïve?"

Chapter Forty-Nine

Jess was so thrilled to obtain an affidavit from Dr. Smith that she could hardly control her exuberance. She called Danni on the way back to the office to give her the good news. Danni's response was, "I never doubted you for a minute."

"Well, *I* did," Jess said. "I think it was Voltaire who said, 'When you're up to your ass in alligators, it's hard to remember that you came to drain the swamp.'"

"Actually, Jess, I think that's your maxim, but it is true, true. And I never doubted you," Danni repeated.

"Thanks, Danni. Yeah, it probably wasn't Voltaire. See you at the office." Jess ended the call on her cell phone and thought to herself once again, "What a wonderful blue sky today! I knew there was a reason I liked this town!"

Back at the office, Jess called Mary Thompson, but there was no answer. Jess had been so excited that she had forgotten the time and realized that Mary was at school. Jess left a message and said she would call back on Tuesday.

Then she checked her messages, and to her surprise, she had a message from Joyce Brown. "Well how about that! There is a god!" thought Jess.

Returning Joyce's call, Jess was actually able to reach her this time. "Hello," Joyce answered.

"Joyce, this is Jess Lamm. I really appreciate you calling back. I really need to talk to you about the affidavit that Lars Hansen signed. He says that you resigned from Peoples under duress because of a drug problem and that you can't be trusted."

"I got your message. I've tried calling him for two days, and he's not answering my calls. That affidavit is just a lie! I can't believe he would say that," Joyce expounded again. "He isn't like that!"

"Joyce, I would be happy to send you a copy of the affidavit. Can I mail it or fax it to you?"

Apparently Joyce was not at all convinced that she wanted to share her location with Jess. "No, e-mail it to me. I'll get back with you."

"It's on its way," said Jess. She was hoping that Joyce really would get back with her. She scanned the affidavit to her computer and sent it to Joyce.

Jess spent a few hours catching up on what seemed like a gazillion phone calls she had been saving up over the last couple of weeks while she was focusing on the problems with the Thompson case. Her concern about the claim for terms had been taking up all her energy, mostly emotional energy. Having hurdled that problem, she had a little more time and energy to take care of the mundane matters.

Next was the affidavit for Dr. Smith. Jess was thrilled with the fact that she had expert support, and she wanted no delay in nailing it down.

Pulling out Dr. Smith's CV to read, Jess was impressed. The list of publications was an impressive forty-nine. It looked like many of them were coauthored, which probably meant that Dr. Smith had a reputation in the medical community that attracted attention. Apparently her name on a paper was a benefit to getting it published.

Jess opened her computer and started with the affidavit that she had originally drafted for John Peterson. In addition to making several changes to substitute Dr. Smith's credentials, she was able to put in the second most important part—that the cardiac arrest was likely not the actual cause of death. She also added the *most* important part:

In attempt to revive a forty-year-old male from cardiac arrest, a large premortem stroke is very unlikely to occur when the patient has no significant atherosclerosis. It is even less likely that such a large stroke would occur with no evidence of embolus or blood clot, as is reported in the autopsy of Brad Thompson. Such a finding is more likely than not a result of the administration of care, which falls below the standard of care of the reasonably prudent medical practitioner in the state of Washington, or as a result of the administration of one or more drugs that do not perform as intended in the body. Such a result would be consistent with an introduction of large amounts of air into the vascular system by administration of counterfeit drug or otherwise...

Jess sent the affidavit off to Dr. Smith with a check for $7,500. She thought it ironic that, if Dr. Smith were called to testify at trial, the amount of her fee would be played up by defense counsel. The whole litigation process is expensive and sometimes frustrating as hell. If defense didn't play such hard ball, the cost of medical malpractice wouldn't be so high. The insurers pay the defense bar to employ scorched earth tactics and then point at the plaintiff's counsel, claiming that they bring frivolous lawsuits.

Now, Jess needed Joyce's help to confirm that there was a code problem. She really didn't believe that Joyce took drugs, and she was glad that Joyce's response confirmed that.

Jess had also been extremely disappointed to learn that Peoples obtained its pharmaceuticals from DRD, a small secondary wholesaler, but she was suspicious that this was not really true. It would be a hell of a coincidence if Peoples didn't receive its bicarb from Unit Dose when counterfeit bicarb explained the events at Peoples so well.

DRD was so new and small, it was virtually impossible to find out anything about the organization online, except that they were located in a small town in eastern Washington, called Toppenish.

"Must be an Indian name," Jess thought. Hopefully, she would be able to find out the information that she needed from Joyce. "Hearing from Joyce was a good omen!" she thought.

Jess decided that she should schedule the deposition of the head pharmacist at Peoples to confirm where the hospital got its drugs. Since Jess didn't know the name of the head pharmacist and wanted to put the responsibility on Peoples to produce the person who had knowledge about the source of drugs, she prepared a 30(b)(6) deposition notice to compel the hospital to produce someone with the information. "Well, 'compel,'" Jess thought. "Baker doesn't seem to feel compelled to produce any info. I'd better schedule it for an early date because we'll probably need at least one trip to the courthouse on this one. Think I will set it for mid-August."

Looking at her watch, Jess saw that it was six o'clock in the evening. Almost everyone in the office had gone home. Jess was startled to hear, "Hey there, what are you smiling about...especially at six o'clock in the office all by yourself?" It was Drew—just in time for a trip to McCormick's.

"I'm on a roll!" Jess thought.

Chapter Fifty

The alarm rang altogether too early on Saturday morning of the weekend following Jess's discussion with Dr. Maggie Smith. The week had flown by partly due to an improvement in her luck on the Thompson case but more due to the fact that Jess and Drew were spending a lot more time together. In fact, when the alarm sounded, Jess was dreaming about making love with him again— her favorite dream of late. She woke up and moved her leg behind her. Right, Drew wasn't there. They had a wonderful dinner the night before, but he had begged off spending the night. He had "a prior engagement early today." Jess had experienced a fleeting moment of jealousy, but Drew had invited her and Reesa to dinner at his condo tonight. "Now that's not at all bad," thought Jess.

Hearing the alarm, Reesa knew that she was entitled to breakfast. She jumped up, stretched, and climbed on top of Jess's hip, purring so loudly that Jess could easily hear her even though Reesa was nowhere near her ear.

Jess had a day at the King County Law Library planned. She decided to spend Saturday on cases other than the Peoples case, and she needed a more general take on the law from sources that she couldn't easily get online. Her plan was to take a leisurely stroll through actual books—"CJS" or Corpus Juris Secundum and "Am-Jur" or American Jurisprudence. "This will be a change. Change is good for the brain," she thought.

"You can burn out on a case as intense as the Peoples case," Jess thought. "But at least it looks like it's coming together." She had received the signed affidavit from Dr. Smith. She was pretty sure that she could avoid dismissal now and get to a jury trial. In order to be successful at trial, however, she needed the information that Joyce Brown had related about trend in codes and verification of Peoples source of drugs.

"At least the trial won't be all that expensive," Jess thought. "We can probably get by with only $75,000 in costs." In addition to Dr. Smith, Jess would probably need an emergency room physician. Depending on what she found out about counterfeit drugs, she might need another expert for that, but what kind? She would certainly need an economist to testify about the income Brad would have earned over his lifetime, had he not died prematurely. She wondered if one of the partners at the accounting firm would help and how much he or she would charge. Then there would be the depositions of Baker's experts, all in the same fields as her experts but with opposing views.

Jess would have to advance all of the $75,000 in costs that it would take to get this case to trial on behalf of Mary Thompson. Even though Mary was not totally financially devastated, as most plaintiffs were, absent a win or successful settlement, it was very unlikely that Jess would be totally reimbursed for these out-of-pocket costs, let alone her probable $100,000 in fees.

Jess thought about the advertisements she saw on television about how greedy trial lawyers are. The insurance companies who pay for those don't tell the public how much their profits are. They don't mention the tens of thousands of deaths, let alone injuries, resulting from medical errors every year.

Jess had never seen a hospital's or doctor's insurer step up right out of the box and say, "You're right. My insured messed up. We will pay you what your client deserves because that's what our insured pays us for. How much do you think is fair?" In Jess's experience, insurers only paid when they had to—usually just before trial—and then only if you showed them that you knew what the problem with their case was.

While Jess was thinking about her pet peeves, she was laying in bed, and most importantly, not feeding Reesa, who'd had just about enough of this inaction. Since Jess wasn't getting up, Reesa took the next step. "Maybe Mom is hard of hearing today," her move indicated. She carefully stepped up the ridge of Jess's body and put her nose in her mom's ear. That was it! That got her attention. With Reesa's nose in Jess's ear, the sound was just a little quieter than a chainsaw. There would be no more sleeping this morning.

Jess was out of bed and into the kitchen to replenish the contents of Reesa's Good Kitty dish. As she washed and filled the dish with the remainder of the can from the refrigerator, Jess thought how appropriate the name on the dish was.

After feeding Reesa, Jess showered, wolfed down an Atkins bar, brushed out her hair, and put on a little mascara and blusher. She wasn't sure she'd have a lot of time later in the day to put on makeup, and she wanted to look good for Drew's dinner.

Jess drove down Second Avenue and turned right into the triangular-shaped parking lot at Second and James. Since it was Saturday, she thought she might find a place to park nearer the only courthouse entrance open today—the Third Avenue entrance. Though the lot was an older open area, it did have a credit card slot for payment and would be much less hassle than driving down into the bowels of the Columbia Tower parking and then hiking down the hill to Third Avenue. She took a spot and paid for the five hours that she thought she'd be there.

As she approached the courthouse, she passed the usual number of homeless wondering the streets outside. In the past, they would have been sleeping on the window ledges and in the foyer at the courthouse entrance. That was until the courthouse had been remodeled to make these areas inaccessible. Although Jess sympathized with the homeless, she was glad they weren't sleeping in the courthouse entrance anymore. She was a little tentative about walking around them. Usually they were reasonable people, just down on their luck. Sometimes, however, they were on the street because of mental illness, either leading to or resulting from homelessness. It was difficult to tell one from the other, and as a woman, she could be an easy target. There had been a few deaths in the area blamed on the homeless, usually the mentally ill.

The King County Courthouse in downtown Seattle had undergone a major remodel after the 2001 Nisqually earthquake. The courthouse hadn't been significantly refurbished for years before that and had lacked modern reinforcements to withstand earthquakes. A number of the judges took issue with the idea of leaving it that way after the quake. "I guess they didn't like waiting for the ceiling to fall in," thought Jess. Along with the retrofit for enhanced earthquake protection, the improvements had included closing off the main entrance foyer, refurbishing the floor inside the Third Avenue entrance, and redecorating the elevators.

The library in the King County Courthouse opened at eleven o'clock in the morning on Saturday. There wasn't the usual rush of people that occurred at nine o'clock on weekdays. Jess was able to get through the metal detector and into the lobby in record time.

"Too bad they didn't make the elevators any faster," Jess thought as she pressed the button to call one of the six elevators situated on each side of the Third Avenue lobby.

Upstairs in the law library, Jess pulled out AmJur and went to work. AmJur is a compilation of law from each of the state governments and the federal government as well. By reading it, a lawyer can get a good start on understanding an area of the law that she hasn't studied in depth before. Contrary to what some clients seem to think, lawyers don't have all the law in their heads; nor is there one book containing a single answer to a particular question. In fact, for most legal problems, there really is no one "answer." Uncle Frank had told her when she was applying to law school, "You can find law to support almost any position." Crazy as it sounds, Jess had found that statement, by and large, to be true.

At about one o'clock, Jess decided to check whether her friend Shelly Riley was in the office today. Jess and Shelly were "good buds," but they both had been so busy that they hadn't seen each other lately. They hadn't had time to sit down and *really* talk since the night that Shelly had to cancel their date at McCormick's. Jess went to one of conference rooms in the library so as not to disturb others and called Shelly's direct dial number at the office. It wasn't surprising to Jess that Shelly picked up.

"Hey, Shelly, long time, no see. I was hoping you would be in today. Are you up for lunch?"

"Well, hey! Good to hear from you. And I sure am! I have a brief that I have to get ready for Monday, and I don't want to come in tomorrow. How about an hour from now at our usual place?" That meant McCormick's, of course. On this Saturday afternoon there would be no trouble finding a table. Unless there is a baseball or football game scheduled, downtown Seattle isn't a hot spot on Saturdays.

An hour later, Jess walked to McCormick's since it was only a few blocks from the Third Avenue entrance of the courthouse. She and Shelly walked in the door at almost the same time. Hugging each other, Jess asked Shelly, "What's up in your life?"

"Same old, same old. Sometimes I get pretty tired of sexual assaults, but I'm glad that I have Jeff to bounce things off of. Otherwise it would be easy to think that the whole world is made of the perverts that I prosecute."

Shelly Riley and Jeff Preston had been dating for a couple of years. They had met in the juvenile department of the King County Prosecutor's office. After they started dating, Shelly moved to the sexual assaults unit because Jeff had been her supervisor in "juvie." Since lawyers spend a lot of time at work, office romances are far from uncommon. Fortunately, Washington State law is practical on the subject. It allows for and even protects office relationships by preventing termination of employment as long as one spouse doesn't supervise the other. Actually the move to the sexual assaults unit had worked out well for Shelly. She was seen as a rising young star in the department. She and Jeff now lived together in a condo on Queen Anne Hill, a mixed but trendy part of Seattle. "Jeff and I are thinking of getting married," Shelly said.

"Shelly, how exciting!" Jess smiled. "Damn, I leave you unsupervised for a month or two, and see what you go and do!"

Jess and Shelly ordered food and drink and caught up on the last few months, including Jeff, Drew, the Peoples case, and Shelly's three cases set for Monday. The prosecutor's office is always overloaded with work. Several cases are often set for the same day in order to comply with the "speedy trial" rule of criminal law. There are a few exceptions to the rule, but it generally requires that criminal cases be started within ninety days of when charges are brought. The system counts on some criminal defendants pleading guilty. Otherwise cases are started and continued to another date for completion. It's a practical way of complying with a requirement that the department and the courts are way understaffed for.

Jess looked at her watch and saw that it was three thirty. "Wow, look at the time! Reesa and I are having dinner with Drew tonight at his apartment in Bellevue. I want to have time to pick up Reesa and find his place. I don't get over to Bellevue a lot."

"That sounds serious—a guy who cooks and likes kitties. Hold on to him, Jess!"

"My plan entirely," said Jess. As she stood and put down cash for her half of the bill, she said, "Damn, it's good to see you, Shelly! Don't stay away so long next time."

"Right," Shelly said wryly, knowing that both of them would get wrapped up in their lives, and it probably would be another month or two before they would find the time to get together again.

Jess walked back toward the courthouse and on to her car, which was going to be hot since it was sitting outside today. Jess turned on the air conditioner full blast and turned east up to Third Avenue and home. The air conditioner was loud enough that she didn't hear anything until she saw movement out of the corner of her eye. Something was moving in the seat next to her!

Jess looked to the right. It was a snake—a *big* snake coiled and ready to strike! Her eyes glued on the snake, she totally missed the red light at Seneca and Third. When she looked up there was a pickup sideways to her in the middle of the street. She tried to swerve but couldn't turn in time to miss it. The snake didn't miss either.

Chapter Fifty-One

Jess didn't remember anything until she woke up in the hospital room. Her head was pounding, and her right arm felt so heavy she could hardly move it.

"Hey, sleepy, are you awake?" Jess thought she heard Drew's voice. She tried opening her eyes, but her lids were heavy, possibly swollen. She couldn't tell why, but they definitely weren't working right. When she saw her right arm, she could tell why it was so heavy. It was swollen to twice its normal size.

Someone took her left hand and gently squeezed it. Jess looked over that way and saw Drew.

"Where am I?" she asked.

"Drew was sitting next to the bed holding her hand. "Harborview Hospital," said Drew. "Say, if you didn't want to come to dinner you could have just called," he joked. But he couldn't maintain the bravado. His voice cracked and his eyes watered. "Damn, I'm glad you're okay, Jess."

"I don't feel okay, but I am glad to hear that. What happened?" Jess asked.

"You had an accident. You were really lucky that you were downtown. The medics got to you within a few minutes. After they got rid of the snake, they were able to treat you right away. You could have had a real problem if you hadn't been so close."

"God, my head…I think the accident affected my hearing. I could have sworn that you said 'snake.'"

"I did. Someone put a rattlesnake in your car. You probably didn't see it until you started driving, and then he was probably as freaked out as you were. Too bad you couldn't talk sense to him."

Jess smiled. Drew really had a good way of making people, especially her, feel like things were not so serious.

"Oh, Jesus, Drew. I don't feel so good," Jess said, feeling as though she could vomit.

"Here, Jess, don't worry, these things are made for that." Drew held forward a ridiculously small pan that hospitals call an emesis basin. If you can't hit this thing, don't worry. We have towels on your bed, and we can replace them."

It turned out that the emesis basin could hold anything that Jess could bring up. Apparently she had been quite a mess when the medics picked her up. She had lost her whole lunch at the scene of the accident, so there wasn't much left.

"Reesa," Jess said.

"Not to worry. I called Paul and Teresa. They got Tommy to let them in your condo. They have her."

"Thanks, Drew." Tears trickled out of her eyes. "I'm so tired." She nodded off again.

The hospital had called Drew since Jess had his phone number and address in her purse. They thought he might know someone in her family to call. It turned out that he didn't, but he did rush down to Harborview Hospital. He had been there since Saturday afternoon, and it was now Sunday morning. Jess had been drifting in and out of sleep or unconsciousness; Drew couldn't tell which. A nurse came in every hour and flashed a light in Jess's eyes to make sure her pupils were even and reacting to light. The CT scan had revealed a concussion, but nothing more. "Even with two black eyes and a swollen arm, and occasionally vomiting she looks beautiful," Drew thought. "I guess there usually is something behind those trite expressions."

Drew was so relieved to see Jess finally wake up. The doctors had said that she would probably be just fine because she had been so close to the hospital when the accident occurred. Drew was glad to see that Jess seemed to be doing the things that confirmed the doctors knew what they were talking about.

Chapter Fifty-Two

Jess insisted on going home on Monday afternoon, even though her doctor had suggested that she stay another day, considering her concussion *and* the snake bite. Jess just wanted to go home but didn't quite feel like she could handle things at the office. Drew took her home, went to the office briefly, and picked up takeout food for dinner that night. He said he intended to work his way through the takeout vendors on the atrium level of the office building and bring food and anything from the office that needed immediate attention each afternoon. Jess appreciated the thoughtfulness.

Monday night when he left, Drew kissed her on the forehead, which was about the limit of sexy contact that she could take. Her eyes were healing, but they still had a wonderful yellow and purple tinge about them. "Too bad the purple isn't on the upper lid. At least that way I could pretend it's eye shadow," Jess thought every time she looked in the mirror. Drew reminded Jess to throw the dead bolt on the door when he left. She didn't need to be told but appreciated the thought. Danger was front and center in her mind.

Coincidentally, shortly after Drew left on Monday night, the phone rang. Jess answered, expecting it to be Drew calling, and said, "Hello, forget something?" The slight attempt at humor went nowhere, and there was no answer. The line went dead before Jess had a chance to look at the caller ID. Under normal circumstances, this would be nothing, but things hadn't exactly been normal lately. She shoved the incident to the back of her brain.

On Tuesday, Jess's second day home from the hospital, Drew had brought veggie wraps and a bottle of Hogue chardonnay. They had enjoyed a glass of wine and the takeout, but it wasn't more than an hour before Jess was exhausted. Seeing the droopy eyelids, Drew said he should get going, kissed Jess on the forehead again, and reminded her to throw the deadbolt. Again, Jess appreciated the thought.

Jess was on her way to bed for the night when the phone rang. This time she looked at the caller ID before picking up. It showed caller "unknown." Jess picked up the phone and answered, "Hello... hello." The response was silence. Jess was irritated. "Is anyone there?" she asked in a voice that showed the irritation. Jess was just about to put down the phone when she heard noise on the other end of the line as though someone was picking up the phone hand piece. In a muffled voice, but distinctively a man's voice, Jess heard, "If you know what's good for you, you'll stay away from Dr. Haseem."

"What? What are you saying?" Jess replied into the phone while she involuntarily moved it away from her ear as though it was the speaker. She noticed that her voice came out much louder than she intended and her heart was thudding rapidly.

"You know, bitch. You know what I mean...snakes are not all we can do." The line went dead. Jess put the phone down hard, as though being angry would make the voice go away. Unfortunately, banging the phone didn't eliminate the voice from her brain. She was so shaken by the threat that she did nothing for a few minutes. Recovering somewhat, she called Drew on his cell phone. He didn't answer, but she left message. "Drew, this is Jess. Give me a call, would you?"

In a matter of minutes, the phone rang again. Jess looked at the caller ID, which again said "unknown." Hesitating to pick it up, she determined she should, since it could be Drew calling back. She hadn't really paid attention before to what Drew's cell phone ID was. She picked up the phone. "Hello?" Jess said in a tentative voice.

Jess was relieved to hear Drew on the other end. "Hi, there! You okay?" Drew asked. "I knew you'd miss me. Sorry, I'm in the car and couldn't get the cell out until after the phone stopped ringing."

Jess hesitated. "Drew, I didn't realize your phone had ID blocking. Have you always had that?"

"Is that why you called? I was hoping for something more," Drew teased.

"No, I'm serious. I almost didn't pick up the phone. Last night when you left, I got an anonymous phone call. I didn't mention it because it didn't seem like a big deal. Tonight, again just after you left, I got another call. This time someone answered just as I was about to hang up. It was a man speaking in a muffled voice, obviously an effort to disguise. He said I should stay away from Dr. Haseem and that he could do more than snakes."

"Jess, I'm turning around right now. I am taking the first exit off I-90."

"No, I'm sure I'll be all right. After all, the deadbolt is locked. I'm so tired, and I really need to go to bed."

"Sweetheart, don't worry about keeping me company. I just want to make sure that you're okay."

"No, really. I'll be okay. I'm just a little shaken. I don't get calls like that every day, and it just shook me that I've received two right after you left. But I'll be okay." The fact that the word *okay* came out twice suggested to Jess that maybe she didn't feel okay.

"Jess, you can't imagine how much this worries me. I really want to come over and make sure you'll be all right."

"No, really, I need to go to bed. I'll see you tomorrow." Jess hung up before Drew could say anymore.

Jess did go to bed but didn't go to sleep. Instead, she lay staring at the ceiling. "Maybe I should have let him come back," she thought. "No, get a grip, girl! Big girls don't need 'big strong men' to protect them." She turned on her side, thinking that maybe a better position would help her get to sleep. As if she felt Jess's concern, Reesa climbed up on her hip, purring up a storm. "Thanks, girl. I can use some loving. I just must be really tired, or I wouldn't let my thoughts run away like this."

Chapter Fifty-Three

On Wednesday, Drew brought takeout food again. Jess wasn't her usual outgoing self. It had occurred to her that her condo had been trashed the day she met Drew. Was it really by chance that they had met at McCormick's that night? It seemed unlikely Drew could have planned it, since she was supposed to be meeting with Shelly that night.

Jess called Danni to talk with her, since Danni's husband knew Drew. Jess thought that she would double-check her impression of Drew. Danni was unavailable during much of the day but called back about four o'clock. "How are you doing? Things are under control here. In fact, I see that you even have the signed affidavit from Dr. Smith. You've done a hell of a job on the Peoples case! It's lucky you have nursing experience. I never would have put that case together."

"It's nice to know I can do something right."

"*Whoa* there Jess! That snake must have poisoned your brain. What's bothering you?"

"I think it's just being here alone and bored all day. I should get back to the office soon."

"Right, and what else? I know you—you don't get down like this unless there's *really* something wrong. Don't give me the boredom story."

"Well, I get plenty of time to let my mind run away with thoughts, and I've had a lot to think about. Since I came home from the hospital, I've been getting anonymous calls."

"You've checked caller ID, right?"

"Of course, and it's blocked. But something else is bothering me. Last night, it wasn't just anonymous; it was threatening. A man's voice told me to leave Dr. Haseem alone—he's one of our defendants in the Peoples case, you know. I don't even think that Mr. Thompson's death was his fault anymore. So why would someone call about that? But in addition to that, the caller said he could do more than snakes. Of course, I thought that the snake was a warning, but it still shakes me up to hear it confirmed. I guess the thing that bothers me most is the timing. I've received two calls, and they came just after Drew left my condo. I know that sounds paranoid, but it seems like a hell of a coincidence."

"So I knew that Drew was helping you out on this case. Sounds like it's more than that, huh?

"Well, yes," Jess said, smiling despite her concern, as she thought about their lovemaking.

"Well, watch out for yourself, Jess. You know he's married, don't you?"

"You mean that he used to be, right? He said he's divorced."

"Well, I know he's been separated on and off for a couple of years, but I don't think he's ever gotten divorced. David plays on the same baseball team with Drew, and sometimes they go bike riding. David says he's never seen a guy who seems less eager to get on with life. He's not sure why Drew and his wife are still tied. If you're spending time with Drew, you're the first that I've heard of…Jess?…Jess? You still there?"

Jess cleared her throat. "Oh, well, I'll talk to you later, Danni. Thanks for the info." She was glad that Danni was on the other end of the phone and not in the room. Her throat had suddenly tightened, and her face was turning red. "How could I be such an idiot!" She was embarrassed for being so trusting. "Wait…I'm not the one who lied! Why am I feeling like the idiot?" Jess said to herself. "Because you are one," she heard the voice in her head respond. "You think you're so wonderful that anyone would just love to spend his time helping you research on a sunny weekend with no ulterior motive? You idiot!"

The conversation with Danni had taken place just forty minutes before Drew arrived, and the conversation within Jess's head hadn't had time to die down. She was stunned and had no time to recover from the sting of the news about Drew before he rang the doorbell. She met Drew at the door with a glass of wine and led him into the living room, where they sat down on the couch. "How did your day go?" Drew asked.

"Well, I would say not so well," said Jess. Then without pausing, she blurted out, "I thought you were divorced!"

A red glow worked its way up Drew's face, and there was a long pause, giving Jess time to think, "For a lawyer, you're mighty speechless."

Drew started to put his hand on Jess's, but she pulled back and stood up. "So what are you saying, or not saying? I assume your silence means it's true!" Jess exclaimed.

"Jess, I'm sorry. I really think of myself as divorced. My wife and I have been separated for two years. We've even started the divorce proceedings. We've attempted a property settlement. Finishing it just seems so final when you've been married ten years."

The words "my wife" really stung. "Well, I've got news for you! It's even tougher to be lied to. And I want to know when you put your cell on ID block. I know I saw your caller ID before. So why is your number suddenly blocked?"

"What are you talking about? I have it blocked so that I can call clients when I am out of the office and not be hammered with return calls. You know clients can get demanding sometimes."

"Really? I could've sworn that it wasn't blocked."

"Jess, why does it matter if it's blocked or not?"

"Because of the anonymous calls I've been getting just after you leave. How would anyone know when you leave? I don't get them any other time. How would anyone know but you?"

"Jess, you're kidding, right? You don't really think I'm calling you anonymously."

"Well, I didn't think you were married either, but it seems you are."

"Jess, it's not me! I swear it! I can understand your reasoning…but there must be another explanation. I would never do that to you!"

It was Drew's turn to stand. He moved toward Jess, and she backed farther away. "Drew, I think you'd better go. You can take the food with you. I'm not very hungry. Please go."

He didn't move immediately. In fact, he stood perfectly still for at least twenty seconds, but in the situation it seemed much longer than that. Jess was clearly not in a talking mood, and it was also clear that there wasn't anything Drew could say that was going to make a difference. "I'm sorry, Jess," he said, as he turned and walked out the door, closing it behind him.

Reesa followed Drew to the door and sat staring at it as though waiting for him to come back. Seeing her, Jess sat down, buried her face in her hands, and sobbed. "Reesa, even you?"

Chapter Fifty-Four

Jess woke up at four o'clock Thursday morning and couldn't get back to sleep. Even though her arm was still a little swollen and her brain was only working at half speed, she decided she couldn't stay at home. She was going crazy sitting around home by herself wondering about a possible connection between Drew and the threatening phone calls. "My god, he could even be associated with the snake in the car," she thought. "How could I have been so gullible?" she asked herself over and over. "Why would Drew volunteer to be so helpful? Does he have some plan to keep tabs on the case? Did he intentionally mislead me about the sodium bicarbonate connection? No, John thought about that, and Dr. Smith agreed. If Drew is behind the threats, why would he mention Dr. Haseem? What was the deal with the intruder on that Sunday night? He could've set that up. The intruder on the elevator video was short and slight—Drew is at least six feet tall. He could have set that up too. Is that why he was so attentive that he knew Joyce Brown's name? Damn, what a chump!" Jess shook her head, trying to erase the thoughts.

As soon as she thought that Teresa and Paul would be up, Jess called and was relieved to find that she hadn't woken them. Teresa confirmed that she and Paul would *love* to take care of Reesa.

Jess just couldn't take a chance with Reesa. As disloyal as she had been the night before, she was family, and it seemed that she was the *only* family Jess had right now. Sure, there was her mother in Minneapolis, but the trip to the hospital had re-impressed upon Jess how big the distance between Seattle and Minneapolis actually is. She just didn't want to think about anything happening to Reesa.

One thing that really got Jess's attention was the fact that there had been no phone call the night before. "What a hell of a coincidence!" Jess thought. But as soon as the paranoid thought flashed by, the voice of reason followed, "And what does that prove?"

As Jess arrived at the office, she was hoping she wouldn't run into Drew. She just didn't have the energy to deal with him now and really didn't know what she would say to him. She walked in and waived though the office window at Danni, who was busy on the phone, as usual. Jess sat down and listened to her voice mail. The cheery automated voice said, "You have…twenty nine…voice mail messages." The pause before and after the message count sometimes made the voice sound human, like it was criticizing Jess for letting the messages pile up.

The first several messages, which played in order received, were hang-ups. "I guess there's an epidemic of those," thought Jess. The fourth message caused Jess's adrenaline to start flowing. "Ms. Lamm, this is Joyce Brown. I got Mr. Hansen's affidavit that you sent. I have been trying to reach him, but I'm getting no return call. I just can't believe he would accuse me of using drugs. I *reported* missing controlled drugs in the ER. How could he say that? Please call me on my cell."

Jess stopped playing the messages and immediately called Joyce back. No answer. "Shock, shock," Jess thought, but she did leave her numbers to call back, at the office, on her cell, and even at home. "It would be a pleasure to have someone call me at home who actually has something to say," Jess thought.

Just then Danni stuck her head around the door jam. "You're back! Damn, it's good to see you! How are you feeling?"

"I'm not a hundred percent, but I can't sit at home anymore. It's driving me crazy."

"Well, I reset the 30(b)(6) deposition that you had scheduled for this week. Baker said that Hansen couldn't make the day you set anyway. We reset it for next Thursday. I checked your schedule, and that looks okay," Danni said. "I penciled it in. I just wanted to bring you up to speed."

"Really! So Hansen is the all-purpose witness," Jess noted. "Thanks, Danni. I really appreciate you following up on that. And wait until you hear this! I also got a call from Joyce Brown. Remember that she was the head nurse on duty the day that Brad Thompson died. Hansen put in an affidavit that said she was fired for using drugs. I sent her the affidavit. I just got a phone message from her, adamantly denying that she ever used drugs, and she's really angry that Hansen said she did. I called her back, but of course, got her voice mail. At least there's one thing looking up."

"Well, hang in there Jess. You'll get to the bottom of it. You always do."

"Thanks, Danni. It is really good to be back. Sometimes this business gets overwhelming though."

"Actually, it may be my personal life that's more to blame. Even Joyce calling back isn't enough to dig me out of the cellar," Jess thought, but didn't say.

"I'm really so sorry to have dropped the news about Drew on you, especially when you feel so lousy. I really wanted to call you back yesterday, but I couldn't think of anything to say. I really don't know Drew, but David seems to think he's a good guy. I know that doesn't mean he's a good guy with women, but it is a start."

"Thanks, Danni. I know you care, and sometimes it is especially nice to hear it. This is one of those times. Thanks…really."

Chapter Fifty-Five

After Danni went back to her office, Jess continued her trek through the remaining voice messages. She was in process of returning calls when her call-waiting showed that Joyce Brown was calling back. Getting off the line as fast as possible—almost hanging up on a new client—Jess was able pick up the call from Joyce.

"Hello, this is Jessica Lamm," Jess said.

"Hello, this is Joyce Brown. I got the affidavit that you sent me, and I've been trying to contact Mr. Hansen about it. There *was* a nurse in the ER at one time that was pilfering controlled drugs, but it wasn't me! I actually brought it to the attention of the nursing supervisor. And I know that Mr. Hansen knew about it, because he talked to me before she was fired."

"Joyce, where are you? Are you still on vacation?"

"Well…," Joyce paused. Jess was afraid she was going to hang up again. "No, I'm back in Seattle. I decided that I need to get back to work. I was also concerned about my reputation. I have my old job back at Renton Hospital, though, so I guess I'm all right for now."

"Joyce, since we last talked, I've been looking into the potential cause of the code problems that you and I talked about. I've even run it by a pathologist who has given us an opinion about what is causing the situation. She thinks that the problem is due to carbon dioxide being released when counterfeit sodium bicarbonate is administered in codes. I would really like to have you review the affidavit that she signed explaining how it works."

"Really? Why would that happen? We have always used bicarb in code situations. Why would it start happening now?"

"We think that Peoples is getting counterfeit drugs. It can happen even when you don't know it," Jess explained. "The drugs can come in packages that look exactly like the genuine drugs. There is virtually no way to tell."

"Well how do you know if the drugs are fake, then?"

"We know partly from the fact that the hospital is having a problem that it didn't have before, which is one of the reasons that I really needed to get in touch with you. You told me about the code problem. It's very hard to get evidence like that before the court without having the person who knows about the situation sign an affidavit. So when you left town, I was very concerned. I am even more concerned that you mentioned Mr. Hansen suggested that you go on vacation. If he knows that you have valuable information and suggests that you go on vacation, that is very suspicious. It's also very suspicious that he knew where you were all of the time and wouldn't tell us about it until the court ordered him to."

"It's hard for me to believe that Mr. Hansen would do such a thing, but I also didn't think he'd lie about me. I'm not sure what to think."

"Joyce, I could really use your help. I really need to have you come in and sign an affidavit so that I can get this information before the court. Otherwise, we may never find out why Mr. Thompson died, and I really don't want that to happen. His widow and child really need your help. It's just not fair that he should die of bad drugs and no one does anything about it. We think that this problem is probably still going on, and others could die too."

"Well, I'll think about it."

"Joyce, I would like to get you a copy of the pathologist's affidavit so that you can know for sure what the she thinks. Can I send it to you?"

"No, I don't want you to. I'm not sure about this." Joyce paused for quite some time. Jess held her breath, again worried that she would hang up and never call back. Finally, Joyce said, "I'll come in and pick it up. I'm going to be downtown anyway."

"When do you want to come in?" Jess asked. "If we're going to be able to file your affidavit, we need it soon."

"I'll come in tonight after work. I should be able to get there by about five o'clock."

"Thank you, Joyce. I'll be here," Jess said, as Joyce hung up.

Jess was thrilled. "Now if she really does come in…" she thought. She was amazed at how much better she was finally beginning to feel. "Getting back in the saddle is good medicine."

Chapter Fifty-Six

It was five thirty on Thursday evening. Jess was on her way out of the office feeling tired but pleased with herself. This time Joyce had been true to her word. She had come to the office at exactly five o'clock, as promised, and picked up a copy of Dr. Smith's affidavit. She wasn't prepared to talk and Jess didn't press her. It was enough that she was thinking about the problem. Again, Jess thought about whether she should serve a subpoena on Joyce and force her to come to a deposition. Again, her intuition told her that would be a bad idea. All Jess said was, "Remember, I really need your affidavit."

As she walked out of her office, Jess almost ran into Drew. She wasn't expecting to see anyone in the office this late and hoping especially that she wouldn't see Drew. Her feelings were so intense that she hadn't had time to come down to earth about the situation. She felt an aching loss, but when she thought about it, she was also embarrassed that she had been so trusting and had allowed herself to believe that Drew was what she was looking for. Running into him caused those feeling to well up front and center again.

"Oh, I didn't know you were here," was all that Jess could spit out.

"I thought that you'd be home." Drew was apparently uncomfortable too. "I was actually going to leave you a note to give you something to think about. I know that my word is low on your list of trusted sources, but please do think about it." Drew gave her the envelope that he had in his hand and then turned and walked back toward his office.

Jess took the envelope and stood where she was in the middle of the hall for a minute. Her feet seemed glued to that spot on the floor. The feelings, whatever they were, paralyzed her body for an instant. "Get a grip, Jess. Walk out and go home," she told herself. "No more stupid statements off the top of your head. This is too important for that."

At home, after picking up Reesa from Teresa and Paul, putting food in Reesa's Good Kitty dishes, and opening a bottle of wine, Jess sat down on the couch to contemplate the letter. It said:

Dear Jess,

I am so sorry that I allowed you to believe that I am divorced. I really do consider myself divorced. My wife and I actually have filed the dissolution action, and we have a draft of a settlement agreement which is essentially done. Until now finishing the divorce has not mattered.

When I said that I lost my cat in the divorce, I did not realize how misleading it would be to someone who really cared. I do believe that you care, maybe mostly because I really care about you. Sorry does not seem to be good enough, but it is the best I can do.

My purpose in spending all afternoon on this letter is not just to tell you that. I want you to know something else, and I hope that you will follow up on it. This morning, I contacted the police again. You know that when I called them after the car "accident" they were not very helpful. Without more to work on, they essentially said that they were going to file a report. At best, I guess they are still working on the boyfriend theory, which seems especially ironic now.

Anyway, I talked to the police again today. I used my connections at the old firm to get to someone who *might* listen. I have racked my brain to figure out why someone would be able to call you when I left your condo. The only thing I can come up with is that your condo is bugged. I ran this by a Sergeant Tobowlski to-day. I don't think that he believes it, but seeing as how he has a recommendation from my old partner that I am not crazy, he is at least willing to supply a guy to check for bugs in your condo. If you are willing to do that, I can put you in touch with him.

Jess, I am so sorry that I hurt you. I also want you to know that I really am working on making the rep-resentation about my marital status true. I know what will run through your mind in response to that, but again, it is the best I can do. I hope that it will be good enough.

Love,

Drew

Having finished the letter, Jess felt paralysis setting in again. She stared out the windows of her condo at the spectacular view, not really even seeing it. Reesa was sitting on the couch beside her and moved over to her lap when Jess stopped reading. She started purring up a storm, her usual response when she could tell that Jess needed kitty love. "It's good to have someone you can count on," Jess thought. She wasn't so sure about Drew, despite his protesta-tions. "Or maybe this is just his version of love," Jess thought wryly. "I'll think on it."

She poured herself another glass of wine. "The hell with mod-eration. Sometimes wine really can clear the head," she thought. She held up the glass of wine and said, "Here's to moderation in all things, even moderation."

Chapter Fifty-Seven

Friday morning Jess woke up to daylight streaming into the window. Since she didn't often allow herself the luxury of lying in bed in the morning, Jess decided to soak in the feeling for a minute, but only a minute. As soon as she began to wake up, she noticed a throbbing emanating from her head. It also seemed to be spreading down to her stomach where it felt more like slight nausea. "My god, my head hurts!" she thought. "Where is the Alka Seltzer when you need it? Sure am glad I left that little bit in the end of the bottle. I might have gotten *really* drunk!"

Seeing that Jess was awake, Reesa climbed up on her hip and started the "purr machine" again. Jess knew that Reesa would shortly be more insistent about getting her breakfast and decided that since Reesa had been so sympathetic the night before, she deserved better than waiting until she got impatient for food. Jess sat up on the edge of the bed and despite her pounding head, walked into the kitchen and filled Reesa's dishes.

Searching through her bathroom closet, Jess located some Alka Seltzer. She needed a double this morning. Since she had made arrangements with Teresa and Paul to take Reesa again today, she delivered Reesa to the next door condo after taking a quick shower and pulling her hair back in a clip. Before leaving for the office she added a little mascara and blush. She was actually beginning to feel better and wanted to look it. She had decided to follow up on Drew's suggestion about checking for a bug. "Obviously couldn't hurt, could it?" she thought. "But what if there isn't a bug?" Jess wasn't sure which would be worse. "Wait a minute, what am I thinking. That would *not* be worse," Jess thought. "I am a big girl! I can live with the truth!"

Arriving at the office, Jess was glad she didn't see Drew. One minute she was thinking that she would tell him how sorry she was for doubting him, and the next she was thinking what a fool she was for thinking that. "Better to find out the facts," she thought.

Sitting down in her chair at the office, Jess fired up her computer and looked up the number of the Seattle Police. She was hoping that she could locate Sergeant Tobowlski without calling Drew. She wasn't sure what she would say to him, and she wanted to make sure that there really was a Tobowlski at the Seattle Police Department. Fortunately, she found out that there was such a man.

"Sergeant Tobowlski, this is Jessica Lamm. My friend Drew Stewart talked with you yesterday. He said that you might be able to run a check for listening devices in my condominium. I know that it sounds strange, but strange things have been happening in my life…You can?…This morning?…I can be there whenever your man can…Ten o'clock today?…You have the address, right?…Just have him press the buzzer, and I'll let him up."

Jess felt a surge of excitement as she put down the phone. Looking at her watch she determined that she had about forty-five minutes to kill before she would have to leave to meet the "Bug Detector Guy." Sergeant Tobowlski had explained that Investigator Kobiyoshi, who liked to call himself "Bug Detector Guy," would come to her condo at ten o'clock this morning. She picked up the phone again and listened to her voice mail messages. This time there were only nine messages—the voice mail lady didn't sound so critical. Unfortunately, there were no messages from Joyce Brown. "Well, it's probably too early to expect a response from her," Jess mused.

Jess arrived at her condominium well ahead of the ten o'clock appointment. She wanted to be sure that she didn't miss Bug Detector Guy. At ten o'clock on the nose, the phone rang, Jess answered, and found that it was Investigator Kobiyoshi. "Take a right out of the elevator," she told him, and pressed the button to buzz him in. Jess was waiting at her condo door as Investigator Kobiyoshi stepped out of the elevator. She was sure that it was Kobiyoshi because he wore a ball cap that said "Police." He also wore jeans and a plaid shirt with a pocket protector full of pens. He motioned to Jess to step out into the hallway. As she did so, Kobiyoshi pulled out his identification and, in a voice so low that Jess could hardly hear it, introduced himself. "Hi. I am Investigator Kobiyoshi, a.k.a., Bug Detector Guy. My friends call me 'Bug Guy.'" In an even quieter tone, Bug Guy leaned toward Jess and said, "Have you been talking about my coming in the location?"

Jess responded in an equally hushed voice, "The location?" Jess was really glad she had taken the time to call Sergeant Tobowlski herself. If she didn't have confidence that Bug Guy was really a member of the Seattle Police, she would have been worried that he came straight off a movie set. He certainly took his job seriously.

"The location, the site, the condo," whispered Bug Guy.

"Oh…," Jess thought for a minute, "no."

"Good, I always like to surprise these guys."

"Oh…," was all that Jess said, again.

"Just follow me and don't say a thing," Bug Guy said as he pushed open the door to the condo. He pulled a handheld device out of the canvas bag hung over his shoulder and began walking down the entrance hallway waiving the device over everything other than flat wall—the light fixtures, wall plugs, vents, etc. Occasionally he would stop and make notes. After about forty-five minutes, just as Jess was getting a little tired of this borderline comedy, Bug Guy turned, tapped her on the arm, and motioned toward the front door. Jess followed him out.

"The location is bugged…one on the back of the bedside table in the bedroom near the phone, of course; another in the kitchen phone; and one under the bench seat in the living room. I also looked for cameras…didn't find any. What do you want me to do with the bugs?"

Jess stared at him. "You have got to be kidding," she thought. "Take them out!" she virtually shrieked, forgetting to continue the cloak-and-dagger charade. Seeing the horrified look on Bug Guy's face, she lowered her voice and said again, "Take them out!"

Bug Guy looked a little disappointed but walked back into the condo. As she followed him, Jess was too stunned to proceed. Her mind was flooded with scenarios of embarrassment and anger. It was one thing to have your home invaded and ransacked. It was another to think of someone listening in on all your conversations, especially private conversations. Jess sat down and took a few breaths to dam the emotional flood. She needed more rational thinking.

Why would anyone want to bug her house? If this was connected with the snake episode, which seemed likely, why would anyone want to hurt her? And where would you get a rattlesnake? Rattlesnakes weren't prevalent residents of the rainy forests of the west side of Washington State. On the east side of the state—in the desert on the other side of the rain barrier created by Washington's Cascade Mountains—rattlesnakes were common. DRD was also located in eastern Washington. What a hell of a coincidence! Well, she felt relieved about one thing. At least there was reason to think that the anonymous phone calls came from someone other than Drew. "Doesn't mean that he couldn't be involved, but he's sure doing a good job of making himself look innocent," Jess thought. Her feeling of gullibility dropped from a ten to a seven on her personal Richter scale.

Bug Guy, having finished the job of removing the bugs, startled Jess by speaking in a normal voice. "We usually take these down to the lab and check them out for further evidence. This is kind of different. This case came through different channels. What do you want me to do with these?"

"What do you mean 'different channels'?" Jess asked.

"Well, Sergeant Tobowlski said that this was a domestic dispute, but we were going to have to go through the motions just in case. I don't usually work on domestic disputes."

Anger crept into Jess's voice. "Oh." she paused. "Just a minute. Do you have Sergeant Tobowlski's number?"

"Sure, here it is." Bug Guy pulled out a pad and one of the pens from his pocket protector and wrote down a number.

Jess dialed and got Tobowlski's voice mail. She left a message to call her and then turned to Bug Guy. "Well you have the stuff now. What would you ordinarily do with it?"

"Well, I would have to set up a case number. I'll have to check with Sergeant Tobowlski." Seeing the angry look on Jess's face, Bug Guy continued, "I'll do that. Right, I'll do that, and we'll get this evidence checked out."

"Thank you," Jess said. She thought that it was best not to say anymore. She showed Bug Guy to the door and closed it behind him. Jess went to her bedside table where she had put Drew's letter and sat down on the bed to read it again. It was difficult to read because her eyes were watering so much.

Chapter Fifty-Eight

Jess didn't go back to work Friday afternoon. She needed time to let her mind settle. She walked down to the Pike Place Market and perused the stalls looking for nothing in particular. The market wasn't nearly as busy this Friday as it was on weekends. She walked on down the way to the piers lining the waterfront. She sat on a bench and found that she stayed most of the day, occasionally feeling guilty about not being in the office but not enough to do anything about it.

On Saturday morning the guilty feeling overtook Jess. She really had to get back to the office after having been out so long after the accident. She thought again about how she hoped to obtain an affidavit from Joyce Brown but didn't feel that she could count on it considering Joyce's past conduct. She wondered if her judgment not to serve a subpoena on her had been right. Dr. Smith's affidavit was good—maybe it would be enough.

Reesa intruded on Jess's thoughts by climbing up on her hip and cranking up the purr machine. "It is good to know that some things don't change," thought Jess. She sat up, petted Reesa, and went to the kitchen for Reesa's food. Reesa walked ahead of her to the kitchen, as if leading the way. She would look back occasionally to make sure Jess wasn't taking a detour. Jess could almost hear Reesa thinking, "Sometimes servants can be so dense!"

Jess took a shower, blew her hair dry and put on slacks, a sexy short-sleeved sweater, and more make-up than necessary for a Saturday. If she was going to the office today—and she had to—she was going to feel good. Sweat pants and tennis shoes didn't make her feel good. She was glad to see that the discoloration around her eyes was gone enough to be covered by make-up. She felt like she was getting back to normal.

Arriving at the office, Jess parked in her usual place on floor F of the garage. Not only was it more convenient to the office, Jess decided that parking in a secure lot was a better idea, at least for now. The thought rekindled an idea in the back of her brain. She was sure that rattlesnakes weren't found in western Washington. Where did that snake come from?

When Jess opened her computer, she decided to do a little research on rattlesnakes. The information that she found confirmed her suspicion. They aren't common in western Washington; in fact, they don't naturally occur there at all. The map that she found on rattlesnakes showed them occurring only in eastern Washington, the dry part of the state. "Hmm," thought Jess, filing that fact in the back of her mind.

Before turning to her voice mail, there was one more search that Jess decided to pursue. She searched for King County cases on Courtlink to see if they—Drew and his wife—really had filed for divorce. There were several Stewarts, but she thought that she could identify Drew's case. "Hmm," she said to herself.

Since Jess had spent very little time at the office on Friday, her voice mail messages would be piled up high, and the voice mail lady was going to be telling her about it. Jess dialed in, and the mechanical lady said, "You have...*fourteen*...voice mail messages."

Jess decided to skim through the messages because she really wanted to know if she had heard from Joyce. After skipping over nine messages, including one from Lorraine and another from Monica at the court in Okanagon County, Jess came to one that caught her attention. "Ms. Lamm, this is Joyce Brown. I have read and reread the affidavits that you gave me. I still find it hard to believe that Mr. Hansen could write those things about me, but

I followed up with my friend in the pharmacy. She told me some interesting things. Please give me a call on my cell. I would like to talk to you about this." Jess punched the save button and quickly skimmed through the rest of her messages, just to confirm that Joyce hadn't left another message.

Hanging up to cut off voice mail, Jess looked at her watch. "Nine o'clock—this has to be late enough to call back a nurse even if she worked the evening shift yesterday. If she's working the day shift today, she'll be at work, and I won't be waking her up." Unfortunately, it appeared that Joyce was at work, or at least that was what Jess was hoping was the reason that she didn't answer. Jess left a message asking Joyce to call her either at the office or on her cell. She finished with, "Don't worry about calling me outside the office. Our deadline is coming up, and I need to talk to you as soon as possible so that we can get an affidavit filed to save the Thompson case." Jess hoped the last sentence would tickle Joyce's sense of responsibility and increase the chances that she would call back. She was beginning to think—or maybe it was just hope—that Joyce's earlier disappearances were more a result of misinformation than irresponsibility.

Having left the message for Joyce, Jess picked up the phone again to thoroughly review her voice mail messages. Focused on her notepad, she didn't see Drew walk past the office window and wasn't aware of his presence until she heard, "Hi, Jess, how are you doing?" Jess looked up and paused before she said, "Uh, fine!" She couldn't think of anything wittier to say.

"Do you feel like talking?" asked Drew.

"Sure, have a seat," Jess responded.

"I talked to Lorraine yesterday. She said that you had gone home to meet the Orkin Man. She gave me a little speech about how you wouldn't have any bugs if you kept your house clean yourself instead of using a cleaning woman. I assumed that meant she didn't understand the type of bugs you were looking for and that you had your condo searched for electronic bugs, true?"

Jess smiled, "Right." She paused and didn't give the information that Drew was obviously looking for.

"Well, don't keep me in the dark. What did they find?" Drew asked.

"They did find bugs, three of them, one even in the bedroom." Jess turned red. "That kind of made me think that you probably didn't have anything to do with their placement, unless you are the jealous type and wanted to see if I had any other lovers." Jess made a joke but neither she nor Drew paid any attention to it.

"Jess, I really am sorry about the other…I really did not intend to mislead you. My wife and I really are getting a divorce. It didn't seem important to finish it until now, and I just didn't find the right time to take back the careless statement that I made when I first met you. The longer I waited, the harder it became to tell you."

Jess thought to herself, "The 'other.' That is what he calls his marriage. Hmm, I hope that means that he really feels guilty, because he should!"

"Well," she said, "I've done some thinking about it. I even did a little research online. I decided that either you are *really* devious and set up a scenario to cover your tracks, or you aren't guilty. I think that putting bugs in my house in order to throw me off when you make threatening phone calls and going to eastern Washington to get a snake is probably a bit much, even though you said you had an appointment the day of the snake event. And I find it hard to believe that you could break into my condo and then appear at McCormick's right afterward after having changed your suit. You might have had to shrink a size or two as well. And by the way, I did look you up online. I see that you and Sherri filed for dissolution over a year ago."

"Sure wouldn't want to try to lie to you!" Drew smiled. He stood up tentatively, hoping that Jess would too so that he could hold her. She did, and she felt warm and satisfying in his arms. The knot in his chest that he had been carrying around for the last few days finally began to relax.

"By the way, Jess," Drew said, "I looked up rattlesnakes online too. I find it very strange that someone would make the effort to bring a snake over from eastern Washington. If they wanted to hurt you, it seems like there would be many easier ways to do it."

Jess shuddered. "My thoughts exactly," she said. "One more thing! What was it that you were doing that Saturday morning? You sure weren't telling me much, and that really got my attention after the fact. I even thought about you driving to eastern Washington to pick up a rattlesnake."

"You are thorough!" Drew said. "I was meeting with Sherri to talk about getting the divorce finished."

"Oh," Jess said. "Glad I asked." She was happy that Drew couldn't see the red in her face as she considered how far down the road of suspicion she had traveled.

Chapter Fifty-Nine

Drew and Jess stood holding each other for a good three minutes. Jess was just beginning to think about how sexy Drew's body was when her cell phone rang. Much as she didn't want to break away, Jess said, "I've got to get that—it could be Joyce. She is so hard to get a hold of."

Pulling away from Drew, Jess looked at the caller ID. It was Joyce, so she answered the phone. "This is Jessica Lamm."

"Hi, this is Joyce Brown. I did a little investigation about what you were telling me, and I think that you might be right. I would like to talk to you about it, but not on the phone."

Joyce sounded so cloak-and-dagger. Ordinarily Jess would have thought that it was overly dramatic, but with her experience in the case, she could understand Joyce's concern. "I'm at the office now. If you want to come down, I'll be happy to reimburse your parking. We can go over what you've found out."

"I'll take you up on that. I can get downtown a lot faster that way, but parking is so expensive. I can be there by about ten thirty. Is that okay with you?"

"Sure. See you then. Be sure to bring your cell to call me when you get here so that I can let you in the building. There is usually parking on Cherry or Fourth this early on Saturday, and you can put your credit card in the slot. I'm not sure if you can get into the building parking on the weekend. I don't think that it was open to the public when I came in."

Jess put down the phone and looked at Drew. "That was Joyce, of course. She's willing to talk. I got a message from her this morning that she has a friend in the Peoples pharmacy that she talked to. We may have hit pay dirt!"

Joyce had given herself forty-five minutes to get downtown. Jess found herself wondering if she and Drew could make love and get put together in that amount of time. "Wrong!" she told herself. "I'm not ready to make love in an office with a window, even if it is Saturday and the office has blinds."

Joyce found parking and called Jess to meet her in the lobby. On the way up the elevator with Jess, Joyce pulled something out of her purse. It was an empty package for sodium bicarbonate injection. She was obviously pleased with what she had found and talked as fast as she could all of the way up the elevator, through the lobby, and into Jess's office. "I showed my friend in the pharmacy Dr. Smith's affidavit—her name is Rosemary. She is just a tech but she's pretty 'with it.' She said that they started getting drugs from a new source almost two years ago—a little after Mr. Hansen came to Peoples. She's seen Mr. Hansen and Mr. Roberts, the head pharmacist, arguing about drugs. She doesn't know what about, but she's seen them in Mr. Roberts's office. Mr. Roberts has saved some of the packages for the drugs and seemed to think that they are important. She's also heard Mr. Roberts mumbling about counterfeit drugs.

"One of the points that they argued about seemed to be where Peoples gets its drugs. She says that they usually get their drugs from a place in eastern Washington called DRD. Here's the address." Joyce held out a piece of paper, and Jess saw that the address was Toppenish, Washington. "But sometimes they come from the main pharmacy center for VAHC, called Unit Dose. Rosemary noticed because they all used to come from Unit Dose, and then they started using DRD too. Like I said, she thought that seemed to be a point of controversy between Mr. Roberts and Mr. Hansen."

They were walking from the elevator as Joyce was telling Jess her new information. As they walked into Jess's office, Joyce pulled up short. She was staring at Drew who was sitting in one of the two chairs opposite Jess's desk. Seeing what she thought was concern on

Joyce's face, Jess introduced Drew. "Oh, this is Drew Stewart, an attorney who is working with me on the Peoples case." The introduction seemed to put Joyce at ease. The way that Joyce smiled at Drew, Jess quickly determined Joyce was no longer concerned, if that was her original response. Joyce sat down in the chair next to Drew and turned to him to continue her story.

"Anyway, Mr. Roberts has been saving these packages, and he writes on them. Just a couple of weeks ago he threw some of them away, so Rosemary pulled a couple of them out of the trash. Mr. Roberts is a jerk; he's always on Rosemary's case. She figured that the packages might be important, and low and behold, one of the ones that Mr. Roberts threw away happens to be a sodium bicarbonate package! Rosemary says that she wants it back, but she gave it to me to show you."

Joyce handed over the empty bicarb package to Drew. He turned it over in his hands, noticing that the word "ingestible" was circled on the package. "Hmm," said Drew, "somebody was looking for counterfeit drugs." Looking at Jess, Drew continued. "In that prior case that I mentioned, I learned that counterfeit drugs are a big problem, of course, but also that one of the ways to catch counterfeit drugs is to identify fake packaging. The counterfeiters try to make the packaging look like the real stuff. The problem is that sometimes they don't do a perfect job. This package looks like somebody used spell check and got the wrong word. It should be 'injectable,' not 'ingestible.' This looks like the owner's manual in my foreign car. Someone wrote this who isn't a native English speaker." Turning back to Joyce, Drew said, "Joyce, since you need this back, can I make a copy?"

Joyce smiled at Drew. "Sure, no problem."

While Drew was out making the copy, Jess said to Joyce, "How about if I make a few changes in the affidavit that I started so that you can sign it? That way we can get your information before the court. One thing that I want to put in is that you don't take drugs. You said that you even brought the missing drugs to the nursing supervisor's attention, right? I think you said that you talked to Mr. Hansen about it too. I'm sure they never wrote you up for anything like taking drugs, right? If this gets to be a big argument, we need to know all the facts."

"Of course, they didn't write me up! I didn't do any such thing! Are you doubting my word?" Joyce asked in a testy voice, as Drew walked in the door with the package and the copy.

Seeing that Joyce was becoming upset, he tried to sooth her ruffled feathers. "Don't worry about that, Joyce. We know that you don't do drugs. We have to put that in the affidavit so that the court will know it too, that's all. If we don't put it in, even if it is obvious to you, the court doesn't know. You saw that Mr. Hansen claims that you did take drugs. That raises the issue. We just have to tell the court that it's not true."

"Oh," Joyce's tone changed dramatically as she smiled at Drew. While Drew and Joyce chatted further about the case, Jess finished the changes to Joyce's statement, ran it out on the printer, grabbed it, and gave it to Joyce to read. Jess held her breath while Joyce read the statement.

While Joyce was reading, Jess thought about their "find." Jess had just about fallen on the ground when Joyce produced the pharmaceutical package. All too often she had seen the average employee who, treated rudely by his boss, showed more knowledge than his boss ever expected. As Leona Hemsley might have said after her conviction, "Never underestimate the power of the little people." Jess was pretty sure that this was an example of the same, but she had also had a couple of false starts with Joyce. She would feel better after Joyce signed the statement.

And Joyce did sign, with no changes! No more worry about having to pay $75,000 to Baker! To Joyce, Jess said, "You would like a copy of this, right?"

"Sure," said Joyce, almost as though it was an afterthought.

As she walked out to the photocopier, Jess mused to herself about how often people seemed to underestimate the importance of their information and how they think proving the facts is a matter of just knowing them. "So often people seem to think that lawyers just go into court, tell the judge the facts, and win the case. If that were true, we wouldn't need judges or juries," Jess philosophized.

As Jess walked back into the office, Drew and Joyce were standing. Drew was shaking Joyce's hand and thanking her for coming in. He had also handed her Jess's card and told her that if anything came up she should be sure to call. Joyce looked a little disappointed but took the card. Jess's woman's intuition told her that Joyce would much prefer to call Drew.

Keeping to her promise to pay for parking, Jess asked Joyce how much it had cost. "Oh, no problem. Glad to be of help." Joyce smiled at Drew again. Jess showed her out of the office and called the elevator for her. Jess thanked her again and explained that there would be no problem getting out the door of the main entrance. The security only worked from the outside.

Walking back into her office, Jess gave Drew a wry smile, "If I had known how persuasive you are, I'd have used you from the start."

"Right, well keep that in mind," said Drew, taking Jess in his arms and kissing her hard on the lips. Jess said, "You know, I've had just about enough of this office today…and I know that Reesa would love to see you. She even moped at the door when you left the other day. It just about broke my heart. How about coming home with me?"

"I'd like that, Ms. Jessica. I'd like that," Drew whispered in her ear.

Chapter Sixty

The Sunday morning sun peeked around a cloud and shot a couple of rays through the bedroom window, intruding on Jess's dream. She had been dreaming about lying in bed with Drew after making what could be best described to her mother—if she were going to mention this to her mother—as "passionate love." She knew better than to open her eyes, since she wasn't ready to hear the Reesa "purr machine." Jess moved her leg to determine whether it had been a dream. "Ah," she thought as she felt Drew's leg, "it wasn't a dream." Jess smiled.

Drew's presence caused other ideas to spring into Jess's mind. First she decided to surprise Reesa and get her breakfast without having to be nudged. Then she slid back into bed beside Drew, reached over, and kissed him on the side of the forehead. He opened his eyes and said, "I was hoping that you were coming back to bed." He put his arms around her, rolled her over on her back, and started kissing her on the neck and chest. "God, she's sexy!" he thought.

About thirty minutes later, Reesa climbed up on top of Jess and Drew. They were lying so close together under the covers that Reesa couldn't tell where one hip ended and the other began—she wasn't all that familiar with the human body—but she was not about to be left out of this family hug. She had her rights!

"Sure am glad that Reesa is discreet enough to know when to join in and when not to," Drew chuckled. Reesa responded with a meow-squeak as if to say, "Of course! Who do you think you're dealing with?"

Being spurred on by the "purr machine" to come out of their reverie, Jess and Drew got up, took a shower, made coffee, petted Reesa, and left for the office. "Who would've thought that going to the office could be so fun," Jess thought. "I don't think I'll tell anyone that. They'd think I'm 'teched' in the head." *Teched* was the label that Jess's grandmother often put on what people now call "emotionally disturbed."

Drew started outlining the questions for the 30(b)(6) deposition this coming week. Since they had already heard from Baker that Hansen would be testifying, Drew could tailor the questions for him. He also decided to throw in a few questions concerning Hansen's knowledge about the location of Joyce Brown. "Fat chance we'll get anywhere with these, but it's worth a try," Drew thought. He could already see Baker coming unglued about revisiting that line of questioning.

The sodium bicarbonate package was a great find, but getting it into evidence at a trial was not going to be easy. Jess and Drew had discussed the fact that Hansen would probably give some vague response to questions about the package, saying that he would have to look into the pharmacy records about where and when the drug was received.

Considering the short time period they had, they thought they ought to cover all the possible means of getting information. Jess set about writing requests for admission—written questions taken to be true if not denied in the specified time period. Ordinarily, a party must answer requests for admission within thirty days, or they are "deemed admitted." Depending on what came up at the Hansen deposition, Jess might have to make a motion requiring Baker to answer the requests for admission in shortened time. They didn't have the usual thirty-day period for response between now and September 14, the date of the summary judgment motion. For sure, Jess wouldn't have a response to the requests for admission before her supplemental response, which was due on August 31.

Regardless of the problems, getting the requests out to Baker might be helpful. They would be a hedge against the tactics that Baker was sure to use. One of the requests for admission would be, "Admit that erroneous word 'ingestible' on the attached copy of sodium bicarbonate packaging is an indication that the drug contained in the package was more likely than not counterfeit." There would be objection after objection to that request, but Jess thought that Judge Pacer would be backing her up that this request required an answer.

In addition to requests for admission, Jess was going to schedule the deposition of Mr. Roberts. Assuming Hansen put them off about where and when the package came from and what the circled word meant, Jess would have the right to take the deposition of an additional person. It would be tough to have a motion heard before August 31 when her response to summary judgment was due, and scheduling the deposition of Roberts would be a hedge. Hopefully Roberts would be more forthcoming than Hansen about the details.

Jess was also sure that Baker would attack her personally, claiming contact with Peoples' pharmacist was an ethical violation. It was lucky as hell that Joyce had taken it upon herself to investigate the situation and even luckier that the package came from a waste basket. That way there would be no basis for a claim that Jess was using Joyce as her agent to do something that Jess—as an attorney for an opposing party—could not. There was almost a certainty that Roberts would be a speaking agent for the hospital on the subject of drugs, meaning that if Jess had contacted him outside Baker's presence she would have committed an ethical no-no.

Taking a package that someone had intended to keep could be a theft. "Pretty unlikely it could be construed as that when it came out of the wastebasket," thought Jess.

Jess knew that these extenuating circumstances wouldn't stop Baker from making the allegation. His approach was always shoot first, ask questions later. This package was going to be devastating for his case, and he would have to try all the arrows in his quiver to keep it from being admitted as evidence. "Score another one for the 'little people,'" Jess thought again.

Drew decided to recheck his recollection about counterfeit drugs. The questioning was likely to be hotly contested, and it would be helpful to have a little back-up information to whip out on Baker when he started getting difficult at the deposition.

Shortly Drew said, "Would you look at this, Ms. Jessica!" He was pointing to the screen with the title "Counterfeit Drugs" prominently displayed. "Essentially what it says is that counterfeit drugs are becoming a bigger and bigger problem. Two sources, although by no means the only ones, are China and Mexico. The feds have a web site to report what might be counterfeit drugs, and under the whistle-blower statute, a person who discovers counterfeit drugs can even get a bounty.

"It's so hard to believe that anyone would actually make counterfeit drugs knowing that they could kill people. I know that it happens because you hear about it on the news—like the glycol in the cough syrup thing that you found online. It's beyond belief that they can't be satisfied with just a little illegal profit."

"I just thought you might need this for the Hansen deposition, and certainly for the Roberts dep. My guess is that those depositions might be a little rancorous," Drew said with a smile.

"Ya think?" Jess smiled back. "I'm sending these requests for admission out on Monday. This case is really going to heat up!"

Chapter Sixty-One

Jess had her requests for admission delivered to Baker's office on Monday, and he received them that afternoon. Since she didn't have to send her response on the summary judgment until the end of August, Jess didn't send the affidavits from Joyce and Dr. Smith with the requests. It was possible that additional information would develop between now and then, and she might want to update those affidavits.

Jess was expecting a call about the requests, and it came at four o'clock. She saw the caller ID and prepared herself for the tirade before picking up the phone. She was not disappointed.

"What the hell do you think you're doing?" Baker yelled so loud that Jess held the phone away from her ear. You keep throwing mud because you have nothing else. You can't impugn the integrity of a reputable hospital like Peoples whenever you want to! Where the hell did you get this packaging? I'll press charges if you have been skulking around Peoples!" Baker was so worked up he couldn't stop long enough to let Jess get a word in, and he hung up abruptly.

"Well, that was a productive conversation," Jess thought. "Asshole!"

In the Washington Mutual Tower, Baker was still seething. "How the hell did she get such a package?" It was becoming more and more clear that he had made a mistake relying on Hansen's assurances, which made him even angrier.

If the package really came from Peoples, Baker could have some trouble. He had a lot of billable time in this case that he hadn't been paid for. Lawyers' billing always lags behind the actual generation of fees since the bill comes out at the end of the month. Then the insurance company pays sixty to ninety days, sometimes even six months, after the bill arrives, essentially causing the attorney to finance payment of their own bill. Of course, insurance companies don't pay late charges. Baker might not get paid for the outstanding bills and unbilled time if he had to withdraw because of a conflict.

Baker picked up the phone again. This time he was a little more under control. He dialed Hansen.

Hansen didn't answer, but Baker left a message that he expected would get a quick response. "I just received a copy of a package that the Lamm woman says came from Peoples. She says that this shows the package contained counterfeit drugs. What is she talking about? I'm going to fax it over to you."

Hansen received the message and checked his faxes immediately. This couldn't be! Hansen picked up the phone and called Guzman. Guzman answered, "Hello, Mr. Hansen. How are you today?"

"I warned you, you son of a bitch!" Hansen yelled into the phone. "You couldn't make enough from the normal markup? You had to use counterfeit drugs? Well now they know. What are you going to do about it?"

"What are you talking about, *Mr.* Hansen?" Guzman responded, the emphasis on "mister" hinting at disrespect.

"That Lamm bitch has produced a copy of a package that is clearly counterfeit. She has circled a typo on it that shows it's counterfeit. You couldn't get someone who could speak English? This is such an obvious error!" Hansen rattled on with disdain, feeling totally justified in his anger.

"¡Oye, *senior*!" Guzman's voice was firmer this time. "If this was so obvious, why didn't you catch it? You knew what the cost split was. "What made you think that you could get the real thing so cheap?" Guzman was glad that he had gone with the lower price level now. He had considered selling Hansen the drugs for one-third or a quarter of list price, instead of one-fifth. That would have given Guzman more profit, but it also would have given Hansen better basis to say that he really thought that the drugs were genuine. Guzman had tried to price his "drugs" for Peoples low enough that they would be suspect, so that someone with Hansen's experience would have to admit suspicion that the drugs were counterfeit. He was pretty sure that he had done that, though it was a little hard to tell. He didn't have any connections in real U.S. drug companies to check.

Hansen told himself to calm down. He had been concerned that this day might come, and he had planned an exit strategy worthy of the Pentagon. Hansen would play the victim of a swindle to separate himself from Guzman and the plant. He could keep his money in his Panamanian bank account. No one would be the wiser—not even Anika. All he had to do was calm down and play out the story.

Hansen told Guzman that he was going to inspect the Toppenish plant. Looking at his schedule, Hansen decided that Wednesday was the earliest he could make it. He and Anika had tickets to the symphony Tuesday night, and he might not get back to Seattle in time if he went to Toppenish Tuesday morning. Even though he sometimes got tired of her naïve little habits, it could be nice to have her father's money in addition to his own nest egg if things went to hell.

After the prior troubles with VAHC, Hansen's motto had become "Redundancy Über Alles!" This phrase was one that Hansen had cobbled together from his days in grad school, and roughly translated it meant "Backup over all." It was a paraphrase from the national anthem of Nazi Germany, meaning "Germany over all." The "Über Alles" was taken out of the anthem after World War II, for obvious reasons.

Hansen wasn't sure how VAHC was going to take this new counterfeit drug problem, even though they had the same damn problem with Unit Dose. He'd had a chuckle when he saw Lamm's affidavit about their problems with Unit Dose. VAHC had been pretty angry with his prior "mistakes." Lars had noticed that people tend to put a gloss over their own blunders and highlight those of others. He was worried about what might happen this time because of his history with the company.

Hansen was also aware that he had another deposition coming up on Thursday. He wanted to be able to say that he had investigated DRD before then. He had to make this look like a real investigation, and taking all day Wednesday would reinforce that image.

So, Hansen told Guzman that he would be there on Wednesday. "Hasta la vista, senior," Guzman responded.

Chapter Sixty-Two

Having initiated his plan with the call to Guzman, Hansen called Baker back. Before calling, he rehearsed his speech of indignation that anyone would attack Peoples' reputation.

Baker picked up the phone and said, "Hello, Mr. Hansen. I assume that you got my message."

"Yes, that Lamm woman is a real piece of work. What does she think she's doing impugning the integrity of Peoples? Of course we don't use counterfeit drugs! I will get to the bottom of this. There will be no problem here. When one acts with integrity, one need not fear the result. I will check this out with our pharmacy, and I am personally going to inspect DRD's plant. I will make sure that Roberts, our chief pharmacist, has made no mistakes."

Baker thought Hansen's statement was a bit pious but wanted to believe that there was no problem. He was relieved to hear that Hansen wasn't shaken. "Be sure to let me know as soon as you have finished your investigation," Baker said.

Chapter Sixty-Three

Roberts was next on Hansen's agenda. As he started implementing his plan, Hansen felt a well of pride that he'd had the foresight to set up a defense. He hadn't thought to do that with the billing "situation" back east, and he wasn't going to be the fall guy this time if anything went wrong. He pulled out the two personnel files that he had in his desk drawer—those of Joyce Brown and Peter Roberts. He had requested them as soon as he had heard about the Thompson suit. Hansen double-checked to see that the reprimands were still there—the ones that he had put in shortly after he received the files. He checked to confirm that his additions still served the intended purpose and that there was nothing he should add. He had also taken the liberty of "revising" the contract with DRD that he kept in his file cabinet by adding Roberts's signature. Everything was in place.

As was his usual routine when dealing with Roberts, Hansen decided to go to the pharmacy to confront him unannounced. It would also help to have a witness to yet another dispute with Roberts. Hansen walked into the pharmacy holding the copy of the package received from Baker. He noticed a pharmacy tech working at the counter. "Fortunate," he thought; he had a witness to yet another argument.

"What the hell is this!" Hansen said as he stormed into the pharmacy waiving the fax he had received from Baker. He didn't really expect an answer and didn't even want one. His purpose was to create a scene. He waived Roberts into the pharmacist's small office and closed the door. "Look at this!" Hansen yelled again. "I told you that I wanted to know if there were any more counterfeit drugs. Where did this come from?" Then lowering his voice, Hansen continued. "I am not paying you $2000 a month to sit and do nothing. I want to know when there is a problem. You never told me about *this* problem." Hansen threw the copy of the sodium bicarbonate package down on Roberts's desk.

Roberts looked at the copy on the desk and then back at Hansen. "Where did you get that?" Roberts asked in a wavering voice, trying to remember when he had thrown that away. Why hadn't he been more careful? Roberts couldn't get past the booming voice in his head telling him how stupid he had been for saving that package.

"That woman lawyer in the Thompson case came up with it. Have you been talking to her?" Hansen asked, continuing his accusatory charade.

"No, sir. I wouldn't be talking with her. I wouldn't do that, sir."

"Well, what *is* this? Why do you have a sodium bicarbonate package anyway?"

"I…I noticed the package. I was looking for counterfeit drugs like you asked me to. I just kept the package in case it came up," Roberts said. "After you told me they were talking about counterfeit drugs in the lawsuit, I decided it wasn't such a good idea to have it around."

"You didn't tell me about this. Were you trying to go behind my back?"

"No, sir, I took care of it. I just started buying the bicarb from Unit Dose. I thought that was what you wanted me to do?"

"What? When?" Hansen couldn't believe what he was hearing. "Maybe this will be a stroke of luck!" he thought.

"I…I don't know. Sometime last year…s-s-s-spring, I think," Roberts said.

"You think! *You think!* You don't know? You can find out can't you?"

"Well, s-s-s-sort of."

"What do you mean 'sort of'?"

This was the question that Roberts had been waiting for and working over in his mind for months now, ever since he had heard about the Thompson suit. Why hadn't he taken the next step to get rid of the old bicarb? He had been alert and changed sources for the bicarb, but at the time it seemed like a lot of work to get rid of the old "drug," and replacing every suspect syringe might have had to come out of his budget. Hell, he wasn't even sure if he could have identified the real from the counterfeit once they were out of the container. He didn't have the personnel to go looking at every syringe of bicarb in the hospital. Besides, it didn't seem to be all that much of a problem at the time. It hadn't been until the lawsuit that he had recognized what a problem it might be. Roberts couldn't find the words to explain what he had done. It seemed so stupid now.

Chapter Sixty-Four

That night when Hansen arrived at home, Anika was there in her usual startlingly attractive loungewear.

"How did your day go, dear?" Anika asked as she mixed his customary martini.

Had he not given it some thought after his conversation with Roberts, Hansen wouldn't have known how to answer that one. Roberts had made a choice that could have saved Hansen, but he had been so inept about it that he probably made it worse. Roberts had changed sources for bicarb but left the rest in the hospital. Now no one knew where the bicarb came from that Thompson was given, and Hansen's possible defense was muddied, maybe beyond repair. After giving it a little thought, Hansen had become a little concerned that if anyone looked into the situation they might investigate the source of money that Hansen paid Roberts for his "extra duties." It didn't exactly come through standard channels.

But Hansen decided that the best course was to proceed as he had been. He had already told Baker about his source of drugs. It might even work out to his benefit. Maybe he could be a hero for having a different source of drugs since VAHC had had the same problem.

All this ran through Hansen's mind when Anika asked what should have been a simple question. "Best to stick with the story," he told himself.

"We had a flap about counterfeit drugs today," he said. "They're a problem, even in the U.S. I've had Roberts on it for some time. I guess if you want something done right you have to do it yourself, though. I'm going over to eastern Washington on Wednesday. I know you don't want to miss the symphony tomorrow night.

"Thank you, dear. I appreciate your consideration. I think you might like the symphony as much as I do," Anika said. She also thought to herself how pleasant it was to see Lars appreciating the finer social events. Her narrow mind pondered once again why it was that Lars continued to associate with immigrants from the junior soccer league. They may be hard-working and maybe even intelligent—Anika had to grant them that—but she believed they all came from plebian, even mongrel families, whereas her obviously much more important family had actually been in America at the very founding of this great nation. When she had married Lars, her father and mother had thrown a tantrum about his working-class background. But he was white, Anika told them, and his rising position at VAHC assuaged their concerns too. The troubled times before they left the East Coast had been a real strain. It was easier here on the West Coast where she didn't see her disapproving, equally elitist friends. Anika would have insisted that she was only thinking about his welfare—the effect on Lars's reputation caused by associating with a lower class—but she knew he didn't like to hear it.

Tonight Lars heard even less of what Anika said than usual. His mind drifted off to the issues at hand. It had been impeccable planning that put him in the situation in which he found himself today.

Hansen had been concerned a little about Guzman's source of pharmaceuticals, but the extra income soothed his concern. Guzman seemed to have a source from his days as a pharmacist in Mexico that yielded the most inexpensive drugs that Lars had ever seen. There seemed to be a connection to China, but Guzman was pretty closemouthed about it.

The important thing was that the appearance of the drugs was quite impeccable, and once repackaged at Guzman's plant in eastern Washington, there was virtually no way to tell that the drugs were not genuine. There isn't enough manpower anywhere to track all the drugs that are used in the U.S. To detect a problem you have to nearly stumble on it, unless you have nothing more to do with your time than study packages to collect whistle-blower bounties. Lars was a little afraid that Lamm might have actually done just that—stumbled onto something.

He was also surprised to learn that VAHC had a counterfeit drug problem, but on second thought, maybe it wasn't surprising. Lars knew from his experience in the industry that counterfeit drugs were more prevalent than one might think. It would be the ultimate irony if Unit Dose happened to tap into the same source of sodium bicarbonate that he had through DRD. If so, they probably paid more for the bicarb thinking it was the real thing. If that were the case, it would be a pity he wouldn't be able to tell the stuffy fat cats on the board about it. He would get a chuckle out of seeing their pious faces drop.

Well, anyway, he had his fallback plan, and it was a stroke of genius. Too bad he couldn't tell anyone about it. Lars had been concerned when his hospital had started having code trouble. All that talk in the news about dangerous food and drug additives from China was worrisome as well, making his arrangement with Roberts look even better.

Roberts had come to him about counterfeit drugs and had been all fired up to go to the fed hotline and claim a bounty for discovering counterfeit drugs. Hansen had pointed out to Roberts that if anyone was going to get a bounty it was going to go to Peoples—actually Hansen had been thinking specifically of the CEO at Peoples. It didn't matter whether it was true, because he had been able to convince Roberts that it was. In any event, Hansen didn't want to have any investigation of People's drugs. "Better," he had told Roberts, "that we point this out to our supplier and get it taken care of. I'll do that. You let me know when you see anything else like this."

Thinking further, Hansen had said, "Now I know that this isn't part of the job that you do here, so I will pay you an additional $2,000 a month." Hansen remembered how Roberts's eyes had widened at the thought. Hansen had been fairly sure that the extra money would keep him quiet.

Hansen was also proud of the fact that he had arranged for the $2000 to come from a dummy company that he had set up. He had listed Guzman as the chief officer. That way, if anyone looked, they would be suspicious of Roberts or Guzman. Apparently Roberts hadn't even noticed, or maybe didn't care, that the source of the extra "salary" was not Peoples. If it had come up, Hansen had planned to tell Roberts that it was just another VAHC subsidiary set up to pay for quality control. A problem might arise if someone with better investigative powers and more interest than Roberts traced the source of the money to the company.

Hansen's plan had been a good one. So far it allowed him to provide the lifestyle he and Anika had become accustomed to. This little glitch was unfortunate, but Hansen believed he had it taken care of.

Chapter Sixty-Five

It was Tuesday, and Jess was trying to catch up on the many smaller things that she had let go while concentrating on the Peoples case. The phone rang, and caller ID showed it as a King County number. Picking up the phone, Jess learned that it was Bug Guy.

"Hello, Ms. Lamm. Investigator Kobiyoshi, a.k.a, Bug Detector Guy, here." Jess wondered if he watched CSI every night.

"Your friends who put in those bugs surely went to a lot of trouble. Those babies are pretty top of the line."

"So how do they work? Was someone sitting outside in a van with earphones on?"

"Actually, that's a different system. This you can just dial in and listen to what's going on, or you can record and play back."

"Can you tell the source of the bugs?"

"Well, this globalization thing really fixes us on that one. You can get these things almost anywhere online, so it's hard to say where they came from. One thing though, whoever put these in was kind of messy for the surveillance business. He left smudges all over the devices."

"What do you mean, 'smudges'?"

"Well, unfortunately I couldn't get any fingerprints, but there was a black residue all over the devices. Well actually, at the microscopic level there were other colors too, but you couldn't tell by just looking. I don't think I've ever seen such a thing on devices. Usually we find nothing on them because the guys who know what they're doing don't want to get caught. They wear gloves. The guy who put these in wasn't so smart but pretty lucky. He left smudges all over the place, but I couldn't find any finger prints. Now the other type of system that you referenced, the listening devices from the van—"

"Bug Guy, wait a minute, what do you think caused the smudges?"

"Right, ma'am. Near as I can tell the smudges are ink. I know that sounds funny, but I double-checked it with my colleague at the lab. Do you know anyone who has a printing shop? That's what this looks like. Someone smudged these all up with ink. I can't imagine anyone who would have such dirty hands."

"Thanks, Bug Guy. I appreciate your help. I'm especially glad that you got the bugs. You do think that you got all of them, don't you?"

"I'm pretty sure about that, Ms. Lamm. If I didn't get all of them, you got some bad people after you. Now the government has some really tricky ways of bugging. They can actually go to the phone company and tap in to the line. You haven't made anyone in the government mad, have you?"

"Not that I know of, Bug Guy. I hope not. Thanks for the information. Let me know if you come up with anything else." Jess decided that she had to cut off the conversation. She just had too many things to catch up. As interesting as this was, she didn't have time to learn about the world of bugging devices.

"Will do, ma'am. Glad to be of help."

Jess thought back on the picture of the intruder in the elevator. She hadn't really gotten a good look at his hands. She doubted, however, that Dr. Haseem had ink all over his hands. That wouldn't work for "hospital clean." That was also another point confirming that it probably wasn't Drew—that was good too!

Chapter Sixty-Six

Lars Hansen never particularly enjoyed the symphony; his mind usually wandered to more important things. He used the time to plan his contact with Guzman the next day. Hansen wasn't really an expert on review of repackaging operations, but he had done some investigation online so he had some idea of what to look for. He'd start with a demand to see invoices to confirm Guzman's source of drugs, and he would inspect the lab for implementation of safety measures to avoid errors in repackaging. He had found enough online to know that you didn't store two strengths of the same kind of medicine next to each other because it would be too easy to accidentally pick up the wrong medicine. Good quality control also meant that you located penicillin away from other drugs to avoid contamination. Many patients are highly allergic to it, making even a little contamination dangerous.

Once he completed his review of DRD's plant, Hansen could report to Baker with some detail about his assurance that there were no counterfeit drugs or that there was no evidence of it at this level at least. He'd say there was no way for him to know about anything further back in the chain. Once the pills were made, if they looked genuine there wasn't much more one could do without testing each and every one. That was unrealistic, but also way beyond his capability and responsibility. Some manufacturers were introducing trackers to help follow the source of medication. But it was far from common and not necessarily foolproof.

Hansen thought that he'd take the contract too, just in case he needed it. He would e-mail Guzman to confirm what to have available for his review in the morning. It would be good to have a paper trail proving his diligence. Maybe he should have sent his list to Guzman on Monday or Tuesday. But the short notice would show how good Guzman's organization actually was.

The next morning, before leaving for Toppenish, Lars checked his e-mails; put on the out of office message; and just to assuage any concern about the use of DRD versus Unit Dose, double-checked the balance in his Panamanian bank account. As it had many times in the past, the balance in his account calmed his concerns.

The drive to Toppenish was actually relatively pleasant, and Lars decided to soak it in. After all, it wasn't like he was responsible for the lab—that was Guzman's job. Lars was just there to make a show of oversight and diligence in his review.

Since it was mid-August, there was no snow on Snoqualmie Pass through the Cascade Mountains, which were covered by a blanket of evergreens and random patches of deciduous trees—yellow, orange, and red. The view was quite spectacular.

As he reached the summit and started the uneven descent into eastern Washington, he was surprised at the parting of the clouds and how bright the sun was. The Cascades really did block the rain and, even more importantly, the humidity that dulled the rays of the sun. Along with the general brightness of the sky, the vegetation became a lot shorter and changed from green to yellow and brown, interspersed with some silvery green of sage brush. The area wasn't as pretty as Snoqualmie Pass, but still, it wasn't bad.

Hansen turned off I-90 onto I-82 at Ellensburg and proceeded on the freeway around Yakima. As he progressed, he noticed that he "wasn't in Seattle anymore." The freeway skirted towns instead of providing an arterial through the city and showed the seedier side of the area. This was obviously small-town America where the promise of jobs would be tantalizing to any local chamber of commerce or city counsel. The road faced the backs of warehouses, big box stores, and rickety houses adorned with peeling paint and rusted cars.

As Hansen proceeded onto Highway 97, the scenery changed to cornfields dotted with a couple of schools, an Indian cultural center, and very small centers of what might have been strip malls if they'd had more than one or two stores. He could see why Guzman located his lab in Toppenish.

Though he knew that the lab was on West First, Hansen thought he would peruse the town first, and he continued into downtown Toppenish. The series of fruit warehouses and payday loan establishments gave way to a refurbished old-time tourist attraction. There were murals everywhere showing the history and scenery of the area, and covered wooden sidewalks were bordered by post railings. The town was making an obvious attempt to attract tourists and probably other business as well.

Hansen turned back to West First Avenue and found what he thought must be the lab. To his surprise, it looked more like a warehouse than a lab. On his drive by, he had assumed that the lab wasn't visible from the main road, but after a thorough search, he could find no alternative to the warehouse at the stated address.

He pulled out Guzman's card to refresh his memory. He had been impressed by the appearance of the plant. It was a brick-covered, two-floor structure that appeared to be about a block long. There was definitely nothing of that sort here.

Pulling up to the entrance of a warehouse, Hansen saw no indication that DRD even operated here. He opened the door to what appeared to be the entrance and found no receptionist and no security, and he even had difficulty finding an office. Stopping a sweaty, weathered-looking man driving a forklift, he asked for the location of the lab. The driver just looked at him, not seeming to comprehend. Hansen said, "Do you speak English?" The man just shook his head and spoke in what Hansen thought must be Spanish, but he wasn't sure. Hansen said, "Guzman?" The forklift driver pointed toward a curtain of clear plastic sheeting strips in the back of the warehouse. Well, they had once been clear but were now old and yellow.

Hansen walked through the rows of cartons that defined a path to the sheeting and made his way through it to the door of the only office he could see. The office had a window, but it was frosted so he couldn't tell if it was occupied. There did appear to be a light on inside. He knocked and heard a response, "Si, venga."

Opening the door, Hansen recognized Guzman sitting behind a desk piled with stacks of papers interspersed with a few old paper coffee cups. "Hello, Mr. Hansen," Guzman said slipping into his businessman's demeanor. "It's good to see you. It's kind of you to visit us after so many months."

Hansen was beginning to feel uneasy about the situation. Guzman had assured him that the lab had the latest in security, technology, and hygiene. This couldn't be the lab. "I'm surprised that this location is your warehouse. I thought we were meeting at the lab."

Guzman smiled and allowed his business facade to fade, "Senior, our labs are in Mexico and China. You Americans have too many red tapes to jump over, and you pay your workers too much. We must keep our expenses under control."

Hansen noticed the slip in Guzman's usually impeccable speech. He wondered if Guzman had committed the error for effect. Hansen was stunned and it showed on his face. "But I understood that your lab was in Toppenish—DRD is in Toppenish."

"I assure you that we are, senior," said Guzman, beginning to smile as he saw Hansen's expression. "We have plants in Tijuana, Mexico, and Hangzhou, China, as well. We are a large organization, Senior Hansen. I wonder if you perhaps simply assumed that our lab was here."

Hansen knew that he hadn't just assumed but had been told that the lab was in Toppenish. Guzman had gone to great lengths to describe the benefits that Toppenish was giving DRD in return for providing substantial employment in the town. Guzman's letterhead showed a picture of a modern-looking building situated in a lovely landscaped area. Had he known that he was dealing with drugs sourced from China and packaged in Mexico, he would have been much more suspicious. He knew that there was a danger of counterfeit drugs in the United States but had counted on the regulatory safety of a local repackaging facility. He hadn't signed up for *this*! Hansen opened his briefcase and pulled out the contract, which he had brought only as an afterthought. Now he was glad he had thought to bring it along.

"You not only told me, but you stated it on your contract." Hansen pulled it out and read the introductory paragraph showing the location of DRD as Toppenish, Washington. At the top of the stationary was the same drawing that appeared on Guzman's card. Wanting to assure himself, Hansen pulled Guzman's card out of his pocket and compared it to the stationary logo. It was the same.

"Senior, I am sorry if you mistook that to mean that we repackage the pharmaceuticals in Toppenish. I have found that Americans prefer to deal with businesses housed in nice-looking buildings and also trust to their government to insure quality control. I always try to supply what my customers desire. I believe you will find that the contract does not assure that we have nice buildings. I do particularly like that building, but I must confess that if you want nice buildings you are going to have to pay more for your drugs, and I won't be able to offer you the kind of rebates that you have been enjoying."

Hansen's face was starting to turn from ashen to red. Guzman had defrauded him. He knew damned well what Hansen thought about the location of the repackaging plant. Hansen remembered what Guzman had told him about jobs in Toppenish. "You said that you had a small staff of twenty in Toppenish and that you would be expanding."

"Oh, yes, senior. We do have a small staff here. Unfortunately our staff did not expand as we had hoped, but we do have a staff of nine. We have two very competent printers who, through the benefits of computer technology, are able to reproduce practically any packaging they may be required to 'correct.' We also have seven very competent warehousemen who organize our products for shipping. I am sure that you would not want us to place our lab in such a facility. We have a fair amount of dust and ink around here. I know that your authorities would frown on the use of such a facility for extensive repackaging. We try to keep that to a minimum at this location, Senior Hansen. And the warehousemen are not skilled in the art of drug manufacturing…or repackaging, for that matter."

"Your plant is where—in Mexico?"

"As I said, Senior Hansen, we are located in Tijuana, Mexico, just across the border from San Diego. We have expanded my old pharmacy to allow cost-effective repackaging. Our major source of pharmaceuticals is Hangzhou, China. As you are probably aware, some of your U.S. drug manufacturers are opening plants in China. That provides my Chinese friends with excellent information as to drug ingredients and appearance. Our chemists are some of the best in China, and they are constantly finding new methods to speed production. With your government's policy to open trade between Mexico and the United States, we have been able to facilitate the import of our pharmaceuticals without difficulty.

"I received your request for invoices sent this morning. Unfortunately on such short notice, I have not been able to obtain those for you. I am afraid that you would have to go to Tijuana to get them, senior. You should be aware that the invoices might be difficult to read, since they are in Spanish or sometimes Chinese. In Mexico, we are not required to keep quite as complete records as you may anticipate in the U.S. However, I will be happy to make available what we have."

Hansen had been listening to Guzman talk on, becoming angrier and angrier. Guzman was essentially outlining how he had defrauded Hansen, as though there was nothing Hansen could do about it. "That isn't the way things are, you scumbag!" Hansen thought to himself.

Lacing his speech with all the disdain that he could muster, he said, "*Mr.* Guzman, you seem to believe that you can lie to me with impunity. You don't know who you're dealing with. I am a reputable businessman and the CEO of a well-regarded institution. You can't simply lie to me and get away with it."

"On the contrary, *senior*, I can and I have. Your greed has put you in a rather awkward situation, senior. You think that I don't know why you came to Peoples from VAHC and the East Coast? You think that you are dealing with some stupid Mexican? Just because I was not born here and don't have an MBA from Duke University does not mean that I am stupid, senior! I know about your past and your need to impress your wife. You will not endanger my operation or your own by causing alarm. You will go home and tell your attorney that you have inspected our operation in Toppenish and that you find it wholly satisfactory. As they say, *senior*, 'You are not in Kansas anymore.'"

"You, sir, will not threaten me," Hansen said. He'd had enough of this insolent Mexican! He stood, packed up his brief case, turned on his heel, and walked out with what little dignity he still had.

Chapter Sixty-Seven

Despite his statements and attempts to maintain his dignity when leaving Guzman's office, Hansen was shaken by the meeting. He "beeped" open the lock on his white Lexis sedan and sat for several minutes while the air conditioning cooled off the car. "It is hot over here," he thought.

In fact, Hansen was so shaken that he couldn't remember how to get back to Highway 97. Leaving the warehouse, he couldn't even remember whether he should turn left or right. Picking left, he soon noticed that his choice of direction had been wrong. The road lead him into central Toppenish, which his prior tour of the town told him was not on the way back to Seattle. Just as he was about to turn around, he saw a sign indicating the way to Highway 97. Rather than continuing as his own navigator, he decided to follow the signs.

Lars was so preoccupied thinking about his conversation with Guzman that he didn't notice that an old, rusted Chevy—with dull blue, peeling paint; a rosary hanging from the rear view mirror; and three very dark men in work shirts—was taking the same route through town. Had he noticed, it probably wouldn't have made any difference. The car was like many others in town.

Following the signs to Highway 97, Hansen came to a T-intersection. He checked his vehicle guidance system and then the sign on the intersection. He noticed loud music coming from the car behind him. He actually felt it as much as heard the music since it was the base that was so loud. Looking in his rearview mirror, he saw that the music was coming from the old, blue Chevy. "Disgusting," he thought.

Deciding that a left turn was called for, Hansen looked left and then right, before pulling out. Before he could move forward, the Chevy pulled up along his left side, blocking his turn. Since it was roughly ninety-five degrees, and the car obviously had no air conditioning, the windows were down. The passenger in the front seat said something to him. Hansen waived him forward to get out of the way of his turn, but the Chevy didn't move. The passenger still appeared to be talking to him.

Hansen lowered the window of his Lexus and yelled, "Move your car!" The music was so loud that, even yelling, he couldn't make himself heard. Deciding that he ought to back up and go around, Hansen looked behind him. In the split second that he took his eyes away from the car to look back, a gun appeared in the window. The motion got Hansen's attention. Seeing the gun, Hansen felt paralyzed. Time went into slow motion. He tried to put his car in reverse, the gun fired, and then there was no more.

The gunman fired several shots in rapid succession, splattering blood all over the white leather seats of the Lexus. After waiting only seconds to see that there was no movement from Hansen, the Chevy drove off.

At DRD, Guzman received a phone call. Seeing the caller ID, he clicked on the phone and said, "Diga."

Giving no introduction on the other end, a voice said, "Terminado, Senior Guzman."

"Gracias," said Guzman, as he clicked off the phone.

Guzman turned to his computer. He signed in to Hansen's Panamanian bank account. "Americans are so arrogant, so greedy, so naive!" Hansen had never noticed the bot Guzman had sent to monitor his key strokes—the hospital apparently didn't have a good security system. Guzman transferred the entire balance from the Panamanian account, minus one dollar for good measure, to his own account. "I may not be able to stay here long," Guzman thought, "but it won't be a total loss. Certainly Senior Hansen is not going to be the cause of my leaving. America really is the land of opportunity."

Chapter Sixty-Eight

Jess heard nothing from Baker until Thursday morning, which surprised her a bit. She had expected a few more scathing phone calls repeating the harangue about defaming Peoples. On Wednesday evening, she had received a call from Baker's office telling her that he needed to reset the deposition scheduled for Thursday afternoon. It came after hours, of course, so that she couldn't get any information as to what possible justification there could be for his unilateral rescheduling. The message said that Baker would get back with her no later than Thursday morning. This cavalier change of the deposition date angered her. She needed to get the information that Hansen had or at least to find out what he knew. How could Baker unilaterally decide to change the deposition date when there was so little time left before she was required to file her response to the summary judgment motion? The only thing that stopped Jess from immediately issuing a scathing e-mail to Baker was the fact that he had already accommodated her by moving the deposition from the prior scheduling due to her "accident." Since the message said that Baker would be getting back to her by Thursday morning, Jess decided that she would wait at least a little while.

By Friday morning, she still hadn't heard from Baker, which wasn't surprising. She opened her computer Friday morning to write the scathing e-mail she'd been composing in her head since Thursday but decided to give Baker until ten o'clock. It was tough to wait, because she was really peeved about the cancellation but also didn't want to waste her time writing an unnecessary e-mail.

As an alternative, Jess signed on to the *Seattle Times* online. What she saw there amazed her and also explained why Baker was having trouble getting his client to the deposition.

It read:

Local CEO Murdered

The apparent subject of random gang violence in Toppenish, Washington, Lars Hansen has died. Mr. Hansen was the CEO of Peoples Hospital of Seattle, who rescued the hospital from bankruptcy, setting a shining example of American entrepreneurship. It is believed that he was visiting Toppenish on a business trip when the tragedy occurred, though the specific business purpose is not known at this time. Toppenish officials expressed their concern regarding the incident and noted in particular that due to their special efforts in the area, gang violence has seen a significant reduction...

The article continued, but Jess found nothing more of help regarding the fate of Hansen. She stared at the article for several minutes. If she hadn't been aware of the eastern Washington connection to DRD, she would have passed the story off as unfortunate but "no big deal." As it was, she could not believe that a shooting over hospital drugs could occur in the US. "These things don't happen in the United States!" she thought.

Finally, Jess printed out the article and walked down to Drew's office. Since he wasn't there, she penned a sticky note and pasted it to the paper, putting it on the middle of his chair so that he wouldn't miss it. The note said, "Can you believe this?"

Going back to her office, Jess decided to call Baker. Asshole that he was, even he deserved a little sympathy over a dead client. Jess dialed his direct line, but as usual the call forwarded to his secretary. Jess introduced herself and asked for William Baker. Per her usual call-screening duties the secretary also asked what the call was about and where Jess was calling from. Sometimes these questions seemed so useless—and this time was really one of them—but Jess knew from experience that if she didn't answer the questions she wouldn't get through to Baker. "This is about the Thompson case and death of Lars Hansen," Jess said.

Baker came on the line, his usual belligerent self. Why had Jess expected otherwise? "Calling to gloat over the situation?" Baker asked.

"I am so amazed!" Jess responded. "Much as I didn't like him, I also think that this is a terrible thing. I am calling to ask if you would like to delay the scheduling for the summary judgment motion."

"You would like that, wouldn't you? Delay doesn't hurt your client. My client still faces the stigma of a lawsuit and now this allegation of counterfeit drugs. Are you going to withdraw your requests for admission? We need to get this thing done."

"I really have no choice but to follow up on those, in particular since I don't have the benefit of Hansen's deposition, and I do have the deadline for response staring me in the face. If you can agree to a delay on my response to the summary judgment, I can give you a delay on your response to the requests. Will, it really does appear that your client was receiving counterfeit drugs. Peoples might be the victim of the drugs as much as my client was," Jess said, trying to talk sense to Baker.

"That's ridiculous!" Baker countered. "As far as I know, your client might even have been involved in a plot to get rid of Hansen. No way am I going to give you a break on this one."

"Will, get a life! I thought that a man's life might make more difference to you than this. You're crazy! See you at the summary judgment motion." Jess hung up so angry that she couldn't sit in her chair. She jumped up and walked toward the door. She was so agitated and moved so quickly that she almost ran into Drew as he was coming from the other direction. He had the newspaper article in his hand.

"Whoops! Sorry. I just got off the phone with The Asshole." Jess had recently gotten so tired of dealing with Baker that she had officially coined him another name. He had the nerve to accuse me of being involved in the Hansen killing. Even a death doesn't turn off his wild-bull imitation!" Jess ranted.

"Jess, I'm more worried about you than Baker. If this is related to the Peoples case, these guys play rough. Your house was already ransacked and bugged. A snake was planted in your car. And they obviously haven't given up on you since they were making anonymous calls! This is really serious, Jess! I don't care if the police shrug this off. They don't have as much at stake in this as I do. I don't want to see anything happen to you over a lousy lawsuit. You don't want to make Reesa an orphan, do you?" Drew threw in the last sentence to lighten up the situation, but he was obviously worried.

The connection seemed so farfetched to Jess that she hadn't really thought about her own safety. Of course, it was hard to believe that the Hansen death was related to the case, but there were a lot of things about this case that were hard to believe. Jess started to say, "I can't…"

Drew cut her off. "Think about it, Jess. I know it's hard to believe, but think it through. If nothing else, humor me or think of Reesa. I am on my way out of the office to meet a client for lunch. I can't cancel the appointment—he's probably already at the restaurant. Think about it, will you, and let's talk about it when I get back. I should be back about one thirty."

Drew walked out and Jess sat down. Hmm…what was Drew saying? He was asking her to drop the suit? There was no way she could do that! There was no proof that the break-in and the snake were related to the suit. Brad Thompson had lost his life, and if she and Drew were right, there was a good chance that what killed Brad could kill others. She couldn't let the lawsuit go.

Chapter Sixty-Nine

Drew didn't actually return to the office until two o'clock. "Damn," he said as he looked in the door to Jess's office. "Finding a place to park down there after lunch is getting worse and worse."

Jess turned around from working on her computer and faced Drew in the doorway. "You have time to talk?" he asked.

"Sure. I was thinking about the situation." Jess paused. "Drew, I know it sounds stupid if you are right that these things are related—and I think that may well be the case—but I just can't let Mary Thompson down. Her husband is dead, and if you and I are right about the cause, others will be dead. And we don't even know for sure that there is a relationship between these events and the case."

"I'm not asking you to drop the case! I'm saying that you should come and live with me in Bellevue. Hopefully, they won't think about where to look for you. I'll sleep on the couch, if you want me too. I just don't want you to stay in your condo alone right now."

Drew's face was so earnest that Jess almost smiled. "So that's what you have in mind!" she said. "Hey, that's clever," Jess joked. "I have never heard that one before."

Drew turned red and looked sheepish. "I know it sounds like a ploy, and I really respect you for how you help people. I know you put your money, heart and soul into it. Just don't get carried away by putting yourself in danger."

Jess stood up and walked toward Drew. "The old 'I'll respect you in the morning.' How can a girl pass up such an offer?" Jess joked again. "Can Reesa come too? By the way, I don't want you to sleep on the couch."

Drew put his arms around Jess and kissed her. "I was hoping you would say that."

Chapter Seventy

Will Baker sat in his office, staring out the window. He was thinking about the Thompson case. The conversation with Jess Lamm was running through his head. He had never had a case where a client had actually been killed. That was shocking. What if there was a connection between Hansen's death and the case?

As he considered the matter, the nagging thought in the back of his mind moved to front and center. He had never really discussed the case with Dr. Haseem as he should with any client. When the case started, it seemed like any other case he'd had for Peoples. The problem here was that the evidence was turning toward bad drugs. It was only when that Lamm woman started digging into what seemed like a ridiculous theory at the time that things began to get stickier. Baker decided that he would schedule an appointment with Dr. Haseem to get his take on Jess's counterfeit drug theory.

Baker found out that Dr. Haseem wouldn't be in the hospital until Sunday, so he decided to try to reach him first thing on Monday. With Hansen's death there would be no immediate way to contact Dr. Haseem at home. Like most physicians, Haseem kept his home phone number confidential in order to avoid emergency calls when he wasn't on duty. Hansen had really been Baker's only contact at Peoples, and Hansen's assistant was about as helpful as a post. She wouldn't or couldn't even give Baker the information about why Hansen had gone to eastern Washington.

As it worked out, it was a couple of weeks before Baker was able to nail down Haseem. At first Haseem was unavailable by phone.

The DDS—doctor defense system, set up to screen doctors from unnecessary calls—worked well, especially when the doctor didn't want to talk. Finally, Baker made an appointment at his office via the ER receptionist, but Haseem didn't show up. At first this didn't bother Baker because he wasn't all that eager to face the possibly difficult session with Haseem either. It was okay with Baker if that meeting was put off due to factors of Haseem's making.

As time went on, it became clearer that Baker was going to have to track Haseem down to talk with him, and the passing time required that he really must, as unpleasant as it might be. He decided to go to Peoples to visit with Haseem in order to make sure that he and Haseem actually got together. They met in a conference room at the hospital. When Baker finally got the chance to sit down with Haseem, his hunch about his difficulty contacting him was confirmed.

Haseem seemed incredibly fearful. Baker's first questions were met with almost one-word answers, and it seemed that Haseem was hiding something. After half an hour of this, Baker turned to Haseem and said, "You know that I'm your lawyer, don't you?"

Haseem just nodded.

"Look, I need to know your side of the story. This Lamm woman is saying that there are counterfeit drugs being used at this hospital. Lars Hansen has been killed. If his death has anything to do with this case, I need to know! I don't know what you are used to in Iraq, but in the U.S. we don't have hospital CEOs die of multiple gunshot wounds!"

Haseem didn't speak at first. The repeating scenario of being sent back to Iraq clouded his mind. It conjured up so much emotion that he could hardly think. Hansen had helped him get to the U.S. He had been the first one to respond to his inquiries about coming to this country, and had pulled strings to get Haseem here. As far as Haseem knew, no colleague of his had been able to come to the U.S. Iraqis just weren't getting into to the U.S. since the war started.

He had been eternally grateful, even if Fatimeh didn't think that Mr. Hansen always had his best interest at heart. Maybe Mr.

Hansen had something to hide, and maybe he was even shifting the blame onto Haseem. He wasn't sure that it made any difference.

Haseem had run into plenty of people in his route from Iraq to the U.S. who claimed to want the truth. Some of them did, and some were just trying to get information to use against him, as far as he could tell. He had discussed this over and over with Fatimeh. She kept urging him to take a chance and tell Baker what he knew.

Fatimeh had actually learned about the U.S. legal system in her work at the school. Granted it was what they were telling the children, but the teachers seemed to believe the story—that was significant. Omar hoped that Fatimeh was right. It was looking less and less like Omar had a choice anyway, since there was no Mr. Hansen to help him any more.

Just as Baker stood up to leave, Haseem turned to him and said, "Mr. Baker, please sit down for a minute. I have something to tell you. You must understand that this is difficult for me. Try to put yourself in my shoes and consider how concerned you would be if you were charged with incompetence in a foreign country, a charge that might send you and your family back home to your death." Baker immediately sat down again. In fact he almost fell down, he was so surprised. He had come to the conclusion that Haseem either did not speak English well enough to communicate or not as smart as one would expect from his position. The change in attitude and ability to speak got his attention.

For the next three hours, Haseem told Baker what he knew about the care at Peoples. Before contacting Haseem, Baker had decided that he would allow him to bring up any mention of a code problem to see if it was an issue for him. Haseem not only brought up the subject, he discussed at length his observations and his determination that the problem continued to this day. The fact that he actually volunteered the information in Nurse Brown's affidavit was disconcerting. In response to a direct question about whether he had seen her affidavit, Haseem looked surprised to hear that there was such an affidavit and then denied that he had seen it. Hansen had been so adamant that there was no code problem. It seemed clear that Haseem was very loyal to Hansen, and he had good reason to be. Haseem's information made it clear to Baker that he had been used by Hansen. "Damn, this a problem!" Baker thought.

Back in the office, Baker mulled over what he had learned in the context of the summary judgment motion pending the next day. He hated to admit it, but he really did have a conflict of interest representing both Peoples and Dr. Haseem. If Dr. Haseem was at fault, this case was a simple act of negligence at most, but there wasn't any proof of that. Jess Lamm had been concentrating on the counterfeit drug theory. She apparently had no expert who was willing to testify that Haseem's care itself was negligent, and the affidavit she presented pointed generally at the hospital on that damn *res ipsa* theory.

Getting into the issue of counterfeit drugs presented a much bigger problem. That would open the way for huge losses, possibly even bankruptcy for Peoples. There would be hundreds of claimants coming out of the woodwork claiming that they had been hurt by bad drugs. Sorting out which ones really received bad drugs would cost millions. Sometimes—hell, in most cases—you might not even be able to tell the cause of injury. The hospital wouldn't have given the counterfeit drugs if they had been labeled "Counterfeit."

Baker sat down and wrote a report about the situation to his contact at Peoples' insurance company. There was no way anyone at Hospital Insurance Corporation was going to read his letter before tomorrow's motion. Baker really had no client contact. Well, there *was* Haseem, but he had no horse power with VAHC or Hospital Insurance, either to get a settlement done or, more importantly, to recommend Baker for further representation of Peoples.

Like many insurance companies, Baker's contact at Hospital Insurance was an overworked, lower-level claims specialist. "Boy there's a misnomer—'claims specialist,'" Baker thought. His contact had no real ability to evaluate a potential danger of a claim to the insured or any financial authority to offer a meaningful settlement even if he did recognize the danger. That meant that the claims "specialist" didn't give much attention to a claim until trial was near—an arrangement that worked out well for Hospital Insurance, if not necessarily for Peoples. It would be hard to convince the insurance company that settling a case early to avoid the public disclosure of "bad facts" was a wise thing to do. The times that Baker had tried to make this clear to insurers, and there had been several, Baker found he was treated like a cowardly alarmist.

Baker had represented Peoples ever since Hansen had taken over. It was his major client, and he wanted to continue the relationship. So he had worked hard to cultivate the relationship with Hansen. Now that he was dead, Baker's main client contact was gone, which could threaten his ability to keep Peoples as a client.

Like the typical firm, each lawyer in Baker's firm guarded his clients like a hawk. Each was paid based on the income the lawyer brought into the firm—the "eat what you kill" method. Losing your major client could ruin your income for the year. It could take months, even years, to build up other clientele. In the meantime, your "partners" weren't all that willing to share.

If Baker really defended Haseem by going along with the counterfeit drug theory, it could be counterproductive to his defense of the hospital in this case and possibly his ability to keep representing the hospital in the future. So he wanted to stay away from the counterfeit drug problem. It wouldn't be productive for his career or in the hospital's interest.

"You never know," Baker thought. "I might get lucky. Maybe the court will dismiss this god-forsaken case, and my problem will go away."

Chapter Seventy-One

Friday morning Jess and Baker appeared at the courthouse early for the summary judgment motion. The actual trip to the courthouse had been quite a new experience for Jess. Drew had delivered her directly to the court since they had driven in from Bellevue together. On that Friday three weeks ago, after talking about it in the office, Jess had filled two suitcases with clothes, packed up Reesa's traveling case and litter box, and followed Drew to his condo in Bellevue. Jess had the impression that Drew wasn't taking any chances that she might change her mind, and that pleased her.

Reesa, of course, moved right in. She loved the view of the forest from Drew's living room window and adopted the windowsill as her personal perch. Jess was wondering if Reesa would want to come home again when the danger was over. She was looking at this living arrangement as a temporary situation, but she wasn't so sure if Reesa, or Drew for that matter, were of the same mind. But that wasn't all bad either.

Seeing Baker outside Judge Pacer's courtroom brought Jess's thoughts back to the business at hand. She had been able to reach Baker only twice since Hansen's death. The first time was when he accused her of being responsible for the murder. The second was when she was finally able to get him on the phone to attempt to reset the 30(b)(6) deposition that had fallen by the wayside due to Hansen's death. Baker had put her off saying that he was trying to determine who the new witness should be at Peoples to comply with the deposition notice. He appeared to be having trouble making client contact since Hansen's death. In any event, he had successfully avoided producing anyone for the deposition, and Jess had a motion pending to compel him to produce a witness. Noting Judge Pacer's previous decision to hear argument on a simple discovery motion, Jess had requested oral argument on this motion to compel, which was also set for today. That was a plus for Jess's chances on winning the summary judgment motion, since it demonstrated that her efforts to discover the facts in the case were once again being thwarted.

Jess's requests for admission were also still pending. She was glad that she'd had the forethought to issue those. Baker was going to have to answer them. It was going to be hard to simply deny them, with the evidence of bad drugs mounting.

A week ago, Jess had received Baker's reply brief, which was his opportunity to respond to the affidavits of Dr. Smith and Joyce Brown as well as Jess's brief. There was nothing new in Baker's reply. It looked like he had pulled out "Speculation Brief 10" and slapped the heading for this case on it. Jess was glad to read the brief. The fact that Baker offered nothing new made it likely that she would be able to avoid dismissal.

Dr. Haseem was with Baker today. Jess assumed that the woman with Dr. Haseem was his wife. Since Jess hadn't met Mrs. Haseem, she couldn't be sure—the stylish blouse and skirt, impeccable make-up and hair, and heck, the lack of a headscarf, was impressive to Jess. Switching cultures like she had, being under the strain of a lawsuit, and looking "made in America" was *quite* impressive. Jess said a polite hello to Baker. He barely gave a response and didn't make any effort to introduce those with him.

Mary Thompson met Jess at the courtroom as well. She was looking pale and worried but her usual resolute self. Jess put her arm around her shoulder and steered her to the counsel table to sit down. The case was wearing on Mary, and Jess was afraid she might fall down if she didn't sit down. Jess had talked to her about Baker's brief and about her positive take on it, but it was difficult to take things for granted when Mary, and even Jess to a lesser extent, had so much at stake.

Dr. and Mrs. Haseem sat with Baker at the other counsel table. There was an additional person in the courtroom that Jess didn't recognize. He was much better dressed—emphasis on much—than the usual court watcher. Generally court watchers either don't have enough to do, feel it's their duty to sit in on court and observe what's going on, or maybe want to get out of the rain. Generally, they are dressed in scruffy clothes and often sport bedhead hair. The unknown visitor was dark complected, dressed in a tailored brown suit and had what Jess guessed was a $200 haircut. Jess also guessed that he was not there because he had nothing else to do or needed to get out of the rain.

Counsel arranged their papers at the counsel table, the bailiff announced the judge, and everyone rose. The judge entered the courtroom and directed those standing to be seated. She announced the case, though it was the only one on the calendar that day, and asked the formal question whether counsel were ready. Of course, they were.

Baker stood as Judge Pacer directed him to begin. He introduced himself as usual. "Good morning, Your Honor. I am William Baker, counsel for Peoples Hospital and Dr. Haseem." Before he could proceed, the judge interjected, "Yes, Mr. Baker, that is a problem. How can you possibly represent both defendants in this suit?" Mrs. Haseem's eyes shot up toward Baker. Being more than occupied with keeping his composure, Baker didn't notice. Jess was pleased to hear the question and lowered her head to read her notes and hide the smile twitching on the edges of her mouth.

Pausing slightly, Baker attempted to resume his argument. "Peoples Hospital and Dr. Haseem have brought this summary judgment motion for dismissal of the case against them."

Judge Pacer was having none of this. Before Baker could say more, she interjected again. "Mr. Baker, you can assume that I have read the pleadings regarding this matter. Due to the fact that Ms. Lamm has offered sufficient evidentiary basis to establish an issue of fact, I am not going to dismiss this case. I find that the plaintiff has provided sufficient evidence to cause this case to go to a jury. Specifically, under the doctrine of *res ipsa loquitur*, the plaintiff has established that Peoples Hospital was in exclusive control of the patient's care, there was a corresponding lack of control on the patient's part to take action on his own behalf to avert injury, and the plaintiff has presented expert testimony that a patient does not die from a massive stroke following successful resuscitation from a cardiac arrest in the absence of actionable fault. This ruling does not exclude the possibility of proof under a product liability theory.

"Now, I don't have sufficient evidence to know what part Dr. Haseem played in all of this. My question to you, Mr. Baker, is this: How can you possibly continue to represent both Peoples Hospital and Dr. Haseem? There is a clear conflict of interest in that dual representation. I advised you at the last hearing that you should consider the fact that there may be a conflict. Now it is clear that there is an actual conflict. I am going to make the assumption that because of the death of your client's CEO, you have not had the opportunity to take care of this situation.

"My concern is compounded by the fact that, as I see the pleadings, it appears that Ms. Lamm clearly points the finger of blame at the hospital and there is nothing specific as to Dr. Haseem. If Dr. Haseem had separate representation, it would be extremely likely that his counsel would be discussing dismissal with Ms. Lamm."

Then, looking directly at Dr. and Mrs. Haseem, Judge Pacer continued, "The potential harm to Dr. Haseem's reputation here is not remedied by the mere fact that the hospital would pay any damage claim. I suspect, in light of Dr. Haseem's status as a foreign national, that this is even more important to him than it is in the normal case. Do you have any questions, Dr. and Mrs. Haseem?" The Haseems were so stunned that even Fatimeh had nothing to say, though her face was beginning to brighten and a smile beginning to spread.

Turning back to Baker, Judge Pacer said, "If I do not receive at least one substitution of counsel, showing that Dr. Haseem has separate counsel in this case within thirty days, I will schedule a show cause hearing on my own accord. This is no longer a suggestion, Mr. Baker. This is now a critical situation. By saying this, I am not making any decision that mere substitution of counsel for Dr. Haseem will be sufficient—it may be that you will have to withdraw from the entire case."

Judge Pacer didn't have to spell it out for Baker. He was risking report of an ethical violation to disciplinary counsel at the bar association. At the show cause hearing, Baker would be required to tell Judge Pacer why she should not submit such a complaint. Baker could be reprimanded or possibly temporarily suspended from the practice of law. There would even be a remote chance that he could lose his license to practice law altogether. Jess thought to herself, "If he weren't so difficult to deal with, I would feel sorry for The Asshole."

Judge Pacer continued, "I can tell you that part of my decision as to what is sufficient change of representation would hinge on the structure of any settlement. It *is* clear that this case is ripe for settlement. Unless the evidentiary picture changes to designate some fault on the part of Dr. Haseem, I am going to assume that you are going to be careful to structure a settlement so as to clarify Dr. Haseem's lack of liability."

Looking to Jess, the judge concluded, "Ms. Lamm, I am also granting your motion to compel production of a witness in response to the 30(b)(6) deposition notice. I will give Mr. Baker thirty days to produce the witness. Mr. Baker, I am giving you thirty days on this issue in view of the unfortunate death of Mr. Hansen. This should be more than enough time to sort out who the proper witness should be. I further expect that the witness will have identified the source of the drug or drugs in question by the time of the deposition. Mr. Baker, since you mention in your response to the motion to compel that Ms. Lamm has requests for admission pending, I will also grant you an additional thirty days to answer those, but only because of the death of Mr. Hansen. Since counsel's proposed order on the discovery motion doesn't speak to these additional rulings, I will ask you to present new proposed orders to the court with copy to Mr. Baker within five days, Ms. Lamm. If the two of you are not able to agree on the terms of the orders, please note them for presentation. Mr. Baker, I am going to assume that you will work closely with Ms. Lamm regarding any concerns that you may have regarding the orders. I will review your proposed order on summary judgment, Ms. Lamm, and consider whether I want to add anything to it."

Once again Judge Pacer stood abruptly, everyone in the courtroom jumped up, the bailiff called, "All rise," and Judge Pacer walked out of the courtroom to her chambers.

Jess was so startled that she just sat there for a moment. Then, turning to her client, she said, "Mary, we did it—our case is alive and well. Mary, I am so glad!"

Mary turned to Jess and hugged her. "No Jess," she said, "you did it. Thank you so much!" There were tears in Mary's eyes.

There were also tears in Fatimeh's eyes. She couldn't believe what she had heard. First of all, she was pleased to see a woman judge, but more importantly, the judge seemed to be concerned about her husband getting fair representation. She thought of the television shows that she had seen. "Is this a great country or what!" was a cry that she had heard. Now she knew where that thought came from. Fatimeh hugged Omar, who seemed absolutely stunned. Tears were streaming down his face. He had done so much to get them here and had worked so hard for Fatimeh and Osman. "He deserves this," Fatimeh thought; but like Omar, Fatimeh had observed that life sometimes did not give what is deserved.

Omar couldn't speak and was clearly overcome with what had just happened. As had been the case throughout their lives together, Fatimeh and Omar worked as a team. When one needed help, the other pitched in. Fatimeh turned to Baker and said, "Are we supposed to be talking with you about what the judge said, Mr. Baker?" He turned red and said, "Yes, please call my office and make an appointment for next week. Here is my card."

Baker gathered his papers and rose to leave. He didn't feel like waiting for Dr. and Mrs. Haseem. They were obviously overcome by the statement from the judge regarding Haseem's liability, and so was he, but in a different way. It was a little harder to throw Haseem to the wolves after having met him and his wife. It was also becoming clear that they would understand what was happening, if he tried to do that.

On his way out of the courtroom, Jess noticed that Baker was interrupted by the court watcher. Baker tried to walk around him, but the court watcher blocked his way. It seemed that the man stood with the specific purpose to talk to Baker, and he was going to do that. As they stood in the aisle, the court watcher put his arm on Baker's shoulder and drew him along into the hallway. It was a strange sight, since Baker wasn't the kind of guy you wanted to touch out of friendliness or affection, and people rarely displayed an air of dominance with him. They were still in conversation when Jess and Mary left, and the court watcher seemed to have Baker's full attention.

Chapter Seventy-Two

Will Baker was sitting in his office gazing out at the water. The view of Puget Sound with the mountains in the background was spectacular, even in bad weather. Today, in September, the weather was clear and sunny, at least right now, which added a sparkling effect to the blue water. Generally this view gave him a satisfied feeling, a confirmation of the hard work and brains that had brought him this far. But today, he was worrying about the conversation he'd had with Guzman outside the courtroom.

As Guzman introduced himself and held out his hand, Baker had been wary despite his friendly and polished manner. When Guzman put his arm on Baker's shoulder, his first thought was to reach up and take it off, but intuition had told him that wouldn't be a good idea.

They had stood in an out-of-the-way corner of the hall outside the courtroom for only a few minutes discussing the motion results and more. The conversation did nothing to allay Baker's concern about Guzman.

Guzman had introduced himself as the CEO of Drug Repackaging and Distribution, who worked with Lars Hansen to supply pharmaceuticals to Peoples Hospital. "I had a meeting with poor Mr. Hansen the day that he died. We have such a problem with gangs in Toppenish," Guzman said. "I was so shocked."

Baker said nothing and Guzman continued, "Mr. Hansen advised me about the claim and the hearing today. Despite my concern over his death, I do owe it to my investors to be aware of the result and to stay abreast of this preposterous charge. Claims like these, no matter how unfounded, can be so difficult to defend if not taken care of as soon as possible."

Again Guzman paused and Baker couldn't think of anything to say. Guzman then asked, "What are you going to do about the judge's instruction on representation?"

"Well, that isn't something that I can really discuss with you since you aren't my client," Baker had replied.

"I certainly don't want to influence how you handle your case. I'm just a businessman trying to protect my business. If you think that money would make this case go away, I would be more than happy to attempt to help, to avoid the cost of a lawsuit against DRD."

"Do you have counsel, Mr. Guzman?"

"I don't, Mr. Baker, but I have some experience with these types of matters, and I know they can cost millions of dollars to defend. I generally like to put my money into settlement rather than attorney's fees. Of course, I would be happy to pay you for your efforts in getting this case settled. I'm sure that Peoples would like to avoid the intrusion of an investigation into their business matters as well."

The reference to millions of dollars in defense costs stuck in Baker's mind. That was so off the scale, at least for this case, or was Guzman talking about a flood of claims based on bad drugs? Maybe it was an attempt at a bribe?

If DRD really was dealing in counterfeit drugs it could be yet another conflict for Baker if he took up Guzman on his suggestion, but maybe not. Certainly continuing the use of counterfeit drugs would be against People's interest, and the hospital would certainly want to know if that were the case. The problem for Peoples would be that the whole world might know about it too, and the hospital could be inundated with lawsuits based on speculation about counterfeit drugs. Certainly that wasn't in Peoples' best interest. Settlement of the case would make public disclosure of the problem much less likely, which would be good for Peoples too. The question was how to get Hospital Insurance Corporation's attention to settle. Baker didn't know anyone at Peoples to contact to who could push the insurance company along. Maybe he could find someone in authority at VAHC to help get this case settled.

Settlement would be good for Baker too. It would take care of Baker's problem with the conflict between Peoples Hospital and Dr. Haseem. The only problem would be figuring out how to structure the settlement now that Judge Pacer had spelled out the conflict in front of the Haseems.

Her speech was something that he had not run into before. "It was really off the scale," he thought, "but so is the rest of this case. My god, a murder over a lawsuit! That doesn't happen in this country, does it?"

Just then Baker's phone rang. The caller ID indicated that it was his secretary, Sally. Baker punched the speaker phone on. "Yes?" he asked.

"Your wife is on the phone, Mr. Baker. She says it's extremely urgent."

"Thanks, Sally. Put her through."

Chapter Seventy-Three

"Will, it's Julia. Marissa's been injured. They're taking her to Overlake Emergency, and I'm on my way. I'll meet you there." The phone clicked to the dial tone.

Will's thoughts about the case vanished. The human mind has only so much attention it can give, and his was now fully occupied. Will hadn't even had the presence of mind to ask how badly Marissa was injured, but he wouldn't have had a chance to ask anyway since Julia had hung up so fast. Rather than calling back immediately, he decided to call from his car.

He grabbed his keys and headed out the door of his office, slowing down only long enough to yell to Sally, "Family emergency. Got to go."

Sally yelled back, "When will you be back?" After the word "when" erupted from her mouth, the rest followed at a whisper, as Sally remembered firm decorum. "No yelling, even if your boss is rushing out the door and people will be asking when the hell he will be back...or something like that," Sally thought.

John wasn't willing to wait long enough to come up with an answer for the question. He pretended he didn't hear and continued walking as fast as he could toward the elevator.

The drive across the I-90 bridge was something that generally gave Baker reason to remember how beautiful Seattle and the surrounding area was, even when the traffic was bad. The traffic wasn't bad today, but he didn't stop to think about the beauty of Seattle. He punched in the number for Julia's cell phone and got her voice mail. "Julia, I'm on I-90. Call me back when you get this message, would you?" He paused and then said, "I love you, Julia."

They had been so thrilled when Marissa was born. "This cannot be happening!" Will thought.

Fortunately, the traffic backup along I-90 from the intersection with I-405 had not yet built up. John was able to get to Overlake Hospital in only twenty-three minutes, although it seemed a lot longer than that. He parked his car outside the emergency room entrance in a short-term parking stall, thinking he'd move it later. Running into the waiting room, he saw Julia sitting in the corner with her head in her hands. He almost tripped he was moving so fast. "Slow down, Will," he told himself. Sitting down beside Julia, he put his arm around her shoulders. "What have they told you, sweetheart?"

Julia looked up only slightly. The sound of her voice was achingly low, confirming the knot in her throat. "Compound fracture left tibia and fibula. Maybe internal injuries. Will, it was a hit and run! Who would do that to a little girl?"

Julia, a nurse, had reverted to the medical description of Marissa's injuries. Will was too upset to try to decipher the code on his own. "Julia, tell me in English, would you?" She jerked her head around as though she wasn't sure whether Will was criticizing her or not. "Sorry," he said, "I don't know what you mean."

"Her left lower leg is broken." The bone is actually...sticking through...the skin." She was so upset that her tongue tripped over the *s*'s as she said the last sentence.

Will turned white and thought he was going to be sick. "Wait," he told himself, "not here."

Julia continued, "They think they can fix the broken bone. It appears to be a fairly clean break." Will wondered how bone sticking through the skin could be a clean break, but he wasn't up to discussing the specifics of the leg any further right now.

"What...what else did you say...internal injuries?" Will asked, feeling like an idiot. Of course he knew what internal injuries were, sort of. "I mean, what does that mean...for Marissa?"

"They can tell that she's internally bleeding from her blood tests, but they don't know where. They have to take her to surgery to find out where it's coming from. Hopefully they can stop it. Will," Julia looked at him, "she...she might...die if they can't stop the bleeding."

Will was stunned. The broken bone sticking out of the leg seemed a lot less important right now. He sat with his arm around Julia as she sobbed silently and as tears streamed down his face. He saw a security guard approaching. "*Shit!*" he thought. "The car."

The security guard said, "Sir, we need to move your car. Since you may not be up to that right now, do you want to give me your keys? I'll park it and get them back to you."

"Thanks," Will said, digging his keys out of his pocket. He really didn't give a damn about the car right now. He was glad he hadn't interrupted the security guard before he got the chance to finish his proposal. His first thought had been to throw the keys at the idiot.

Chapter Seventy-Four

It was Monday morning, and Will was back at the office. The weekend had been a life-changing event for him. He had come to realize that there were some things that he couldn't control. He and Julia had spent the night at the emergency room and then in Marissa's room after surgery. Fortunately, the doctors had been able to stop the bleeding. They had removed Marissa's spleen and set her leg. She was even going to be able to go home today or tomorrow, since Julia was a nurse. Julia could give her the IV antibiotics that she needed to take care of the probable infection in the leg resulting from the bone sticking through the skin. Every time Will thought about Marissa's leg, he became nauseated.

The police were looking for the hit-and-run driver, but they weren't very encouraging. According to Marissa, it was a big, blue and brown car. Probably a blue car with rust on it, the police thought. No one else had seen the car.

It was *so* lucky that they lived on Mercer Island, and their neighbor had seen the mangled bike lying on the ground as she was coming home from grocery shopping. She had alerted Julia, and they called 911. In other circumstances, Marissa might have bled to death before she was taken to the hospital. All weekend—well, once he had been able to think, and that wasn't until he'd been told that Marissa should recover fully—Baker had been thinking about how final death is. "Such a cliché," he thought, "but potentially losing someone you love makes you understand." He tried to block out the picture of Mary Thompson. It was hard to do, and that also made it hard to think.

Baker's agenda for the day included reporting the outcome of the summary judgment motion to Hospital Insurance. He also needed to give them the information about new counsel. He thought again about how withdrawal from the case would effect his financial position. Better pull out Lamm's answers to interrogatories and look at how much they are claiming in damages. "It's sure to be way off the scale," Baker thought, "but it would be a starting point for settlement."

As Baker was about to go to the file cabinet to find Jess's interrogatory answers, Sally rang him. Punching the speaker button, Baker answered, "Yes?"

"A Mr. Guzman is on the phone. He says that he talked to you in court last Friday after the summary judgment motion."

Much as Baker really disliked Guzman, he thought he should take the call. If Guzman was really willing to throw money into the pot for settlement, then he might be helpful. "Transfer him in, Sally," Baker said.

"Hello, Mr. Baker," Guzman said. "How was your weekend?"

Baker thought to himself that his weekend was his own business, and he wasn't about to discuss Marissa's injury with Guzman. Unfortunately, he really couldn't think of much else to say, so he said, "Well, it wasn't as enjoyable as it could have been. My daughter was injured, but she's going to recover."

"Well, I'm really sorry to hear that," Guzman oozed.

Again, Baker thought about how intrusive Guzman's inquiry into his personal life felt.

"How did it happen?"

"It was a bike accident, a hit-and-run kind of thing," Baker forced himself to answer.

"My goodness, how awful for a seven-year-old!" said Guzman.

Baker's head snapped, and his heart started to race. "I don't think I told you that she was seven years old," Baker said, trying to keep his voice even.

"Didn't you? I'm sure you did. Otherwise, how would I know?" Guzman said.

Baker said nothing, but he was very sure that he knew how Guzman knew Marissa's age. Baker was totally out of his realm.

"This does not happen here…at least not on Mercer Island and certainly not over a lawsuit!" Baker thought to himself.

After a long pause, Guzman began again. "I am sorry, Mr. Baker. This seems to be painful for you. Maybe we should get down to business." Without pausing, Guzman continued, "My company is prepared to supply a large part of any settlement. As I said, we are familiar with lawsuits and how expensive and intrusive they can be, even to the lawyers sometimes."

The veiled threat didn't elude Baker.

Guzman continued, "Making cases go away is sometimes the best thing to do, even when the cases are unfounded."

"I'll have to discuss this with my client, Mr. Guzman. I'm assuming you are thinking in terms of several million dollars. You know that Brad Thompson was a rising young accountant in a regional accounting firm. Settlement isn't going to be cheap."

"I understand, Mr. Baker. My companions are businessmen. They realize the value of money. My company would also be very grateful to you as well for getting this matter settled."

Baker felt as though he was going to pass out. Steeling himself, he said, "I do have to go, Mr. Guzman. I have your card, and I will call you back after I make a few calls." Not giving Guzman any further opportunity to speak, Baker hung up the phone and bent over from the waist. Even though he was sitting, he was afraid that he was going to faint. "You bastard," he thought. Then he thought about Marissa's leg with bones sticking through the skin. He couldn't stop himself—he lost his breakfast all over the beige carpet in his office.

Chapter Seventy-Five

It was Tuesday morning and Baker was back in the office after going home sick the day before. He had spent the rest of Monday with Marissa and Julia. Marissa was able to go home Monday afternoon, and Baker was glad he could be there to help Julia get her home. He couldn't remember the last time he had appreciated being with them so much. Marissa looked so small and fragile.

Baker hadn't been able to bring himself to tell Julia about Guzman. He'd never in his life felt so helpless, so unable to control a situation. He didn't know how Julia would react to finding out that Marissa's accident was connected with his work. He just wanted the situation to go away.

He sat down to write a status report to Hospital Insurance. The first part was easy—the court had denied the summary judgment motion. The next part was *not* easy. Denial of summary judgment meant that unless this case was settled, there would be discovery into a potentially catastrophic area of counterfeit drugs. Should he tell Hospital Insurance that? If someone in authority found out about counterfeit drugs at Peoples, they might cause Peoples to stop buying from DRD, especially since Lars Hansen was no longer there to make the decision. What would Guzman do about the loss of a major source of business? He had already shown that he knew how to take action, and Baker didn't want to risk that again.

After giving it some thought, Baker decided that he had to report the situation. It was his duty as a lawyer to pass information of this type along to his client. For now, though, Baker decided that he was only going to report the situation to Hospital Insurance. His contact there would probably file the report without even looking at it, but at least Baker could say that he'd sent the information to someone. Finally, Baker sent the report off by e-mail, labeling it "high priority."

"That will ensure that the message will be the last one opened," Baker thought wryly.

Baker also considered contacting someone in VAHC's central management since that was the closest thing to a real client contact that he had after Hansen's death. The danger of this case should be brought to their attention. Again Baker decided that he couldn't take the chance that they would end the business relationship with Guzman. He decided that he could use Hansen's death as an excuse for not contacting his client directly. That would work … at least temporarily.

What Baker did do was call Jessica Lamm to explore the possibility of settlement. He dialed her direct line, and she picked up. "Hi, Jessica, this is Will." There was a long pause on the other side, long enough for Baker to think to himself, "Apparently she's expecting me to criticize." Baker was aware that the last few times they had talked had been less than cordial, and he knew this might make settlement harder.

If Jess could have read his mind just then, she would have said, "Ya think, Asshole?"

"My client is pounding me to see if we can get this case settled," Baker said. "They are aware that you can make life difficult for them investigating the counterfeit drugs theory. Much as I tell them that the idea is a bunch of crap, I can't tell them that it won't cost them a lot of money. They think I'm just trying to get them prepared so I can run up attorney's fees. Can you get me a number that I can pass by them?"

"Sure, Will, I'll send over a settlement proposal. I also have a draft order for Judge Pacer's ruling. I'll send that over too."

"Sounds good. I'll take a look at it and get back with you. Talk to you later." Baker and Jess hung up.

"Amazing," Jess thought, "how Baker is such a chameleon—from asshole to charmer in one trip to the courthouse. I wonder if he's s really serious about settling or just wants to show his client that he tried," Jess thought. It had been her experience with Will Baker that he didn't really talk settlement until they were walking up the courthouse steps for trial. She wasn't sure that was his or the insurance company's doing. "Only one way to find out if he's serious this time," Jess thought. She sat down to write her settlement demand.

A week later Baker was still considering what to do to push settlement of the Thompson case. Jess had sent him a demand for a structured settlement of $2.5 million down and a yearly payment for the next twenty-five years starting at $230,000 but increasing for inflation. The 2.5 million would cover Mary and Madaline Thompson's loss of companionship and support. The settlement demand seemed really reasonable. Baker actually thought from observing Mary's demeanor that she and Brad had been really close. He thought about how Julia would have felt if he had died. He didn't want to think about that or Marissa growing up without him.

The demand for $230,000 per year was also probably reasonable. This was close to what Thompson's net annual income would have been, if he had lived, and of course the income would rise over time.

Ordinarily when considering settlement value, Baker would discount the damages by the risk—a fifty percent chance that the plaintiff would lose the case would mean that the settlement value would be fifty percent of the likely damages. The problem here was that it looked like Jessica Lamm was going to build a rock-solid case, and Peoples needed to get this case settled soon. The settlement value would be actual damages.

Guzman was calling Baker every other day to check on settlement progress, and he was becoming bolder in his insinuations. That alone told Baker that the counterfeit problem was bigger than just the one or two drugs that Jessica Lamm had discovered. No reputable pharmaceutical wholesaler would threaten injury, but Baker was paralyzed to do anything about it.

Chapter Seventy-Six

The Haseems and their new attorney had just left Baker's office. Baker had been able to convince his immediate contact at Hospital Insurance that it was necessary to hire separate counsel only after he had the transcript of the summary judgment hearing printed to prove Judge Pacer's instructions. He had explained to his contact that either they would have to obtain separate counsel, or he would have to withdraw from the case entirely. The insurer would then have to pay for new counsel to get up to speed on the facts of the case. That, of course, would cost thousands of dollars extra in defense costs, which was the clincher for Hospital Insurance. Baker was pleased he had avoided the possibility of having his own bills ignored, at least for the present.

The Haseems were at first startled by the fact that their new counsel had the same last name as the plaintiffs in the lawsuit. Richard Thompson had explained that the surname "Thompson" was just a common English surname and that he wasn't related to the deceased Brad Thompson. Mrs. Haseem had insisted on looking at the phone book to confirm the number of Thompsons in Seattle, and she and her husband were satisfied after that investigation.

Thompson and Baker had discussed the facts of the case prior to meeting with the Haseems. Thompson agreed with Baker that the best way to deal with the conflict was to attempt to put together a settlement between Peoples and the Thompsons and an outright dismissal of Dr. Haseem. The idea was that any damage to Haseem's reputation would be remedied by the fact that he had been dismissed without payment of even a nuisance settlement.

Thompson explained the proposal to the Haseems. Their only concern was when the dismissal would occur and what a "nuisance settlement" was. Thompson regretted bringing up the term in light of the fact that it didn't figure in to the current plan. The Haseems were a little suspicious of what was going on, perhaps rightfully so, and demanded explanation of everything.

Thompson explained that a nuisance settlement had nothing to do with the character of the settling party but was related to the amount of the settlement. A nuisance settlement is a relatively small amount of money, roughly equivalent to the cost of continued defense of the case, and in this case, defense of the claims against Dr. Haseem shouldn't cost much more, maybe $10,000. Since insurance companies aren't so worried about reputations, they often enter into small-dollar settlements in return for dismissal of the claims against a defendant, but Judge Pacer had made it clear that protection of Dr. Haseem's reputation was going to be an issue in this case. Both Haseems seemed satisfied with the plan.

Then the Haseems wanted to know when the settlement would occur. That wasn't something that Baker or Thompson could say for sure, because it wasn't something they could necessarily control. No plaintiff's lawyer, especially an experienced lawyer like Jessica Lamm, would dismiss the claims against Dr. Haseem on the mere request of his lawyer. Lamm would be suspicious that Baker and Thompson had an ulterior motive, since liability hadn't been legally established. What if it turned out that Haseem had some responsibility for the fact that Peoples used counterfeit drugs or that he actually committed some error that Lamm didn't know about yet? Even with a dismissal without prejudice, which theoretically would allow Jess to refile a claim against Dr. Haseem, the new requirement that a plaintiff have a certificate of merit before filing might make it difficult or impossible to *successfully* refile the case.

Much as Baker wanted Haseem's dismissal, he knew it wasn't going to happen unless it was part of a package including enough money to pay for the death of Mr. Thompson. Surprisingly, when

Baker and Thompson discussed why Jessica Lamm wouldn't be likely to dismiss claims against Haseem until they had a settlement of the entire case, the Haseems seemed to readily understand. "Possible double-cross" was the phrase they used. That was certainly within their frame of reference. The Haseems weren't totally happy about the lack of finality but wanted to be kept informed of progress on settlement.

Richard Thompson agreed and explained that now that he was representing Dr. Haseem, he would give regular status reports. He invited them to call him whenever they had a concern about what was going on. "What a country!" thought Fatimeh, as she and Omar left the office. "We have our own lawyer reporting to us."

What Will Baker didn't discuss with Thompson or the Haseems was Baker's concern about how to get his client to consent to settlement. He was going to have to give some reason for settling. Even if Guzman paid the whole settlement, the hospital would have to know why. Consent wasn't a problem for Guzman, but it was for Baker, and he couldn't figure out a way to obtain Peoples' consent to settle without disclosing the counterfeit drug problem. Every time he thought about that, he also thought of Marissa with the bone sticking out of her leg.

Chapter Seventy-Seven

Jess was finding that Bellevue was a nice place to live. Since she and Drew drove to the office together, they could use the carpool lane on I-90, which allowed them to move at what seemed like warp speed compared to the one-passenger cars stacked bumper to bumper at rush hour.

Reesa was settling into her new home too. Drew had started feeding her whipped cream when they had coffee in the morning. Reesa was becoming quite used to the pampering and reminded her "servants" if they forgot the treat. Jess was becoming more and more certain that getting Reesa to come home after the danger was past was going to be difficult. "That's okay," she thought, since she was no longer in such a hurry to get home either. Living with Drew was better than she had expected.

It was a Friday morning, two weeks since the summary judgment motion, and a little less than that since Baker had asked for a settlement proposal. Just as Jess expected, nothing was happening with the settlement. Baker had been almost easy to work with on the order that she had prepared and presented to Judge Pacer for signing. What really had gotten Jess's attention was the lack of the appearance of separate counsel for the Haseems. "How can Baker be so arrogant as to ignore Judge Pacer's instructions? He has such an obvious conflict situation!" she had thought several times.

Musing about Baker as she was sitting at her computer, Jess looked at the *Seattle Times* online. She had been wondering if anything was being done about the murder of Lars Hansen and had been checking the news daily for more. "My god, there it is!" she said to herself. The article read:

Counterfeit Drug Connection to Peoples Hospital

Working around the clock with the FBI, the Toppenish Police have arrested a suspect in the alleged murder of Lars Hansen, CEO of Peoples Hospital and well-known Seattle philanthropist. Toppenish Police announced today that they have arrested Ricardo Guzman, the CEO of Drug Repackaging and Distribution, located in Toppenish, Washington, for the alleged murder and for trafficking in counterfeit drugs.

Toppenish Police Chief, Juan Gutierrez, confirmed that he was contacted by the FBI two weeks ago, shortly after the death of Mr. Hansen. Police officials allege that the motive for the murder was to avoid disclosure of the sale of counterfeit drugs to Peoples Hospital of Seattle. The FBI has had an ongoing investigation of the activities at DRD for possible import of counterfeit drugs, which appears to have had an increasing connection to local gang violence in the eastern Washington town.

Investigators allege that Guzman imported counterfeit drugs from China via Mexico. Guzman represented his operation as a drug repackaging plant in Toppenish. Though a legitimate activity, repackaging has at times been connected with counterfeit drug distribution, as well. See related story, Drug Repackaging.

Mr. Guzman had been courted by the Toppenish City Counsel upon his arrival in the town because his business promised high-skilled jobs for the area. Further investigation of Mr. Guzman revealed that he had illegally immigrated to the U.S. following investigation of a drug distribution enterprise in Mexico, allegedly resulting in multiple deaths related to counterfeit drugs. The Mexican investigation was halted when Guzman's license was suspended, and he claimed to have gone out of business. The FBI alleges, however, that Guzman merely moved his plant and that it is fully operational in Tijuana, Mexico. The FBI has notified Mexican authorities and is awaiting response.

The FBI further alleges that Mr. Guzman imports counterfeit drugs from China and that the bulk drugs are repackaged into containers imitating genuine pharmaceuticals in Tijuana. The operation is alleged to be part of the ever growing multi-billion dollar counterfeit drug industry in the U.S. The FBI claims that after repackaging, the drugs have been imported into the U.S. under relaxed restrictions of the North American Free Trade Agreement, NAFTA.

The FBI cut short its investigation due to the apparent rising violence connected with Mr. Guzman's operation. There were reports of increasing association with Toppenish gang members, including such activities as drug transport and intimidation of parties attempting to investigate the activities of DRD. See related story, Gang Violence in US. The FBI declined further comment on specific allegations, citing an ongoing investigation...

"The 'undocumented pharmacist,'" Jess thought to herself. The story continued, but she needed no more information. She printed out the story and also saved a copy on her computer, which she e-mailed to Will Baker. Walking out to the printer, she picked up the hard copy to show Drew.

At the Washington Mutual Tower, Baker was considering his discussion with Richard Thompson and the Haseems. The second conversation with Thompson alone, which occurred after the Haseems left, caused Baker the greatest concern. Thompson had stayed to give Baker a private heads-up that if they couldn't settle the case within the month, he felt compelled to bring a cross claim on behalf of Haseem against Peoples. Though he sympathized with Baker's position, Thompson felt that if he failed to bring a cross claim against Peoples, he would be exposing himself to a claim of legal malpractice. "He might be right," Baker reluctantly admitted to himself.

Yet one more pressure to get the case settled, and Baker could do nothing about it. As he sat at his desk staring in the direction of Elliot Bay, he wondered how he had allowed himself to get into a position where he was trying to avoid the disclosure of counterfeit drugs for protection of his family. He decided that when he got out of this mess, he was going to do something different with his life.

After sitting for twenty minutes, trying to make his head work despite the guilt hormones surging through his body, Baker finally turned to his computer. "Damn, another e-mail from Jessica Lamm. Damn that woman! Doesn't she have anything better to do than rub my nose in it all day?"

Baker opened the e-mail, which had an attachment. Jess had also written a note in the e-mail. "I thought that you might find this interesting. We should talk."

"Bitch!" Baker thought. "She just can't stop."

Baker opened the attachment and read the headline, "Counterfeit Drug Connection to Peoples Hospital." The headline grabbed his attention immediately, and he quickly read the article until he arrived at the part that Guzman had been arrested. He couldn't believe it! The sense of relief was overwhelming! No more danger to his family, well probably. No more reason to hide what he knew about possible counterfeit drugs. Heck, everyone knew. He felt the vice around his head release, and he was able to think again. The release also seemed to allow his tear ducts to open. He closed his office door to preserve his dignity.

Shortly, Baker pulled himself together. The first thing to do was to send this news article to his client, his real client—VAHC. They would understand the significance, and they could put pressure on the insurer to settle. That was what should happen, and he now thought that he might be able to make it happen.

Before doing anything else, Baker thought that he would go home. He wanted to see Marissa and Julia. He had developed a healthy dislike for his work since this case had taken a bad turn, especially since Marissa's injury. He hadn't been aware of how much his drive for success had twisted his priorities. He wanted that to change, and he hoped that he could make that happen too.

Chapter Seventy-Eight

Picking up the Guzman article, Jess walked down the hall to Drew's office. Looking through the window of Drew's office, Jess thought, "Good, he's here, and he's not on the phone."

"Got a minute?"

"No problem," he responded.

"You are not going to believe this!" she said, as she placed the hard copy of the *Seattle Times* story in front of him.

Drew read it carefully saying nothing. Jess was surprised that it took him so long to read the article, and she began wondering if she had missed something in the story. There was no exclamation of relief, not even a high five about the impact on the Thompson case. As she was about to speak, Drew looked up.

"Jess, I am happy this guy is caught, but you aren't thinking that this is over, are you? What if he gets out on bail? Who's to say he won't try to get rid of a few people who have evidence against him? He's tried it before. And what if he gets off? He seems to have done that down in Mexico. If the snake in the car didn't convince you, Hansen's murder should have. Didn't the snake in the car send a message? How do we know that this is the right guy? You said the anonymous caller told you to stay away from Haseem, not DRD."

Jess looked at Drew. "From the beginning I figured that the reference to Haseem was a red herring designed to steer us away from the drug theory. If you met Dr. Haseem, you would think that too, and when you meet him and his wife, you don't really have any doubt. I don't believe that Haseem is involved in anything like this...and Guzman is an undocumented pharmacist and illegal alien. You think they're going to let him out on bail? He has no ties to the community! The flight risk is tremendous. Taking away his passport is going to mean nothing to him. He probably doesn't even have one! And he has killed people. I'll call the district attorney. There is no way he's going to get out on bail!" Jess paused, and then continued in a softer tone. "I can't stay scared the rest of my life, Drew."

Drew said nothing for several seconds. "You're right. I don't want you to be scared, but I don't want you dead either. I especially don't want you to move back home. I think you should stay at my place at least a little longer, well much longer. If you die on me, I'll never forgive you! Jess, I want you to stay with me forever." Drew stood up as he spoke and started to walk around the desk.

"Well, I don't want you mad at me, and I surely don't want to be dead. I like your place—hell, I love you! You know that I'll have to consult with Reesa, though. Actually, I was worried that she wouldn't come home with me, so I don't think it's going to be a problem." Jess stood up as she spoke and met Drew at the end of the desk. "Ugh, this is awkward. I don't know what to say."

"I do," Drew said, as he put his arms around her and kissed her on the forehead. "Like Mrs. Reagan would have said, 'Just say, yes.'"

Epilogue

Drew and Jess were making the drive across the I-90 bridge from Bellevue to Mercer Island on their way into the office, and as usual, they were whizzing by the other barely moving cars. The day was sunny and bright, and Jess thought that there had been more than the usual number of those days lately.

Jess had moved all of her clothes to Bellevue with the idea that she and Drew would give this a "real try." As Jess suspected, Reesa was *really* settling in. She seemed to be awfully eager to sit on Drew's lap whenever he sat down. "Ungrateful child!" thought Jess.

As he drove, Jess began telling Drew about the miraculous transformation that Baker had made. "He not only changed his job, he also changed his attitude," she said. "I no longer feel the need to yell 'asshole' at the phone after I finish talking with him. He moved from his old firm to a newly created position as 'house counsel' at Peoples Hospital."

"Well, that's something. Doing prevention rather than clean-up," Drew said, knowing that the term "house counsel" refers to a lawyer working "in-house" to provide easy access to legal advice about a variety of issues, including advice that can prevent lawsuits.

"Baker tells me he's working with the new CEO that VAHC sent out. They want to have better oversight of the CEO to prevent another rogue like Hansen. No more side deals on drug purchases...well, other than the ones that the system normally provides. And no more cover-ups of odd circumstances at the hospital. All incidents are going to be reviewed by hospital committee again. It turns out that even the head pharmacist knew that some of the drugs were counterfeit; he was fired and a complaint was lodged with the state disciplinary board. It seems he's going to get a long—maybe permanent—vacation. Can you believe that Hansen was actually paying him to keep silent?

"Joyce Brown is back at Peoples. Her file was purged of the fake reprimand that Hansen slipped in. She called me just to thank me for being so persistent with her so that she found out about Hansen. Actually, I'm not so sure that was her only reason for calling. She did ask me about whether you were still working with me on the case. She sounded a little disappointed when I said no.

"Dr. Haseem will be dismissed from the case as soon as we get the settlement terms ironed out. Baker tells me that a report will be placed in his personnel file to make sure that there is no mistake about his liability, or lack of it, in the Thompson death. Baker has even offered a reasonable amount to settle the case.

"He hasn't totally left the "dark side," though. He did try to slip a provision in the settlement docs that would prohibit Lamm Patrick from taking counterfeit drug cases against Peoples in the future. I actually think it was his version of a joke since it was set out as an additional paragraph that you could hardly miss. I was going over the language with him in our conference room, and I started to remind him that it was an ethical violation to try to restrict the clients that an attorney can represent. He actually smiled and said, 'Never hurts to try.'"

Author's Note

This story is purely fictional, but the factual background related to the health care and drug industries is based on report of information as told or confirmed in reputable sources, many of which can be found online. In addition to the references stated in the text, further information for those who are interested is set forth below.

But first the reader should be aware that, as demonstrated in this book, the development of a medical malpractice case is a long, arduous, and expensive process, the successful conclusion of which is a result of combining scraps of information discovered over time with knowledge of the significance of that information. Though insurers characterize plaintiffs' lawyers as ambulance chasing ghouls, there is another side to the story, one which should tell the American public that we have a broken health care system that needs fixing.

As mentioned in the book, out-of-pocket costs to bring a medical malpractice case to completion are staggering, making it extremely unlikely that a medical malpractice case would be undertaken without significant consideration. Each case requires proof by medical and other experts which cost a minimum of $75,000 for a simple case and up to $150,000 for a more complex one. In a very complex case, which would likely be larger than a two person firm such as Lamm Patrick could handle alone, the advances can be up to $300,000 or more.

There are huge expert witness fees. A large medical malpractice case can require five, even ten, doctors *on each side* because there are a variety of medical issues to cover. There are nonmedical experts on physical therapy, vocational rehabilitation, occupational rehabilitation, economic damages, and other issues, and each side has a set of these experts. All of these witnesses must be paid to study the facts, develop their opinions, and have their depositions taken by the other side. Aside from the fees charged by expert witnesses for testifying, the depositions themselves are expensive since they can go on for hours or days. This money isn't repaid to the victim's lawyer unless the victim wins or settles.

The cost of each expert is astronomical when viewed by the average person. A nurse/paralegal might review files for $150 to $300 per hour, while most medical doctors won't work for under $500 per hour, if they will even talk to a victim's attorney. Many treating physicians—those who have treated the claimant but against whom there is no malpractice claim—will either not speak with the victim's counsel at all outside a formal deposition, or they will require a large nonrefundable retainer up front. Even physicians who agree to offer opinions about the care regarding the defendant doctor or hospital on trial will want large retainers, probably $5,000 to $10,000, unless they have worked with the attorney before. Of course, this cost must be advanced by plaintiffs' counsel.

There is a strong feeling among many, including the author, that the United States health care system is strained, perhaps broken, leaving professionals caught in the middle of this system and exposed to liability potentially beyond their control. See, for example, the author's notes in Robin Cook's *Marker* and *Crisis*.

In any event, the fact that there are numerous unnecessary deaths from whatever cause is well documented. A study published in the *Journal of the American Medical Association* in 2003 confirmed the results of a 1999 study by the Institute of Medicine that found that medical errors caused 98,000 premature deaths per year. Note that the medical community acknowledges this number, which would appear to many as shockingly high. An independent review by HealthGrades Patient Safety in American Hospitals set the annual number of mortal errors at nearly twice that amount. Source: "In Hospital Deaths from Medical Errors at 195,000 per

Year USA." *Medical News Today*, August 8, 2004. http://www.med-icalnewstoday.com/articles/11856.php.

There is also evidence of medical errors causing lesser injury and increased cost of care, to the extent that Medicare has refused to reimburse for medical care made necessary by medical error. The Bush administration acknowledges that this change will save about $20 million per year. Other sources set the figure at much higher, citing savings by Michigan hospitals alone in the amount of $246 million over three years by reducing blood stream infections through better catheter care. Source: Pear, Robert. "Medicare Says That It Won't Cover Hospital Errors." *New York Times*, August 19, 2007.

The other concern of this book is intended to show the reader the out-of-control system of pharmaceutical production, which adds unnecessarily to the expense of health care delivery. The facts regarding the huge play in pharmaceutical cost are taken from government studies, which can be found online:

Department of Health and Human Services. "Prescription Drug Coverage, Spending, Utilization, and Prices." Report to the President, April 2000. http://aspe.hhs.gov/health/reports/drugstudy.

Committee on Government Reform. "Prescription Drug Pricing in the United States: Drug Companies Profit at the Expense of Older Americans." Prepared for Rep. Henry A. Waxman. November 9, 1999. http://oversight.house.gov/documents/20040629104049-62473.pdf.

The astonishing situation confirmed by both of the above sources is that drug companies won't even share their pricing system with the United States government.

Reports do confirm that U.S. pharmaceutical companies appear to be thriving; the ten top drug manufacturers reported a twenty-seven percent increase in profits year over year for the first six months of 2006 as compared to 2005, $39 billion to $31 billion respectively. Keep in mind that this is only half a year's profit and considers only the top ten producers. Authorities assign this increase to the benefits realized from the drug industry as a result of the Medicare drug program. Source: Committee on Government Reform. "Pharmaceutical Industry Profits Increase by Over $8 Billion After Medicare Drug Plan Goes Into Effect." Prepared for Rep. Henry A. Waxman. September, 2006. http://oversight.house.gov/ story.asp?ID=1108.

One would assume that the huge expense of drugs would guarantee quality, but that does not appear to be the case. The *New York Times* reports that the Food and Drug Administration is woefully understaffed and does not have personnel with the training to deal with rapidly developing technologies necessary to inspect pharmaceuticals being imported from foreign sources. Source: "The FDA in Crisis: It Needs More Money and Talent." *New York Times,* February 3, 2008.

As of 2003, the FDA estimated that up to 40 percent of drugs imported from Mexico were counterfeit. Source: Hileman, Bette. "Counterfeit Drugs." *Chemical and Engineering News* 81, no. 45 (November 10, 2003): 36-43. http://pubs.acs.org/cen/coverstory/ 8145/8145drugs.html.

The source of counterfeit drugs is not limited to Mexico, as explained in a companion story to the *New York Times* article referenced above, "Another Danger Made in China," *New York Times,* February 3, 2008.

Finally, it is important to keep in mind that one of the reasons for the prevalence of counterfeit drugs is increasing foreign trade without adequate U.S. government oversight of imports. If we could depend on foreign governments to adequately oversee their own industries, perhaps we could provide adequate protection with fewer additional FDA inspectors than *New York Times* article cited above suggests. However, the evidence indicates that this is not the case. Some may remember the report of the execution of Zheng Xiaoyu, former head of the Chinese equivalent of our FDA, who was convicted of taking bribes from the Chinese pharmaceutical industry that he was tasked to regulate. The investigation leading to discovery of the bribery was sparked by a Chinese whistleblower, Zhang Zhijian, who rather than being credited for coming forward with the information, was jailed for nine months, lost his job, and as of 2007 couldn't get another job. Source: Cha, Ariana Eunjung. "Safety Falters as Chinese Quiet Those Who Cry Foul." *Washington Post*, July 19, 2007. http://www.washingtonpost.com/wp-dyn/content/article/2007/07/18/AR2007/07/18/AR20070771802768_p.

According to a Chinese attorney quoted in the article, who represented relatives of victims of alleged poisonous drugs in China, the fact that some whistleblowers are jailed stems from the view that "company enterprises are people's gatherings. You can't punish everyone in the company for problems caused by some individuals."

One final note: The res ipsa theory that is quoted in chapter 24 was taken from *Zebarth v. Swedish Hospital Medical Center*, 81 Wn 12, 489 P 2d 1 (1972).

I hope that you not only enjoyed this book but also found that it helped you understand our medical care system and the contribution that hard-working nurses, doctors, and even the much-maligned lawyers make to the well-being of the American people. I believe that the health care system needs fixing, and with your help, we can do it.

S.J.R